VELVET BLUES

PATRIK BANGA, EMIL
CINA, EVA DANIŠOVÁ,
GEJZA DEMETER,
OLGA FEČOVÁ,
ILONA FERKOVÁ, VĚRA
HORVÁTHOVÁ DUŽDOVÁ,
MÁRIA HUŠOVÁ, MARTIN
KANALOŠ, STANISLAVA
ONDOVÁ, KVĚTOSLAVA
PODHRADSKÁ, ZLATICA
RUSOVÁ, MARIA
SIVÁKOVÁ, MICHAL
ŠAMKO, MARKÉTA
ŠESTÁKOVÁ

VELVET BLUES

THE TWENTIETH CENTURY IN THE STORIES OF CZECHOSLOVAK ROMA

Edited
by Karolína Ryvolová

English translation
by Alex Zucker

KHER
KAROLINUM PRESS

KHER, z. s.
Veverkova 1172/33, 170 00 Prague 7, Czech Republic
www.kher.cz, nakladatelstvi@kher.cz

Originally published in Czech as *Všude samá krása* (Nothing but Beauty Everywhere) and *Samet Blues* (Velvet Blues), Prague: Kher 2021

KAROLINUM PRESS
is a publishing department of Charles University
Ovocný trh 560/5, 116 36 Prague 1, Czech Republic
www.karolinum.cz, redakcenk@ruk.cuni.cz

Edited by Karolína Ryvolová
Copyedited by Karolína Klibániová
Layout and set by Čumlivski&Horváth
Printed in the Czech Republic by Karolinum Press
First edition

A catalogue record for this book is available from the National Library of the Czech Republic.

This publication was supported by the Ministry of Culture of the Czech Republic and the foundation Bader Philanthropies, Inc.

ISBN 978-80-246-6267-1 (Karolinum)
ISBN 978-80-87780-49-7 (Kher)
ISBN 978-80-246-6268-8 (pdf)
ISBN 978-80-246-6269-5 (epub)

CONTENTS

INTRO-DUCTION

The volume in your hands is an anthology of contemporary short stories written mostly by Czech and several Slovak Roma from a region which was once Central European Czechoslovakia. It is a selection from two previous anthologies, *Všude samá krása* (Nothing but beauty everywhere, KHER 2021) and *Samet Blues* (Velvet blues, KHER 2021), which generated much interest upon their release and to this day rank among the publishing house's bestsellers.[1] The foundation of KHER, a press which caters exclusively for the needs of Romani writers, in 2012 was motivated by the belief that writers of Romani origin – due to their dramatic past linked especially but not exclusively to their merciless persecution during World War II, traditionally low social status and ongoing structural discrimination – enjoy a much harder position in the society to let their voices, stories, and grievances be heard.

The stories in the above-mentioned volumes are primarily dedicated to the writers' loved ones and their shared past in the pre-war ethnic settlements of Eastern Slovakia, their new homes in post-war Czech towns, and the surprising reality of post-1989 transition with its opportunities, but more importantly challenges and disillusionment. In the telling of these deeply personal stories these writers inadvertently convey a much more general picture of the Roma's twentieth century history.

The rise in neo-Nazism, which swept through the former Eastern Bloc countries following the fall of the Iron Curtain with its street violence, pogroms, and deaths, resulted in mass migration of the Roma to the West, where they would become an invisible minority, safe from physical threats and open to the advantages of equal rights. It is impossible to ascertain how many Czech Roma have left the Czech Republic since 1997, when the first wave of Romani migration hit primarily the UK and Canada, but to a lesser extent also the Netherlands, Belgium, Germany, and others. What we do know from eyewitnesses and authority reports is that these families

1 Alex Zucker's English translation of Patrik Banga's "Žižkovite" previously appeared in The Book of Prague (Comma Press, 2023). Mária Hušová's "Where to Now?" is published in this volume for the first time and did not appear in the original Czech-language anthologies.

have blended into their host countries with remarkable ease, adopting their language, joining the job market, and entering children into the local schools, where they go on to become brilliant students, proving the Czech education system with its badly concealed practice of segregation discriminatory and ultimately crippling.

This new generation of Western Roma have partly lost their Czech and Slovak, which have been replaced by the local majority languages, but have retained their Romani as the language of the home and community. The chief intention of the present collection is to provide these Roma with their own ethnic literature which has flourished in their homeland in their absence and thus help them cherish and sustain their cultural background. To this end, all stories written originally in the so-called Slovak Romani are printed in Romani with an accompanying translation in English. English as the lingua franca of the world has been chosen as the main language of this anthology to make the literature of the Roma most accessible to audiences around the world.

Mainstream populations across the globe are the second envisaged readership of this book. It aims to provide them with the fact of the very existence of Romani letters and aid the development of an understanding for, and a sensitivity to a people scattered around the world but bound by a common Indian origin.

Velvet Blues has been chosen as the volume's title despite the collected works speaking of a whole array of topics and periods. The editors felt that it best describes the Czechoslovak Roma's hope that their destiny is following a positive trajectory with a natural climax in the post-Velvet Revolution freedom of the new democratic country. That this has failed to happen is a tragic paradox and a source of ongoing sadness for the local Romani communities.

The selection of the seventeen stories is the result of a long chain of debates between KHER editors and the Czech-to-English translator Alex Zucker, whose job in this book stretched far beyond the usual transposition of one language code to another. Not only did he offer his expertise as to what Western audiences might be interested in and able to relate to, he also tirelessly battled on, trying to capture culturally specific terms and situations pertaining to the Roma. For his devotion to the project and willingness to deliver at any cost, KHER editors would like to express their heartfelt thanks.

The afterword entitled "The Untold Stories of Czechoslovak Roma" provides the factual and historical background to the development of a minority literature in an oral language. It is a case study of how the Roma began to write in the Czech Republic but will suitably serve as an illustration of similar processes in other countries with a significant Romani minority around the world.

BRAVE ROMANI WOMEN

BY ZLATICA RUSOVÁ

When I first started writing this war story, I wondered if it was the right thing to do. Should I or shouldn't I tell these Roma's stories? Shouldn't the suffering these people went through remain hidden away in the heart and memory of my mom? But then I found out that young Roma nowadays know hardly anything about World War II. I found it heart-wrenching, given how much the Roma suffered. Young people have no idea how many of us died in the concentration camps. Some were shot in front of their families, many were dragged away and never came home again, and no one even knows where they're buried.

What I want to write about now, though, is Romani women and children. I want to tell you about the people my mom grew up with. She started talking about them one day when two young people came to see me, wanting to know more about Romanes, the Romani language. As we got to talking, the conversation turned to World War II. And with tears in her eyes, my mom began telling the story I'm going to share with you now. It was the first time my sister and I ever heard it from her.

One night the mayor of the gadjo village woke them up: "Roma, as you know, there's a war on. The Germans are coming, you need to hide. Find yourselves a hiding place and don't come out until they're gone. Only God knows what will happen next."

"All right, but where? There's too many of us. I don't know any place where all of us would fit," replied the vajda, our Romani mayor.

"You'll have to find it yourselves. We can't hide you in the village. The farmers are saving the cellars for themselves," said the mayor, and with that he walked away. Everyone was anxious. They were very afraid for their children and families. Feverishly they pondered where they might hide.

That afternoon some young boys went to tell the vajda they had found a hiding place.

"Where?"

"In a cave. We used to go there to roast stolen hens, geese and ducks. We can hide there. There's plenty of room, the whole settlement can fit."

"All right, boys. Let's pack up everything we're going to need. People, take all the food from your house, duvets, warm covers, and proper clothing. Make sure to bring warm layers for the children, they're going to need them. The cave is made of stone and we're in the middle of winter."

The women gathered up all the essentials and set out. The whole way they wept: "What's going to become of us? We'll freeze to death in this cold! And when the Germans find us, they'll shoot us!"

When they came to the cave, they were amazed at how big it was. Then the older Roma remembered they used to slake lime there. The vajda ordered the people: "Women and children to one side, men and young boys to the other. In the middle we'll make a firepit so we don't freeze to death here."

Winter that year was harsh, although it didn't snow. The Roma survived in the cave as best they could. The grown-ups ate as little as possible to leave enough for the children, and saved as much water as they could. They had hardly any, in the woods there was none. They would have had to fetch it from the village, but they couldn't go there. It was just as the mayor said, that same day the Germans arrived. Toward evening, the Roma spotted them by the woods, but the Germans didn't dare enter the forest—they were afraid. The Roma were lucky.

During the day, some women cooked and some women helped, they shared the work as best they could. It all had to be done without a word, and even the children knew they had to be quiet while they played. When evening came and it was clear the Germans weren't patrolling the woods anymore, the Roma traded stories about all they had been through and how the musicians used to play at weddings and dances. But they laughed only under their breath, the fear was stronger. When Maňa told her story, though, they couldn't hold back anymore and howled with laughter.

Maňa was a bit slow. Cracked in the head as folks used to say. Didn't have all her marbles. She didn't speak too well, granted, but she was very cleanly and loved children. She could easily play with them all day long, so children adored her. She was fairly chubby, but had a charming face and skin like porcelain. They had lots of fun with her, but she was also trouble, since even her own mother didn't know how to explain to her that she wasn't allowed to leave the cave during the day.

One evening, once the children were asleep, the women were trying to figure out what to do, since they had a shortage of flour, potatoes and fat, and no bread left at all. The children were pleading for bread. But worst of all, they had run out of water. There was enough left for maybe two days. The men debated what to do: "Someone has to go down to the village and find out what's going on. Maybe there's a way to bring some water back." The vajda sent a few young men to scout it out. But it wasn't long before they were back.

"It won't work. There are soldiers everywhere, patrolling in pairs."

"If it won't work, it won't work. If only it would snow tonight. If it doesn't snow, I don't know what we'll do."

There was also one sickly little boy among the children. A Romani woman had taken him in from the orphanage in the hope that he would recover with her. But the cold cave and the hunger weren't doing him any good, in fact he was worse.

"What are we going to do with him if he dies?"

"We'll bury him somewhere around here, and after the war we can move him to the settlement."

The women pondered how to help the boy. They started cutting back on their food rations and giving him more of theirs. But with drinking water the situation was worse. They had run out and it still hadn't snowed. The children wanted to drink and there was nothing to give them. The women were at a loss. "What are we going to do?" they said. "The children won't make it without any water. They're going to die!" When the children went outside to pee during the day, by the next day it was frozen. Then the children broke the frozen pee into pieces with a spoon and ate it. They didn't realize where they had gone to pee, they thought they were just eating ice. Their parents didn't tell them what it was or the children wouldn't have had anything to drink. They knew it was the only way for the children to survive. The grown-ups went to a hole where their predecessors used to slake lime. There was frozen water on the surface and lime underneath. They divided it up so there was enough for everyone.

One evening some of the young boys came running into the cave and warned everyone to be quiet, they'd seen soldiers coming into the woods. "What kind of soldiers?" the vajda asked. Some said it was Germans, others said they'd heard Russian. So the vajda made a decision: "We're all going to lie down and no one say a word. Then we'll see what's going on."

After three hours, they heard someone outside speaking Russian. Then came the deafening sound of gunfire. The Russians had set up a Katyusha rocket launcher on top of the cave. Whoever had pillows and duvets covered their heads with them, to keep from going deaf. The soldiers were firing down on the village of Šivetice. As soon as they realized the shooting had stopped, the women wiped soot on the young girls' cheeks, to make them unattractive, and wrapped their heads in rags, for fear the soldiers might take them away and rape them. Everyone knew the Russians did that. Then the women and young girls hid. They even rubbed Maňa's cheeks with soot and hid her. After about an hour, someone lifted up the rug hiding the entrance to the cave and a Russian soldier walked in. He announced something in Russian and after a moment it dawned on them what he had said: "The Germans are gone, don't be afraid, they ran away."

Then some other Russian soldiers came in and started looking for something. When they found the girls hidden beneath the blankets, they took them away, soot-faced and all. As the mothers wept, the soldiers tried to reassure them, gesturing to indicate they were only taking the girls to help them peel potatoes. They took Maňa, too. Her mother tried to communicate that Maňa was sick, that she wasn't right in the head. But it didn't do any good. They took almost all the girls, leaving only the little ones.

When the Roma came out of the cave, they saw dead soldiers, wounded horses and discarded rifles. The women sat down on the cold ground and started weeping. So much sorrow and suffering, so many dead young people!

"Come on, folks, let's see what's going on with our girls!"

The whole way no one said a word. They were all afraid what they might find. What they saw horrified them. The girls were in shocking condition. They had been raped, every last one. Maňa was worse off than any of them.

When she heard the people from the settlement coming back to the village, she crawled out of her hiding place and wailed at the top of her lungs: "Mommy, mommy, they gave me a boo-boo!" Her mother collapsed on the ground beside her, hugged her to her chest, and burst into tears. All of the Romani people wept, they had never seen something so awful.

The first one to come to his senses was the vajda. "All right, Roma, time to stop moaning! We need to do something about it, we can't just leave them like this! Men, we'll divide up the work. Some of you go back to the cave, there are wounded horses there, the rest of you go find wood. We need to heat some water and give the girls a bath, then we can clean up too. But first we've got to fix them up." He walked away with tears in his eyes.

The women, weeping, attended to the girls, doing what had to be done. Only afterwards did they see to their own needs. What had happened could never be forgotten. The girls stripped off their clothes and the women burned them. They were so ridden with lice that when you put your hand down their bosom, you came out with a fistful of lice.

Once they had cleaned themselves up, they sat down to a meal the women had cooked for them. Their plates were piled high, but even though everyone was famished, the food stuck in their throat.

It took a long time for the girls to get well again. Some of them became pregnant. They not very nicely nicknamed the children "Russkies." You can still sometimes hear Roma say it to this day. But Maňa had it worst of all. Three months later, she died in great pain.

The story I told you today is one that actually happened. I intentionally left out the name of the village. Why? Because some of those women are still alive. My hope is that this might move some of you young people to think about what Romani women suffered through during World War II for the sake of their children and families.

ROMANE ROMŇA

ZLATICA RUSOVÁ

Kanak kezdinďom te írinen pal akala Roma, gondolinkerás, či kerav láčhe. Gondolinkerás, sjom te írinen, vaj na sjom te írinen pal akala Roma? Gondolinďom mange, n'élas akale Romengero pháripen, so préko džiďile, te áčhen míra dajorake čak andre lakero jílo te goďi? Pandik ájom pr'odá, hoj o terne manuša románe na džanen pal o dúto máriben, majna ništa. Olestar mange juminďa andro pháripen o jílo. Mer o Roma báre but préko ligene. Hoj but lendar múle andro lágri, but lendar múle khére angil o fajti, mer sle livinkerde, hoj buten ligene, u frima lendar ále khére, vaj na džanen, kaj hine párunde.

Musaj te phenav, hoj akána kamav te írinen pal o romane romňa, ta pal o romane čhavóre. Kamav tumenge akána te vakeren pal o Roma, maškar save ávri barija míri daj. Kanak vakerlas pal akala Roma, avka čak vaš odá, hoj ále ke ma dúj terne manuša, so kamle te džanen buter pal amári romaňi čhib. Sar vakerahas, avka peja lav pal o dúto máriben. U avka kezdinďa míri daj te vakeren, jasvenca andro jákha, pal akadá, so tumenge kamav te vakeren. Adá šunďam míra pheňaha angutno.

Jekfar rataha len uštaďa o starosta andal o gav: „Romale, džanen, hoj hin máriben. Kampel pe te garuven, aven k'amáro gav o Ňemci. Rakhen tumenge than kaj tumen garuvena. U na sikaven tumen, kím adaj éna. So éla dureder, odá džanel čak o Del."

„Láčhe, čak kaj? Sjam báre but. Na džanav, kaj amen sjam te garuven, na džanav ase thanestar, kaj resťamas savóre," phenďa amáro vajda.

„Odá tumenge musaj te rakhen korkóre. Andro gav tumen na sjam, kaj te garuven. O pinci pumenge o chulaja mukenkeren vaš pumenge." Odá phenďa u geja het. Pharone lenge sja, i dar sja bári vaš o čhavóre te vaš o fajto. O Roma savóre gondolinkernas, kaj pumen garuvna.

Pal o dílo ále o terne čháve pal o vajda, hoj rakhle than, kaj pumen savóre garuvena.

„Kaj?"

„Andro barlango. Phírahas odoj le kachňen, le papiňen, te le kačken te pekenkeren, so čorahas. Odoj amen garuvaha. Hin odá báro, resaha odoj savóre Roma."

„Láčhe, čhavale, javas amenge te keden, so amenge

kampola. Romale, keden upre savóro: o chában, so hin tumen khére, keden tumenge o duchni, o pokróci táte, te o táte gada. Keden upre le čhavórenge o táte gada, mer odá lenge kampola, o barlango hin baruno, u hin jevend."

O Romňa kene upre savóro so kampija, u mukle pumen pro drom. O Romňa cele dromeha rovenas: „So amenca éla? Andr'akaso jevend faďinaha! U te amen o Ňemci rakhena, livinkerna amen!"

Sar ále ko barlango, amulinde, savo hin odá barlango báro. Akor ále pr'odá o phúre Roma, hoj jon odoj valekana téle čhorkernas o vapno. O vajda phenďa le Romenge: „O romňa le čhavórenca džana pro jek ódalo, o murša le terne čhávenca pro áver ódalo. Maškare le barlangoske, keraha jag, te na adaj faďinas."

Odá berš sja o jevend báro. Čak o jiv na sja. Avkake o Roma dživenas andro barlango, sar pe delas. Chanas so jekfrimeder, čak le čhavóren t'ovel buter, te le páňiha cidenas te ikrel so jekdureder. Mer te o páňi sja len frima u andro veš páňi na sja. Musaj te gelehas andro gav, u odoj naštik džanas. O starosta sar phenďa, avka sja, mek odá ďives ále andro gav o Ňemci, mer kijaráťi dikhle le Ňemcen pašal o veš. Andro veš andre n'ále, mer daranas. Adá sja le romengeri bach.

Préko ďives o Romňa tavenas, valesave šegitinenas, ulavkernas sar pe delas. Musaj te sle bilaveskero, u džanenas odá, te o čhavóre kanak pumenge khelenas, te na len šunďol. Kijaráťi kanak džanenas, hoj paš o veš náne o lukeste, pumenge o Roma vakerenas, so préko džiďile, kanak phírnas te bašavkeren, o bijava, o bále. No t'avka hasanas polóke, mer i dar sja bareder. No kanak vakerelas i Maňa, odá ávri na ikrenas o Roma, u hasanas avka, hoj o ódala len dukhanas.

I Maňa, odá sja terňi čhaj, so sja nasváji. Avka, sar pe phenel romane, nasváji sja pro šéro. Na sja lake andro šéro savóro avka, sar élas t'oven. Na džanelas láčhe te vakeren, so pe musaj te phenen, sja báre žúži, u kamlas báre le čhavóren. Le čhavórenca peske khelelas te celo ďives. U o čhavóre la báre kamenas. Sja báre thúji, no o muj la sja báre šukár. O tešto sja la parno sar porceláno. Avkake préko laha džiďile but hasaviben, no te bríga, kanak lake i daj na džanlas te den andri goďi, hoj ávri naštik džal préko ďives.

Jekfar kijaráťi, o čhavóre má sovenas, u o romňa pumenge vakerenas, so te keren, má sja frima járo, krumpji, žíro u so na sja, avka máro. U odá mangen o čhavóre. Ále te pr'odá, hoj frima hin o páňi. Šaj ovel, hoj hin pre dúje ďivesende. So te keren, vakernas pumenge o murša: „Élas te džan valeko andro gav. Élas te džan te dikhen, so pe odoj kerel. Šaj ovel, hoj pe delas te páňi te anen." O vajda bičhaďa le terne čháven andro gav, či te del te anel páňi. No báre sik ále pale.

„Na del pe, o lukeste hine vígik, phíren po dúj džéne."

„Te pe na del, ávka pe na del. Lošalo újomas, te aja rat pejas jiv. Te na perla, na džanav, so keraha."

Maškar o čhavóre sja jek cikno čhavóro, so sja nasválo. Lija peske le jek romňi andal o lelenco. Lija peske le, hoj paš late pe dela pro than. No o barlango leske láčhipen na kerlas, aňi i bok. U sja pr'odá na láčhe.

„So leha keraha, te merla?"

„Párunaha le valeka adaj, te éla pal o máriben, thovaha le préko andro gav," phenďa o vajda.

O romňa gondolinkernas, sar te šegitinen le nasvále čhavóreske. Kezdinde pumenge te devkeren frimeder chában. U devkernas le nasvále čhavóreske. No goreder odá sja le páňiha. Má o páňi na sja. O jiv na peja. O čhavóre mangenas páňi u páňi má na sja. Má na džanenas, so te keren. So keraha, phenenas pumenge o romňa, bijo páňi o čhavóre ávri na ikrena. Merna! O čhavóre, so ávri mutrenas préko ďives, odá faďinlas, u o áver ďives le rojenca phagernas u chanas o faďindo muter. O čhavóre na džanenas, kaj mutrenas, gondolinenas, hoj chan jégo. O daja te o dada le čhavórenge na phenenas, so chan, čak te na mangen páňi. U džanenas, hoj čak avka šaj préko dživen. O romňa te o murša phírenas andri chev, kaj o phúre Roma čhorkernas o vapno. Upral sja o faďindo páňi, u telal sja o vapno. Chanas avka, te áčhel sakoneske.

Jekfar kijaráťi našle o terne čháve andro barlango, hoj t'ovas bilavengero, mer dikhle, hoj andro veš aven o lukeste. O vajda phučja: ,,Save lukeste?" Jek phende, hoj dikhle Ňemcen, ávera, hoj šunde te vakeren Rusika. Vaš odá phenďa o vajda: ,,Savóre amenge džaha te pašjon u ovaha bilaveskero. Dikhaha, so pe kerla."

Pal o trin ori šunde te vakeren Rusika. Pandik báro

livišágo. Pro barlango o Rusi thode i Kaťuša. Savóre amenge thoďam keril o šére o perňici, o duchni, kas so sja čak t'ovel amenge o šéro andreučhardo. Te na ovas kašuke. O lukeste livinkernas téle pro Šivetovo. Sar o romňa dikhle, hoj o lukeste má na livinkeren, kormoha lenge andre kerde o muja, t'oven džungale. Devkerde lenge pro šére kendova, mer daranas, te na len keden o lukeste, mer odá kerenas. Le terne čhajen, romňen téle chudkernas. Te la Maňa andre kerde kormoha u garude. Vaj pali jek óra valeko vazdňa o pokróco, so sja andreučhardo o barlango, andre ája jek Rusiko lukesto. Valeso vakerlas u pandik ájam pr'odá, hoj phenďa: „Má o Ňemci adaj náne, ma daran, ništa."

Pandik ále te ávera Rusika lukeste, u kezdinde valeso te roden. Te rakhle le čhajen, rakhle tel o duchni, te melalen len kene. O daja rovenas, sar dikhle o lukeste, hoj roven, sikavkernas, hoj džan te kušen o krumpji. Lile te la Maňa. I daj sikavkerlas, hoj hin nasváji, sikavkerlas hoj hiňi diliňi. No na šegitinďa. Lile majna savóre čhajen. Mukle čak ole ciknen.

O Roma, kanak ávri ále andal o barlango, dikhle le bute múle lukesten, livinde grasten, dikhle but puški. O romňa bešte pri šudri phuv u kezdinde te roven. Aci bríga, aci pháripena, aci múle terne manuša.

„Romale, javas te dikhen, so hin amáre čhajenca!"

Savóre cele dromeha khére džanas bilaveskero. Daranas, so dikhena khére. So dikhle, sja valeso báro. Le čhajen rakhle báre erďavone. Savóre sle téle chudkerde. I Maňa sja pr'odá jekgoreder. Sar šunďa, hoj o Roma aven khére, cidlas pe pal i phuv andal o khér ávri. Rovlas pro celo kirlo: „Mamo, mamo, kerde mange bibi!" Lakeri daj peske bešťa ke late pri phuv, ciňa peske la pro kojin u kezdinďa te joj te roven. Savóre Roma rovenas, asi bríga mek na dikhle.

Angutno ája ke peste o vajda. „Romale, ma roven má! Kampel lenca te keren valeso, naštik avka oven! Muršale, ulavas amenge i búťi. Valesave džana ko barlango, odoj sle livinde grasta, ávera džana kaštenge. Kampel te taťarkeren páňa, kampel le čhajen te nanďarkeren, te amen musaj te nanďuvas. Angutno kampel te den le čhajen pro than." Jasvenca andro jákha geja het.

O romňa rovibnaha dine le čhajen pro than, kerde keril lende, so kampija. Pandik kerde keril pumende. Sja odá valeso aso, so pe na dela te biskeren šoha. O gada, so téle hajinde pal pumende, labarkerde. Sja andre lende aci džuva, hoj kanak denas o vast pal i brek, lenas ávri džuva.

Sar pumen žužarde, bešte ko chában, so o romňa táde. Savórenge sja keno, no o chában na kamlas téle te džan le kirloha, u ája sako bokhalo.

Žibut pumen o čhaja sasťarnas. Valesave áčhile khabne. Lengere čhavóren džungalone vičinenas ,,Ruso". Te akána maškar o Roma šunďol, hoj valesave manuša pumen vičinen Ruso. No jekgoreder sja pr'odá i Maňa. I Maňa pro trinto čhon báre dukhende múja.

Akadá, so tumenge akána genďom, vaj írinďom, hin čáčo. O gav na kamav te írinen naveha. Soske? Mer valesave romňa mek dživen. Vaš odá tumen terne manuša gondolinkeren, so sle o romane romňa andro dúto máriben vaš o čhavóre te vaš o fajto.

RUN FOR IT MARGITA!

BY KVĚTOSLAVA PODHRADSKÁ

MARGITA

"Run for it, Margita! Quick, run!" my sister Olga whispered urgently into my ear, dragging me deeper into the woods so we could hide in the thicket.

"What for?" I asked, surprised.

"Stop asking questions and run!" Branches and tall grass whipped at our skin, but we didn't let them slow us down. "I saw Germans on the road. If we run this way, we'll make it home before them," my sister explained after catching her breath a little.

As we crashed through the door of our wooden cottage, the terrified look on our faces made it clear to our mother that danger was on the way.

"Upstairs, quick, under the hay, and be quiet!" We lay down by the rafter where there was the most hay, hearts pounding in our throats. Hugging each other helped us calm down a bit. Soon we heard a banging on the door and our mother's voice.

"I'm afr—," I whispered, and Olga covered my mouth with her palm.

"Are you alone? Where is your husband, your family? Have you seen any partisans?" the soldiers bellowed at my mother.

"I'm here alone, my husband went to burn lime. Partisans? Here? What would they be doing here? No one comes here all year long," said Mr. Trnka, the teacher from our primary school in Matysová, interpreting my mother's answer for the Germans. We heard one of the guards walk to the stove and lift the lid on one of the pots. Potatoes bubbled away inside. The guards scanned the room.

"Where do those stairs go?" one of the soldiers asked. "Hello, did you hear what I said? What's up there?" he asked again, pointing to the opening in the ceiling and placing his tall boot on the first step.

"Nothing, just the attic, hay, the gate's outside, on the other side of the house."

"Then why do you have stairs in here?" the soldier asked.

"When I make mattresses, I fill the canvas with hay. This way I have it handy, so I don't have to go outside at night," our mom responded calmly. The teacher translated, making sure the Germans understood.

"Let's go," the commander suddenly ordered. He was probably hot from standing by the stove.

"You can come down, girls. They're past the roadside cross now," our mom called up to us, and we came down the stairs, still trembling with fear.

"I spotted those Germans at the crossroads, and we ran for it right away. We don't have any wood," Olga informed our mom.

"Never mind, the main thing is you made it home in time. If they had seen you in the woods, they might have picked you up, and God knows what might have happened. They're still searching for partisans."

"We do have mushrooms, though," said Olga, proudly pointing to our basket, and she began to clean them to put in the soup. My mom sat down on the bench by the stove and you could see there was something on her mind.

"When will this all be over? When will they leave us in peace so we can live without fear again? Come here, Margita, my precious child."

"I'll be twelve soon," I proudly declared, kneeling at her feet. But my mother gave a worried sigh. "You two are all I have left." Our older sister Anna had moved away the year before to live with her husband in Legnava.

"You know, a few girls have gone missing, and those German officers hurt them. I have to keep you hidden so they can't do anything bad to you. You mustn't go into the woods by yourselves. Tomorrow the two of you will go with your grandma to clean at the church, maybe you'll get some cheese curds in return," our mom said, wiping her tears on her apron.

The wooden Greek Orthodox church meant everything to our grandma, she believed that as long as we kept praying, we would make it through these hard times. Sometimes, when the wooden stairs needed scrubbing, she would take us granddaughters with her, and in return we would get some food to take home with us. Olga preferred going to work for the Ruthenian farmers in Stará Ľubovňa, but I liked it in the church. When we were lucky, we came home with enough flour to bake bread for two weeks, then we got eggs and vegetables for helping out on some other farm—there were several of them around Matysová. But most of all, I would have liked to go back to school. When would our lives go back to the way they were before?

OLGA

"You hear that? Someone's knocking at the door. Who could it be at this hour?" wondered our mom.

"Don't go anywhere, stay in bed!" our dad ordered us in a hushed voice.

"It isn't the Germans, they wouldn't have knocked," I whispered to Margita.

"Who is it?" my father asked in a firm voice.

"Atkroy dver, pazhalusta, ya ranyenyi."

"It must be a Russian," my mom said to my dad. "Be careful!" My father picked up a wooden cane and slowly opened the door. A young man fell straight onto our floor.

"Pomoshch, pomoshch," he begged, and in the light we saw that his whole body was covered in mud and blood.

"Come, get up." My dad lifted the man by his right arm, since his left side was wounded, and hauled him up to the attic.

"What happened? Who are you?" From downstairs we heard our mom asking the soldier questions in Ruthenian. In between moans of pain, he answered that he was Russian and had been separated from his unit during an air drop.

"Vodu, vody dai piit, pazhalusta." I leaped out of bed for a tin mug and was up in the attic quick as a flash. My dad had taken off the soldier's coat and was inspecting his bleeding wound.

"He probably stabbed himself on a branch. We need to stop the bleeding. Bring me a cloth and some water," my dad said, looking at me. Once I had delivered them, he sent me back downstairs and my mom tended to the Russian's wound.

"Now listen carefully. We've got a Russian soldier here.

You know what the Germans would do to us for sheltering the enemy and lying to them." My dad gave us a deadly serious look to make sure we grasped how dangerous this was for all of us. "We can either throw him out, or keep him for a couple days, till his wound heals up and he gets some strength back. Which will it be?" My dad gave us an inquiring look. We exchanged glances without a word. We were all well aware what awaited us if the Germans were to find him here.

"We would all have to act exactly the same as we did before he burst in here," my mom decided.

"All right then, he stays, and we all keep our mouths shut, not a peep from anyone, hear that, girls?" said my dad. He instructed us that no one but him was to go up to the attic.

"Good thing we're the last cottage in the village and no one has to walk past us on their way home, right, Olga?"

"Right, Margita, we know, but still we have to be careful," I reminded my sister, just to be sure, before we both fell asleep.

Apart from my dad, no one went up to the attic. Mornings, before he went off to the woods, where the men logged timber for the Nazis, he tended to Sergei, and evenings he checked to see if his wound was healing up. My grandma got her hands on a little bottle of yellow powder, luckily we had plenty of sheets to make bandages with. The whole week, we all acted the same as always.

"Today in the woods I found out the Nazis are looking for a Russian lieutenant," my dad said, and we all perked up our ears.

"That's our Sergei, right, Dad?"

"Yes, Olga, that's him. I'll go and have a look at him, you girls go lie down," he said, but this time he stayed up in the attic longer than usual.

"Sergei wants to leave the day after tomorrow, in the evening," my dad announced to my mom when he came back downstairs. "I'll deliver him to the partisans and they'll take him to his unit."

"But Gabo," my mom asked, "do you even know how to find the partisans?"

"Every man that works in the woods knows that, honey.

Now go to sleep," my dad smiled at her.

Early the next morning he went off into the woods, and came back before the German patrol that supervised the men working in the woods. My mom spent the day kneading dough for bread. We didn't have much flour left, but she knew Sergei was going to need some food for the trip.

"I spoke with Matuš. The partisans know where Sergei's unit is," my dad informed my mom when he came home from work. "Tomorrow, once it gets dark, Matuš will be waiting at the agreed location."

"It's awfully dangerous, do you have to go with him?" I heard my mom say anxiously.

"I do. Sergei doesn't know his way around here. If the Germans got hold of him, it would be bad for us too," my father said, thinking out loud.

"Spasiba. Balshoye spasiba." Sergei emotionally thanked my mom, telling me and my sister goodbye with his eyes. As he walked off into the dark with my dad, I felt like I was going to cry. I imagined them cautiously treading their way through the darkened woods, and meeting up with the brave Matuš at the arranged location. Sergei shook hands with my dad, and the two of them wordlessly hugged farewell.

"Why has Dad been gone so long? He should have been back ages ago."

"He'll come, don't worry. They have to be careful, you know," said my mom, reassuring both me and herself. She was too worried to fall asleep. She prayed for my dad to return, and I prayed silently along with her, next to my sleeping sister.

When my dad still hadn't returned by morning, we were sure something had gone wrong. We set out for Matysová to ask my uncle Ďula if he knew anything. The Germans were chasing each other around the village square on motorbikes, they even had a dog sitting in one of the sidecars.

"What are you doing here, woman? Run along home! They took your Gabo away! The men were talking about it this morning when they went logging. They said they caught him outside last night. What was he thinking, going outside so late like that? You know we aren't allowed out of the house after dark," my uncle said. My mom burst into tears.

"Where did they take him to, Ďula, where?" She hid her face in her hands.

"I don't know exactly, but they said to a work camp. Run along home and don't go asking around anywhere, you'll only make more problems for yourself. What if they take you in too?" my uncle Ďula said.

Our grandma, who lived with my uncle, found out from him what had happened and came to see us. "The nearest work camp is in Hanušovce, here in the Prešov region. They've got men locked up there building train tracks and dams. The parish priest told me, and he knows everything."

"Auschwitz is a long way away, isn't it?" my mom asked my grandma.

"That's in Poland, hopefully Gabo is still here somewhere, we just have to pray for him and trust that he'll come back to us," my grandma said, her eyes overflowing with tears.

MOM

I didn't lose faith that Gabo would come back to me, that we would all live together again like before. Early the next morning, the girls and I went into the woods to gather firewood, we were running out. I hadn't had any news of him, none of the men from the woods knew a thing. Every second or two, my eyes kept wandering to the path leading home, just in case my husband returned. We had a frugal Christmas as usual, but on top of everything else, it was also unbearably painful, every time I thought about the fact that he wasn't with us.

It was awful when the Germans drove all the men, women, and children from the village into the woods to make round logs for trenches. The Germans stood over us, weapons in hand, shouting and pointing machine guns at us. The Roma were beside themselves with fear. I was scared to death they would shoot us, you could hear the weeping from all sides. Finally, after seven days, they told us we didn't have to go into the woods anymore. The men could begin to dig trenches. The ground was frozen solid, they had to burn firewood to loosen up the soil.

We took work wherever we could find it. For a little flour, potatoes, and lard, we would work all day if we had to.

After mass one day, I went to my mother's. "People are saying the fighting between the partisans and the Russian units is getting closer," my brother Ďula remarked.

"You don't see the Germans in the area so much anymore, and some of them are leaving, the parish priest said," my mother added. For the first time in ages, I felt a flicker of hope in my heart that Gabo might return, but then panicked that I might have jinxed it.

"Mommy, Mom!" Olga shouted, bursting into the kitchen one day with the news she had heard on the farm that Soviet rifle corps units had broken through to Hanušovce.

"Hanušovce? Our daddy might be there!" Margita cried in excitement.

On January 24, the Soviets liberated Matysová.

I was out in front of the house with my daughters stacking wood when someone shouted to us from the cross at the crossroads: "Girls! My girls!"

He had returned! I sank to my knees and burst into tears.

"Dad, Daddy, Dad!" My daughters ran over to him and gave him a hug. I thanked God he'd heard our prayers and our family was together again.

"At long last, I'm here with you," said my husband, clutching me in his arms. He was nothing but skin and bones. We wept with joy.

"Were you in Hanušovce, Daddy?" Margita asked.

"Yes, my dear Margita, but in my heart, I was here at home with all of you."

We piled a plate with as much food as we could, but after going hungry for so long, Gabo couldn't eat it all, he had to take it slow and in small portions. He told us that on his way back from the partisans, after bringing Sergei to them, he was stopped by the Germans. They didn't believe that the only reason he was walking around the woods in the middle of the night was because he'd had a quarrel with his wife. They took him to Hanušovce, and he was this close to being sent to Auschwitz like the others before him.

A little while later, Olga suddenly said, "There's a car pulling up to our place."

"Our place?" I said in surprise. My husband was asleep, still recovering.

"Soldiers, but not Germans, their uniforms are different," she said, reporting what she could tell from a distance.

The car came to a stop in front of our door and out jumped a group of noisy Russian soldiers. "Zdrastvuyte, Gabo, mamo!"

"Sergei, is that you?" I said.

"Da, eto ya, Sergei Vladymyrich Gorki, sto syedmy strelkovy batalion Gordeeva. My Ganushovice i Matysova asvabadili," he said with a salute. I translated for my family: "Yes, it is I, Sergei Vladymyrich Gorki, of the 107th Rifle Corps, Commanding Officer Gordeev. We liberated Hanušovce and Matysová."

"Gabo, we brought food for your family," I translated what Sergei had said as the soldiers carried sacks of flour, potatoes, and preserves into the kitchen, along with other provisions the Germans had taken from the farmers for themselves.

At long last, we could look forward to some much-deserved peace and quiet.

This story is dedicated to my parents, Margita and Gabriel Dužda, who, unlike many millions of others, survived the Second World War.

DENAŠ, MARGITKO!

KVĚTOSLAVA PODHRADSKÁ

E MARGITKA

„Denaš, Margitko! Sig denaš!“ zoraleder mange ňisostar ňič phenďas e pheň u cirdľa man andro bareder veš, te pen te garuvas andro bare kraki.

„Soske, Olgo?“ phučav latar u čudaľinav man.

„Ma phuč u denaš!“ O kraki the e uči čar amen labarel, aľe na denašas polokeder. „Dikhľom pro drom le Ňemcen, sar denašaha kadarig, avaha khere sigeder sar jon,“ phenel mange goďaha, sar čino chudľa o dichos.

Fejs rozruginďam o vudar la drevnicatar u amare muja la dake phende, hoj pes vareso kerel.

„Upre, sig andro phus u čiten!“ Pašľuvas peske paš o tramos, kaj hino o phus nekučeder, o jila amenge maren dži andro kirlo. Jekhetano obchudľipen amenge čino šegetinďa. Takoj šunas durkiben pro vudar the la dakero hangos.

„Darav m-,“ cichones phenav u e Olga mange thoďa e burňik pro vušta.

„Sal korkori? Kaj tiro rom? Kaj e fameľija, dikhľal le partizanen?“ vičinen pre daj.

„Som kadaj korkori, o rom geľa te labarel o vapnos. O partizana? Kadaj? So bi kadaj kerenas, ňiko kadaj na avel, sar hino o berš baro,“ prethovel o sikhľardo o Trnkas andal e obecno sikhaďi Matisovatar le ňemcike slugadženge la dakero vakeriben. Šunas sar jekh slugadžis geľa ke špareta, hazdľa upre e chip. Andre piri taďon o gruľi. Rozdikhel pes pal e kuchňa.

„Kaj džan kale garadiči?“ phučel o dujto slugadžis, „Hej, šunes, so hin kodoj upre?“ u sikhavel pre chev andro plafonos the uštarďa uča cirachaha pro peršo garadičis.

„Ňič, oda ča o pados, o phus, o vudaroro avral, pal oki sera le kherestar.“

„Soske tut hin o garadiči kadaj?“ kamel te džanel.

„Sar kerav o štroki, rakinav andre cacha o phusa. Paš o vasta hine, kaj na mušinav te phirel rači avri,“ phenel amari daj, sar te ňisostar na daralas. O sikhľardo prethovel the dikhel pre lende, či leske achaľuven.

„Džas het,“ rozkazinďa ňisostar ňič o veliteľis. Šaj les has kerado, sar terďol paš e špareta.

„Aven tele, čhajale, imar hine pal o kerestocis," vičinďa pre amende e daj u amen mek daraha džas andre kuchňa.

„Daje, dikhľom le Ňemcen pre amaro dromoro u takoj denašahas. O kašta amen nane," phenďa lake e Olga.

„Oda ňič, mištes, hoj denašľan khere. Te tumen dikhlenas andro veš, šaj bi tumen lenas u o Del džanel, so bi pes tumenge ačiľahas. Ča furt roden le partizanen."

„Aľe o chundruľa amen hin," baripnaha sikhaďa e Olga pro košaris the chudľa len te čhingerel andre zumin. E daj peske bešľa pre lavkica paš e špareta u has pre late te dičhol, vareso lake phirel pal e goďi.

„Kana kada savoro imar preačhela, kana amen imar dena smirom the pale peske dživaha, kaj te na daras! Av ke mande, Margitko, čhajori miri."

„Sig mange ela dešuduj," phenav baripnaha u bešav pro khoča paš lakere čanga. E daj cirdňa phari voďi. „Imar san ča tumen dujdžeňa." E nekphureder pheň e Anna koda berš geľa pal peskero rom andre Ľegnava.

„Džanes, hoj varesave čhajora imar našľile u kola ňemcika slugadža len vareso kerde. Mušinav tumen te garuvel, te tumenge vareso džungalo na keren. Andro veš imar korkore našťi džan. Tajsa džana la babaha te pratinel andre khangeri, šaj chuden ciral," phenďa e daj u khosľa peske o apsa andre leketa.

Predal amari baba has e kaštuňi greckokatolicko khangeri but angluňi, pačalas, hoj kada pharo dživipen predživaha. Varekana amen cikne čhajoren lelas peha, sar kampolas te čuchinel o kaštune garadiči, u vaš kada peske khere anahas varesavo chabenoro. E Olga lošaha phirelas pal e buči ko rusinska gazdi andre Puraňi Ľubovňa, aľe mange pes andre khangeri pačisaľolas. Sar has amen bacht, ta anahas o aro u pekahas o maro, so amenge ľikerelas he duj kurke, o jandre the e želeňina chudahas vaš e buči pro aver statki, so has pašal e Matisova, u kerahas odoj. Aľe igen rado bi pale phiravas andre sikhľarďi. Kana ela amaro dživipen pale sar has anglo mariben?

E OLGA

„Šunes, vareko durkinel pro vudar. Kavka rači, ta ko oda šaj avel?" čudaľinel pes e daj.

„Ňikhaj ma džan, ačhuven andro haďi," poloke hangoha amenge phenďa o dad.

„O Ňemci oda nane, jon bi na durkinenas," dichinďom la Margitkake andro kan.

„K'oda?" phučľa o dad zorale hangoha.

„Atkroj dver, pažalujsta, ja ranenyj."

„Oda ela Rusos," phenel e daj le dadeske, „de pozoris!" O dad lel andro vast kaštuňi bakuľa, polokes phuterel o vudar. Terno murš perel takoj amenge pro dili.

„Pomošč, pomošč...," mangel u amen sar labolas e momeľi dikhas, hoj hino but melalo la čikatar the ratvalo.

„Ušťi the av." O dad les chudľa tel o čačikano phiko, bo oki sera leske ratvaľi, u cirdel les pro pados.

„So pes ačhiľa, ko sal?" šunas telal, sar e daj la rusinsko čhibaha phučel le slugadžistar, savo stukinel andre dukh, u jov lake phenel, hoj hino Rusos u peskera jednotkake našľiľa, sar chučiľa le padakoha tele.

„Vodu, vody daj piť, pažalujsta." Chučiľom andal o haďos vaš e trastuňi kučori the maj som pro pados. O dad leske imar čhiďa tele o gerekos u dikhel pre ratvaľi chev.

„Peľa prosto pro konaris, kampol te z'ačhol o rata, džan anen o patave the o paňi," dikhel pre ma o dad. Sar leske diňom, bičhavel man tele u la daha leske e chev ratinen.

„Šunen man mišto, hino ke amende rusiko slugadžis. Džanen, so amen užarel, te les garuvaha the chochavaha le Ňemcen," dikhel pre amende o dad zorales, kaj te achaľuvas, hoj amen savoren šaj murdaren. „Šaj les čhivas avri, abo les šaj mukhas varesave ďivesa kadaj, te leske e chev čeporo sasťol u avla les čino e zor. Ta so phenen?" o dad amen le jakhenca mangel, so leske phenaha. Dikhas pre peste the na vakeras. Džanas mišto, so amen užarel, te les o Ňemci kadaj rakhena.

„Oda amenge kampola te ľikerel pes kavka, sar angloda, sar kij'amende peľa tele," phenďa e daj.

„Ta mištes, ačhela paš amende the amen savore ňič na vakeras, ňikaske aňi lav, šunen, čhajale?" zorales

amenge phenel o dad u mek amenge phenel, hoj pro pados pal leste phirela ča jov.
„Mištes, hoj sam agorutňi dreveňica u ňikas avres pal amende nane o drom, na, Olgo?“
„Hat, Margit, sem savore džanas, aľe the avka kampola pes te ľikerel,“ mek pale phenav la pheňake u so dujdžeňa zasovas.

Ňiko aver sar o dad pro pados na phirelas. Tosara kim džalas andro veš, kaj o murša kerenas le nacistenge o kašta, bajinelas pal o Sergejis u rači les džalas te dikhel, či leske o skaľaripen sasťol. E baba stradľa cikno caklocis šargone praškoha pre kajse skaľaripena, o patave amen hin pre bacht buteder. Calo kurko pes ľikerahas avka sar andre aver ďivesa.
„Adaďives šunďom, hoj o Ňemci roden le rusika poručikos,“ phenďa o dad u amen ča dikhľam jekh pre aver.
„Oda jov, amaro Sergejis, dado?“ phučľom.
„Hat, Olgo, oda jov. Džava pal leste te dikhel, džan peske te pašľol,“ phenďas o dad, aľe akana pro pados ačhiľa buteder.
„O Sergejis kamel paltajsaste te džal het,“ phenďa o dad la dake, sar aviľa ke amende tele. „Džava leha ko partizana u jon les ľidžana ke leskeri jednotka.“
„Gabo, u tu džanes, sar len, le partizanen, te rakhel?“
„Ta sem savore murša, so kerenas andro veš, džanas, daje. Imar sov,“ asandžila pre late o dad.
Sig tosara geľas andro veš u aviľa pale sigeder, sar avile o ňemcika šingune, so pro murša andro veš merkinen. E daj zakerďa o chumer pro maro. But aro imar amen nane, aľe joj džanel, hoj le Sergejiske pro drom kampol varesavo chaberono.
„Vakeravas le Matušiha. O partizana džanen, kaj le Sergejiskere manuša,“ phenďas la dake o dad, sar aviľa andal e buči. „Tajsa sar perela e rači, užarela amen odoj, sar amenge phenďam.“
„Joj, sar me darav, kampol tuke kodoj te džal leha?“ šunav sar e daj daral.
„Ta kampol leske te sikhavel o than andro veš. O Sergejis amare veša na džanel, te les o Ňemci chudenas, oda bi elas namišto the predal amende,“ duminel o dad hoj savore te šunen.

„Spasiba, baľšoje spasiba,“ šukares la dake paľikerel o Sergejis u o jakha čhivel the pre amende. Džan le dadeha andre kaľi rat u mange pes kamel te rovel. Andro šero mange hin, sar džan kale vešeha polokores pro than, so peske phende, u akana pes dikhen the le zorale Matušiha. O Sergejis le dadeha peske dine o vasta u bijo lava pes obchudle.

„Kaj o dad hino ajci, daje? Imar leske kampolas te avel pale.“

„Avela, ma dara, džanes, hoj našťi siďaren,“ phenel e daj polokes mange the korkori peske. O pharipen pal o dad lake na del te sovel. Modľinel pes, hoj te avel pale u me paš o than, kaj sovel e Margitka, man modľinav laha.

Sar o dad calo rat na aviľa khere, imar džanahas, hoj pes vareso ačhiľa. Geľam le dromeha ke Matisova pal o bačis Ďulas, či vareso na džanel. Pal o gavoro o Ňemci džan le motorkenca u lenca andre sajdka bešel o rukono.

„So kadaj keres, romňije, dža khere, ta sem tuke ile le Gabos! Tosara vakerenas o murša, sar gele andre buči andro veš. Chudle les, hoj rači avri. Ta so geľa kavka rači avri? Ta sem džanen, hoj na troman andal o kher,“ čudaľinel pes o bačis. E daj chudľa te rovel.

„Kaj les ile, kaj, Ďulo?“ u o vasta thoďa pro calo muj.

„Na džanav mištes, aľe hoj andro bučakero taboris. Dža khere u ma dža ňikhaj dureder te phučkerel, te tut nane mek bareder pharipen. So te lenas the tut,“ phenel lake o bačis o Ďulas.

Aviľa pal lende e baba, sar le Ďulastar šunďa, so pes ačhiľa. „Nadur bučakero taboris hino kadaj ko Perješis andre Hanušovca. Kampol lenge so nekbuter muršen pre buči pro štacijonos the pro prehradi. Phenelas mange o rašaj u jov džanel savoro.“

„E Aušvica dureder, na?“ phučľas e daj la babatar.

„Andre Polčiko, ta šaj avel o Gabos kadaj ke amende, modľinaha pes vaš leske, u pačaha, hoj amenge avela pale khere,“ phenďa e baba u andro jakha lake demade o apsa.

E DAJ

Has man zor te ľikerel avri the užarel, bo pačavas, hoj mange o Gabos avela pale, hoj savore dživaha jekhetane sar anglal kaja bibacht. Sig tosara le čhajorenca phirahas andro veš pro kašta, bo o jevend mek sikhavelas peskeri zor u o kašta amen imar na has. Na džanavas pal leste ňič, ňiko le muršendar andal o veš tiš ňič na džanelas. Sako čiros mange o jakha dikhenas pro drom, so džal ke amende khere, či o rom na avel pale. Amari Karačoňa has čorikaňi sar akor has savoro, aľe mek upreder igen dukhaďi, savore duminahas, hoj amenca nane.

Bari bibacht has, sar jevende o Ňemci savore muršen, romňijen the le čhaven andal o gav cirdle andro veš, te keren o kašta pro zakopi. O Ňemci terďuvenas le puškenca andro vasta, gravčinenas u prosto pre amende ľikerenas o samopaľa. O Roma igen daranas. Igen daravas, hoj amen viľinena, o roviben has te šunel pre savore seri. Paľis eftato ďives amenge phende, hoj imar andro veš na kampol te phirel. O murša imar šaj chudle te chanel o zakopi. E phuv has faďimen, labarenas upre o kašta, hoj te avel kovleder.

Phirahas pal e buči, sar pes ča delas. Vaš o čino aro, gruľi the žiros kerahas maj calo ďives.

Geľom pal e omša ke daj. „Vakerel pes, hoj o partizana le Rusenca traden pašeder u pašeder," phenel maškar o vakeriben o phral o Ďulas.

„Le Ňemcen imar nane kavka te dikhel pašal amende u varesave džan het, phenelas o rašaj," andre duma pes thoďa the e phuri. Pal o baro čiros mange has pro jilo čeporo feder, imar pačavas, hoj o Gabos avela pale, aľe avka daranďiľom, ča te oda hin čačipen.

„Dajori, daje!" chučiľa jekh ďives e Olga andre kuchňa, hoj paš o gadže šunďa, hoj andre Hanušovca aviľa rusiko jednotka streleckeho sboru.

„Hanušovcate?! Odoj bi šaj elas amaro dad!" vičinďa lošaľi e Margitka.

24. januariste o Sovjeti tradle het le Ňemcen khatar e Matisovo.

Kerahas le čhajorenca o kašta, sar pre amende pašal o kerestocis vareko vičinel: „Čhajale, mire čhajale!“

Aviľa! O pindre man na šunenas u rovav.

„Dado, dadoro, dado!“ o čhajora chudle ke leste te denašel the obchudle les. Paľikerav le Devleske, hoj amen šunďa u sam e fameľija pale jekhetane.

„Imar mištes, hoj som tumenca,“ phenel miro pro kokal šuko rom u kikidel man le vastenca. Rovas lošatar.

„Salas Hanušovcate, dado?“ phučel e Margitka.

„Hat, Margitko, aľe cale jileha somas tumenca khere.“

Anďam le Gaboske so nekbuter chaben, aľe jov našťi chalas, ča polokes the čineder chabenoro, bo imar čirla ajci chaben na chaľa. Vakerelas amenge, sar les chudle o Ňemci, sar avelas pašal o partizana, sar ľidžalas le Sergejis. Na pačanas leske, hoj pes halasinďa la romňaha u geľa avri rači andro veš. Ľigende les andre Hanušovca u but na kampolas, hoj the les bičhavenas sar savoren anglal leste andre Aušvica.

„Vareko avel ke amende le motoriha,“ dikhľa e Olga.

„Kadaj ke amende?“ čudaľinav man. Mro rom o Gabo sovel, mek kidel upre e zor.

„O slugadža, aľe na ňemcika, hin len aver gada,“ phenel paľis e Olga, so dikhel dureder pro drom.

O motoris ačhol paš amaro vudar the avri chučkeren vikaha o rusika slugadža. „Zdrastvujte, Gabo, mamo!“

„Sergej, oda tu?“ čudaľinav man.

„Da, eto ja, Sergej Vladymyryč Gorkij, sto sjedmyj strelkovyj bataľjon Gordejeva, my Ganušovice i Matysova asvabadili,“ u čhinďa le vasteha.

„Gabo, anďam tuke chaben predal e fameľija,“ prethoďom, so vakerel, u o slugadža andre pitvora hordinenas o gone le areha the le gruľenca, o konzervi the aver chabena, so o Ňemci ile le gazdenge predal peste.

Ta akana amen imar užarel ča e bacht.

Kada vakeriben irinďom mire
dadeske the la dake la Margitake
the le Gabrieliske Duždovenge,
save predžiďile o dujto baro
mariben u aver miľijoni manuša
čore mule.

MY DEARS

BY EVA DANIŠOVÁ

People used to call my grandfather Barovčák. My grandmother usually called him "a beggar and a whoremonger." They both had a very hard life, like every other Rom. One day this, another day that. I loved my grandpa very much, since he and my grandma raised me together.

He wasn't living at home with us when I was born, since he had stayed in Opava. That was where he and my grandmother lived, but the two of them had a terrible fight and she ran away from him. She simply got on a train and rode it to Česká Třebová. My mom was already pregnant by then and went with her. Then I was born and they took care of me together. When my grandfather found out where we were, he came after us. I was about two months old at the time.

My grandmother told me the whole story. One evening my grandfather appeared out of nowhere, knocking on the window and shouting: "Haňa, it's me, Janoš, are you there?" Then suddenly he heard a child crying and thought: What is this? My grandmother let him in, but wouldn't talk to him. She was mad because he had stolen money from her back in Opava, which to her was as bad as killing her, because she was a clever homemaker and knew how to stretch one crown into ten. The poor thing saved all that money and never got to enjoy it. She just loved counting it over and over again. She kept it hidden away, and whenever my uncle, my mom's brother, needed money, my grandmother was more than happy to give it to him. She loved my uncle more than anything else in the world; she would have laid down her life for him. She didn't have any other children, just my mom and my uncle.

So my grandpa walked into the house and asked: "What's going on, Haňa? Whose child is that?" My grandmother still wouldn't talk. My grandfather thought that I was hers, that she had had a child with another man. He didn't know my mom was expecting. My grandma was still young back then, thirty-eight or so. My grandpa didn't know what to do next. He was furious. He started swearing like mad. Then he got up and walked toward her like he was going to beat her. "May every illness on earth devour you," he said, pronouncing a curse on her. "You ran away from me, now you've got a child with another man, I'll kill you! Tell me who it's with, so I can kill him too!"

My grandma was tiny compared to my grandpa, just a thimble of a thing, but she stood her ground. She laughed, but she knew it was no time for jokes, given what a hothead my grandfather was. So she said: "Don't be silly, Barovčák. This is our little girl Julie's daughter. Evie, we call her."

My grandpa got even more enraged, since he hadn't realized my mom was pregnant. "So where is our little Julie if this is her child?" he said. "How come she isn't here with her? You can both go to the devil!" My grandma didn't know what to say, since my mom had gone to a dance. "She'll be right back," she told him.

So the two of them sat together waiting for my mom. Unfortunately, it took so long, my grandpa didn't believe my grandma anymore. He started back in with her again, calling her names and cussing her out. In his eyes, my mom wouldn't have left me there like that. She wasn't worried about me, though, since I had been more my grandmother's than hers ever since I was born. She told me that when she was pregnant, my grandma bought her sweets and desserts, and she would always explain: "It's not for you, it's for little Evie in your belly." From the moment my mom got pregnant, my grandma knew it was going to be a baby girl named Eva. She had never really liked my mother much, since my mom was too much like my grandpa.

My grandpa paced back and forth, swearing and cursing the two of them; he still had no idea what the story really was with the little girl. He was worried about my grandma, because he loved her. He was jealous of her being with other men, but meanwhile he never saw a skirt he didn't chase. He had three wives in his life. One before my grandma, then my grandma, and then another one later on, after my grandma stopped living with him. His last wife was a young woman, and by then he was advanced in age, but he still had a child with her. In short, my grandpa was a man about town, and not only that but really handsome, he had an actor's looks. He knew how to read and write, which in those days was unheard of among Roma. Everyone loved my grandpa, only my grandma couldn't stand the sight of him. Whenever she talked about him, she would curse him up and down. Sometimes just for show, but sometimes she was deathly serious.

My grandpa and grandma started to argue again. She even got a few slaps. My dear sweet grandmother just sat and sobbed. She didn't know what else to say to make my grandfather understand. I was still a baby, so she didn't want any shouting. So the two of them went on arguing until my mom came home.

The moment she walked in the door, my grandpa asked her how she could have a child without telling him, and peppered her with questions. My mom explained the whole thing. She was afraid of him, since he had gotten in a fight with my father's family back in Opava. He didn't want my mom to live with my father. She begged him not to be angry with her: "I was afraid of you, Dad, because you didn't like him. I was afraid you would throw me out of the house, that's why I didn't tell you. But now I've got a little girl, just look how pretty she is, look at what a beautiful girl she's growing up to be." When my grandpa heard this, he burst into tears, picked me up in his arms, kissed me all over, and fell in love with me on the spot.

The way it worked out in the end, I stayed with my grandma and grandpa. My mom didn't live with us anymore after that.

I don't know which of them loved me more, my grandma or my grandpa, since as far as both of them were concerned, I could do no wrong. They never said a single hurtful word to me. They gave me so much love I still draw on it today. A lot of time has passed. Both of my beloved grandparents are with God now, but they live on in my heart, and every day they give me strength. When I close my eyes, I hear my grandpa playing the fiddle, I see him sawing wood, having a laugh, I hear him talking.

THE TIME MY GRANDPA TERRIFIED ME

As a little girl, I grew up with my grandmother and grandfather. They took really good care of me. They loved me with all their hearts and fulfilled my every wish even before I opened my mouth. There were times it was pretty comical, since the two of them hardly had an idyllic relationship—they argued constantly. My grandpa was on a disability pension and also had an income from the anti-fascist resistance, since he fought with the partisans during the war. On top of that, he went around the neighboring villages, buying domestic animal skins. With all the time he spent around people, he knew who raised what animals, who needed what, and whenever someone wanted, say, a stud for their rabbits or cow, or needed to sell a goat or horses or what have you, he would act as middleman. Thanks to that he never had to get a job. My grandmother felt taken advantage of, since she worked hard on construction sites and my grandfather, in her opinion, was just slacking off. It made her angry that whenever he had money, he just squandered it, since, unlike him, she kept track of every crown.

It often happened when my grandpa was broke that my grandma would refuse to give him money for tobacco. Also, she would criticize him for eating too much, and do all sorts of things to get even with him. For instance, she would go into town and buy me a chocolate bábovka. Then she would wait till my grandpa was home, sit me down at the table, cut the bábovka, and urge me to take a slice. I was still too young to understand, so I just sat there, stuffing my face with cake. I had no idea that, just before that, my grandma had cursed my grandpa that if he took a piece of the bábovka, his hand would fall off. My grandpa just smiled, and when he had money, he went

into town and bought me something my grandma liked, and the situation would repeat. They settled their scores through me, though I didn't realize it at the time. For me those days were like a holiday, since we never had very many treats at home.

But their disputes fell to the wayside as far as I was concerned. They stuck together when it came to me. I loved them both the same, but in my eyes my grandpa was more progressive, more educated, so I enjoyed spending time with him. Thanks to him, we had all sorts of modern conveniences at home, like a gramophone and fairy tales on black vinyl records, and a little lamp with pictures that spun in a circle when it lit up. It wouldn't have made it through the door if it had been up to my grandma. She was much more traditional. She liked telling stories in the dark and told all sorts of hair-raising tales. She was good at drawing listeners in with her performance. I also witnessed more than once that she knew what was going to happen before it took place.

What she liked most was to start telling scary stories at dusk, just as night began to fall. Once, when I was seven or eight, she called me into her room. She was lying in bed and tucked me in nice and cozy beside her. I don't remember if I did something wrong that day, but my grandma told me a story about what happens to children who don't do what they're told. She said she saw a man who snatched up little rascals in a sack and took them away. She described what he looked like—he carried a big sack with an axe over his shoulder and at first sight you could tell he was bad.

I lay next to my grandma in terror. The whole atmosphere was heightened by the autumn twilight and I was on the verge of tears. I could hear my grandma's words in my head, warning me not to be naughty or that bad man would take me away. Just then, I heard a noise from the kitchen and a man who looked just like my grandmother had described appeared in the doorway. My grandfather had been in the kitchen, listening the whole time. He wanted to join in the performance, so he put a slice of potato in his mouth with a space carved out like a gap between his teeth, and sprinkled his face with flour, put the string bag from the potatoes on his head, dressed in a long winter coat, picked up an axe, and stepped into the room.

I think my grandma was as startled as I was. But I was so frightened I had a hysterical fit. They couldn't calm me down and had to call the doctor. When the doctor came, he gave me a shot and I fell fast asleep. My grandma argued about it with my grandpa for a really long time. And for a while after that, she told me nothing but nice fairy tales. But once I got a little older, I couldn't avoid her stories about dead people and scary ghosts.

THE LITTLE GIRL WITH THE SNOTTY NOSE

When I was little, my grandmother worked for a construction company that built paneláks in cities. She was in charge of rough cleanup after the construction workers finished a building, washing the windows, the doorframes, the floors and the stairs. She worked herself to the bone, poor thing.

When I was about to enter first grade, my grandma had a job in the next town over. That meant she couldn't go to the school with me at eight a.m., so she said to me: "Evie, you're a big girl now. Tomorrow morning I'll take you to school early. Just wait outside till it opens, then go in and ask where your classroom is, all right?"

It was still dark when my grandma woke me in the morning. It was only five a.m. But she had to catch the train to work, what else could she do? She dressed me in red overalls with buttons on the shoulders and pockets in front. They were really nice. Instead of a blouse underneath, I wore a boy's flannel shirt. My grandma gushed lovingly: "Look how gorgeous you are, my precious little thing!" To her I was just as beautiful as all the other Czech girls. We were poor, so I wore hand-me-downs and almost never got anything new. Plus my grandmother had a quirky way of dressing me. She was in such a rush, she just had me put on whatever came to hand. She couldn't have cared less whether or not my clothes matched, just as long as I wasn't cold and had something on my head. A beret or a scarf, it made no difference.

Once I was ready, she slipped a piece of bread spread with lard in my pocket, set me down on the steps in front of the school, said goodbye, and hurried off to the train. In the morning it was chilly, so after ten minutes or so, my nose started to run. I didn't have a handkerchief, so I had to wipe my nose on my sleeve.

As I sat on the steps, alone in the dark and the cold, I broke down sobbing. So my nose started to run even more. Soon I had a potato instead of a nose. I sat there in a heap of misery.

The other children stared at me in bewilderment as they started walking into school with their parents. A girl in overalls with snot running out her nose. Some of the moms knew who I was, since I had gone to nursery school with their children, so they brought me inside with them. They told me where I should go, and that made me feel much better.

Then they called us all into the gym, for a welcome speech by the comrade principal. There we found out what we were going to need for school and what our parents should buy us.

I was still little, but I knew perfectly well my grandma could never buy me all those things. It made me feel sorry for myself. Surrounded by parents showing off their dressed-up children, I looked like the poorest little snot-nosed orphan you ever saw. The whole thing made me break down in tears all over again.

Just then, noticing someone tall standing next to me, I lifted my gaze and saw my grandpa. He gave me a wink and I knew everything would be all right. My grandfather took me by the hand and squeezed it tight. By then he was no longer living with us, but he had made a point of coming to see me, so as not to miss my special day.

After school, he walked into town with me and bought me everything I needed. Not only that, but he also got me white knee socks and a skirt. At long last I looked like all the other girls. So that was my first big day at school. I still remember when my grandma saw what my grandpa got for me, she bought me plimsolls to go with the skirt so there could be no question about her fashion sense.

THE PACKAGES

My grandmother was a very hardworking woman. Early in the morning each day, she left the house with a cart to make the rounds of her turf, then returned home around noon to hastily cook a quick meal, and set out again in the afternoon. For lunch she usually made do with boiled potatoes and fried onions, or some sort of unidentifiable soup thickened with flour and milk. She would regularly return home with a fully loaded cart.

The people in town knew her, so whenever someone had old things they needed to get rid of, they would turn to my grandma, who was grateful to accept them. To them it may have been useless old junk, but to her it was treasure she could turn into precious coins. I often heard her say: "Today I'm going to see a fancy lady who's going to give me some clothes." Other times it was toys or bedding, for instance.

My grandma's biggest entrepreneurial harvests came just before Christmas and Easter. She had no need for any of those things, but she knew just what to do with them. She built a business on cleaning out households. Women gave her things washed and ironed, and my grandma just gave them a quick once-over and packed them in a box. Then it was my turn. Since she was illiterate, she entrusted me with the task of writing letters with great ceremoniousness.

"Evie, come here. We're going to write a letter to Helena in Slovakia." But she didn't say it to me in gadjo language; she didn't know Czech that well. She spoke to me in Romani. In her eyes, I was as good as a university graduate, since I knew how to write.

I think she was already counting the crowns even as she dictated the letters to me. So I would sit down and write what my grandmother dictated:

Dear Helena,
It's me, Haňa, writing to you. I'm sending you a package. Sell this green skirt for 5 crowns, the black sweater for 10 crowns, and the bedding for 25 crowns. I'm sending you beautiful things, so do me a favor and sell them and send me 320 Kčs for the whole package. Say hello to my brother for me and send me the money by the fifteenth of this month.

This brief letter, intended to make my grandma money, was then inserted into the package, which my grandma wrapped and tied with a glint in her eye. With every package she sent, her joy increased. There were times when we sent as many as five a month. In short, my grandmother was every inch an entrepreneur. She even bought me a special marker for writing addresses and, later, a booklet of postal codes, which I still have. I remember the postal code for our settlement in Slovakia to this day.

When it came to the fancier things, my grandma would pick them out and send them to my aunt. She dutifully saved the money she earned from the packages, and as soon as she decided she had enough, she would send a telephone-call notice to my uncle and aunt, so she could proudly transfer the money to them. In those days, a telephone-call notice was the ultimate in communication. My grandma would go to the post office and order a call with my aunt in Slovakia, or her son or daughter-in-law, who lived in Bruntál. Then they would get a telegram saying what time they were supposed to be at the post office. The operator would instruct them to step into the booth and connect the call.

On days when she had a telephone call, my grandmother would begin to prepare for it in the morning. Over and over, she would repeat to herself what she was going to say, to make sure she wouldn't forget. A telephone call was a miracle of technology for her, and she would happily wait for a call three or four hours. She didn't pay much attention to the time written down, so we usually spent the whole afternoon at the post office.

I don't think she really trusted the connection, since she always shouted so loudly into the phone that they probably could have heard her even without it. The women working at the post office would warn the other customers in advance that "the lady is going to use the telephone," and direct them to the counters farthest away, since the soundproofing on the call booths was too weak to block my grandma's voice.

You couldn't see her, but you sure could hear her. Beware if she wasn't satisfied with someone! Then the booth would really shake, and the people in the post office would be treated to one of her monologues, since she wouldn't let the other person get a word in edgewise. I suppose she thought, I'm paying for it, I'm going to get my money's worth!

Most of her calls were about selling the things in the packages. The moment that anyone failed to pay on time, my grandma would order a call. Eavesdropping from outside the booth, anyone who didn't know the dialect would have been baffled: "Listen here. I'm sending my brother a sweater and you a black skirt. Sell all the rest of it and send me the money. I'll wait till the fifteenth." It wasn't so much the words she used as the way she said them: the rhythm and accents sounded all wrong—less Slovak than a mix of Polish and Rusyn.

One time I was on the other end of a call, with my aunt in Bruntál. My grandma wanted to talk to her on the phone and I happened to be spending my holiday with her. I thought, since my aunt was young, we wouldn't spend the whole afternoon at the post office. I was wrong. My aunt, knowing what my grandma was like, wanted to be at the post office on time. So right after lunch, we went and once again waited outside the booth for my grandmother's call.

On a recent visit to my aunt's, she and I were reminiscing about the telephone-call notices and sending the packages, and feeling sorry my grandma was no longer with us. I'm sure if she were alive today, she would be conducting business on the internet!

ZAJDA

My grandma often hauled things around in a canvas sheet on her back. If the canvas, which was just whatever she happened to lay her hands on, was strong and colorful, then we called it a zajda.

We used to go on visits to my uncle's, and we never made the trip without a zajda. Whatever my grandmother found or got from someone, she would save to give to my uncle's family. Before we left, she spread the zajda out on the ground, loaded everything in, tied the two opposite ends firmly together, and it was ready to go. Then she would walk around the bundle with reverential respect.

The bigger the zajda, the happier my grandma was. The only thing she used a bag for was her keys. She had a light, nylon bag that she would put them in, then tie the ears of the bag in a knot. She carried her money tied into a corner of the tarp. She would swing it up on her back, pull two of the corners over her shoulders, hold them tightly against her chest, and then we could head out. When my grandmother boarded the train with that enormous zajda on her back and the other passengers saw it, they cleared right out of her way.

Even I was often surprised at how much she fit in there. I remember the look of mischievous glee on my grandmother's face when she told my aunt, her daughter-in-law, to untie the zajda and take out the polka-dot dress she had brought for her. The moment my aunt caught sight of the fabric, she could hardly wait. She had always wanted a dress like that. As she pulled it out, bit by bit, a rubber snake fell out that looked like it was alive. My aunt was in total shock and my grandma roared with laughter. "Don't worry, it's just a toy," she said, reassuring my aunt, but my aunt refused to come anywhere near the bundle again after that.

So my grandma walked up to the zajda and one by one she pulled out all the things that she had brought. "This is for Jozífek, this is for Bango, this is for Buchta." My aunt had eight children, so it took my grandma a lot of work to find something for everyone. Most of the things she got from people in our town, sometimes she found things by the garbage bins, and then again sometimes she bartered with the Russian officers' wives. After clothing came groceries. My grandmother brought my uncle canned food from the Russian army depots: delicious ham, sardines, pork and beef, pasta, sugar and similar delicacies. Once she was all done, she ceremoniously folded up the canvas and put it away in the bag with her keys. She carried it with her everywhere. While running errands around town, she often stumbled across things that could come in handy for someone in the family, and at times like those the zajda came in handy.

One time she even carried me in it to the emergency room. I was eight at the time and apparently I had a fever. We never had a thermometer at home, but my grandma decided it was serious, so she spread the zajda out on the bed, put a pillow on it, laid me on the pillow, wrapped me up, and swung me onto her back. We lived just under fifteen minutes away from the health center, but still it was an incredible feat on her part.

One time when my grandma came with the zajda to see me in the hospital, the other patients thought she was bringing me a TV. I had jaundice and I was in the infectious disease ward with a strict diet. The only part of the delivery they allowed me was a sack of tangerines, and my poor grandma had to drag the whole bundle back home.

FASHION BOOTS

My grandmother may have been small in stature, but people went scurrying when she began to shout. When it comes to Roma, I'm convinced intonation expresses much more than words. When my grandma let loose with her "Yi! Yooi! Aiee! Yoy!" I knew just what she meant. She didn't have to add another word.

Everyone on our street was well acquainted with her vocal repertoire. My grandma never hid her emotions, she wouldn't hesitate to walk around town cursing out whatever made her mad at the moment. So there were times when she would walk home singing beautifully, and other times she just swore under her breath. Sometimes she would curse, stopping passersby and loudly complaining to them in a mishmash of Czech and Slovak: "Listen here, ma'am, I go to work, I take care of my girl, my beggar of a husband gives me no money at all, and when I want them to get our little Evie into preschool, they say they don't have time. It's nothin but Jarmilka here, Jaruška there, but I gave them a piece of my mind! 'Yi, you don't have time?! All right then, call in your manager, I'll tell him how you sit around here drinking coffee, painting your pretty little nails, and for a worked-to-death old woman like me, you don't have time?!' You should've seen how busy she got then, the little Barbie doll, she was all, 'Yes, ma'am, I'll call the preschool first thing in the morning and make sure your girl has a place!'"

My grandma didn't bother waiting for a reaction and continued on her way home. In the next street over, the passersby could still hear her feisty shouts: "I'll show you, you don't have time! Me, worked-to-death old woman and you, yi, a Barbie doll! You think you can throw me out of here?"

By the time she got home, she realized she had actually won, and little by little her raging changed to a gentle crooning. In the end, she walked in the door with an ear-to-ear smile, humming her favorite song, "Na tarki, na tarki, s košarikom na tarki," about picking berries, dancing, and shaking off the troubles of life. Then at the end of the song, she summed up the whole incident with the words, "I'll show her!"

All of the town officials considered my grandma half deranged. She didn't know how to read or write, and when they spoke to her using formal, official Czech, she didn't understand. This often led to miscommunications. My grandmother didn't know how to react, and when she asked, "What you are saying?" the officials didn't know how to respond.

I remember at one point the National Committee—the local government body under the Communists—was giving subsidies to help retired people pay for winter footwear. My grandma was retired by then, so a neighbor told her about it. On important occasions, whenever she needed to visit a government office or some place like that, out came the lice comb. My grandma lit the stove, sat down on the chair beside it, and untwisted her long thin braids, interwoven with colorful lace. Then she took the lice comb and proceeded to brush out her hair with it, even though we never had lice at home. It was a habit of hers when she was worried or anxious, before an important meeting, or sometimes just so she wouldn't forget the ritual. She sat for a while humming a tune to herself, then in a loud voice she delivered the speech she had prepared for the official at the National Committee: "Well, I came for shoe money, seein as I've got nothing to walk in. You gave some to my neighbor, so I want some too." And she also had a response ready, just in case: "Yi, if they don't give me the money, I'll smash that office to pieces!"

The next day my grandma set out for the office. The woman at the National Committee said she was eligible for a subsidy, and told her to buy some shoes and bring in the receipt. My grandmother was satisfied, but since she was also stingy, she tried to figure out a way not to buy the shoes and still get the subsidy. "What do I need new shoes for? These loafers I have are still fine."

Hearing my grandma say that, I seized the opportunity. I was maybe eleven at the time, and I had seen some lovely fashion boots in the shop. They were light and thin, with laces and a low heel. They weren't meant for kids, obviously, but I really wanted them. I begged my grandma to buy them for me, since she didn't need any shoes. At first she said nothing, but then I think she realized it wasn't a bad idea for her to save on shoes for me, which she would have to buy anyway. So we set out for the store.

Inside, my grandmother headed straight for the shelf with the tuleňky: felt winter boots, with fur trim and a rubber sole. Of course she grabbed a pair that was at least two sizes too big for me, so they would last me a long time. "Ai-yi, Evie, these'll keep you warm!"

I immediately started sobbing that I didn't want those, I wanted the fashion boots in the window. I wouldn't try on the tuleňky and said it was mean of my grandma not to buy me the other boots. I paid no attention to her arguments that those boots were for grown-ups, they were flimsy, I would slip and fall in them and I'd be freezing cold. I just stared accusingly at her with weepy eyes.

My grandma gave up and went to ask how much they cost. She came back in a state of shock. The tuleňky were 160 crowns and the fashion boots 699: the most expensive pair of shoes in the store. It was the price of a luxury automobile from my grandma's point of view. She had never bought anything so expensive, and she only bought the most basic, cheapest things for me. She had never spent such a large sum in her life. The poor thing just stood there shaking her head in disbelief. Finally it dawned on her that the National Committee was paying for the shoes anyway, and we ceremoniously carried the boots home.

My grandma carefully tucked away the receipt and I put on the boots and walked around the room. After a few minutes, I asked if I could go out sledding. In my new fashion boots, naturally. My grandma didn't much like the idea, but finally she gave in, and I marched proudly through town, pulling my sled behind me. The boots were slippery, just as my grandma had warned, but boy, was I cool!

I had sledded down the hill a few times, when suddenly I noticed red grooves in the snow from where I'd braked. I looked down at my beautiful new boots and started to howl in dismay like my grandma. The black had completely peeled off the back and there were red scrapes showing through underneath. The boots were completely ruined and all I could do was cry. I shuffled home dejected, hid the boots in a corner of the hallway where my grandma wouldn't see them, and whimpered to myself in secret all evening long.

Little did I know what would happen the next day. My grandma took the receipt that showed what she had paid and went to submit it to the office. The lady from the National Committee was very nice. She handed my grandma back a slip to give the cashier, entitling her to a subsidy of 200 crowns.

Naturally, my grandma started to argue with the lady. "So first you tell me you'll pay for shoes, and now you give me two hundred crowns?"

"But we told you it was just a subsidy!"

"I know, but I paid 699 crowns for a pair of boots, what am I supposed to do now?"

"Well, there's nothing we can do. That's all that we can give you."

"Yi! I paid all that money, and I'm just a poor old woman! Yoy, what am I going to do?"

My grandma walked out of the office moaning and groaning. She continued to complain at home, rehashing the whole thing in detail. Then she disappeared into the hallway and came back holding my boots. Seeing the damage I'd done to them in just a single day, her howling turned relentless.

After a few days of me slipping and sliding, freezing in my scraped-up, ruined boots, my grandma went to buy me the tuleňky I had so detested, two sizes too big, of course. The fashion boots hung around our hallway for a while, until finally my grandma tossed them in the stove with a befitting curse.

MIRE KEDVEŠNE

EVA DANIŠOVÁ

Mire papus vičinenas Barovčak. E baba les nekbuter vičinelas „kuduš the kurevňikos“. Has len pharo dživipen, avka sar savore Romen. Jekhvar kajso, jekhvar ajso. Kamav te phenel, hoj le papus igen kamavas, bo man la babaha ľikerde avri.

Sar uľiľom, ta na has o papus khere, bo ačhiľa andre Opava. Bešenas odoj, aľe miri baba lestar denašľa het. But pen dujdžene halasinde, joj bešľa pre mašina the avľa andro foros Česká Třebová. Miri daj has manca imar phari, the tiš laha gejľa. Paľis uľiľom u ľikerenas man jon dujdžeňa. O papus pes dodžanľa, kaj hine, ta avľa pal e baba. Mange akor has vaj duj čhon.

E baba mange kada sa vakerelas. Jekhvar raťi o papus avľa, durkinelas pre blaka, vičinelas: „Haňo, sal adaj, oda me, o Janoš!“ Akana šunel te rovel cikne čhavores, phenelas peske: Ta so oda?! E baba les mukhľa andre, aľe duma leha na delas. Has pre leste but rušľi, bo akor Opavate lake o papus čorďa varesave love, oda sar te la murdarďahas, bo joj has bari gazdiňa, džanelas ňisostar te kerel love. Čori, šoha ňigda pal ole lovore na chaľa, ča len ginelas upre, garuvelas the sar kampelas mire bačiske, mira dakere phraleske, ta ľidžalas leske. E baba ňikas pro svetos na kamelas avka sar les. O dživipen vaš leske delas. Na has la buter čhave, ča miri daj th'o bačis.

Ta o papus avľa andre the phučel latar: „Ta so, Haňo, kaskero čhavoro?“ E baba duma na delas. O papus duminelas, hoj som lakeri. Hoj hin la avre muršeha čhavoro. Na džanelas, hoj miri daj has manca phari. Akor mek e baba na has but phuri, has lake vaj trandatheochto berš. O papus imar na džanelas, so te kerel. Kajsi choľi chalas. Chudľa lake te rakinel. Ušťiľa upre, hoj la marela, chudľa la te koškerel: „Ta tu lubňije, sukrovica the morovica tuke te marel pro nakh, mandar denašľal, avre muršeha tut presuťal, akana hin tut kadaj cikno čhavoro, imar me tut murdarav! Phen, kastar hin tut kada čhavoro, džav, murdarav the les!“

Miri baba has cikňori, ajso štumprľikos, aľe na delas pes leske. Asalas tel o nakh, aľe imar daralas lestar, bo miro papus has baro beng, sar chalas choľi. Ta e baba leske phenel: „Barovčakona, ta so diliňaľos avri, sem oda la Julkakeri čhajori. Vičinas la Evička.“

O papus mek buter chudľa te rušel, bo na džanelas, hoj miri daj phari. Phenel la babake: „U kaj e Julka, te oda lakeri čhajori? Sar oda, hoj nane paš late? O benga tumen mi len, so tumen dujdžeňa pratinen!“ E baba na džanelas, so leske te phenel, bo miri daj gejľa akor pre zabava. „Maj avela,“ phenďa leske.

Ta užarenas so dujdžene mira da. Kampľa či na kampľa, miri daj na avelas pale. O papus imar la babake na paťalas. Pale pes laha halasinelas, košelas, rakinelas lake. Phenelas peske, hoj miri daj man kavka na mukhľahas. E daj pal mande na daralas, bo imar ciknorestar man e baba vaš ňič pro svetos na delas. Sar has e daj phari, ta lake e baba cinelas cukrici, torti the phenelas lake: „Oda na cinav tuke, aľe la čhajorake andro per.“ La da e baba but na kamelas, bo has čhiďi pro papus. Čačes, joj imar džanelas, hoj me oda avava. Imar andro per man vičinelas Evička.

O papus phirelas upre tele pal o kher, koškerelas so dujdžeňen, la baba the mira da, bo na džanelas, kaj hin o čačipen. Daralas pal e baba, bo la kamelas. Thovavlas la avre muršenca, aľe les korkores has ajci lubňa, kaj zijand te vakerel. Has les trin romňija. Jekh mek anglal e baba, paľis mek aver, sar leha e baba imar na dživelas. Pro phuripen mek dživelas terňa džuvľijaha the čhavoro les laha has. Miro papus has baro špekulantos, aľe šukar murš, sar hercos. Džanelas te genel the te irinel, oda has akor maškar o Roma baro čudos. Sako les rado dikhelas, ča miri baba na! Sar pal leste vakerelas, ta les ča košelas. Varekana kamukeri, varekana čačes.

O papus pes chudľa pale la babaha te halasinel, the lake pekľa vaj trin pal o muj, pal o šero. Miri somnakuňi baba čori ča bešelas the rovelas. Imar na džanelas, so leske te phenel. Na kamelas vika andro kher, bo somas cikňori. Kavka pen odoj halasinenas, kim na avľa miri daj.

Sar avľa andro kher, ta o papus latar phučelas, sar oda, hoj hin la čhavoro, soske leske na phenďa, kada the koda. E daj leske sa phenďa. Tiš lestar daralas, bo o papus pes Opavate marďa le Romenca, ola fameľijatar, khatar has miro dad. Na kamelas, hoj miri daj leha te dživel. E daj les mangelas, te pre late na rušel: „Dado, me tutar daravas, bo na kamehas les, daravas, hoj man čhiveha andal o kher avri, ta našťi tuke phenďom. Akana imar man hin čhajori, ta av, dikh pre late, savi šukar, sar amenge barol.“

Sar kada o papus šunďa, chudľa te rovel, iľa man pro vasta, čumidelas man, minďar man kamelas.

Paľis avka dopejľa, hoj ačhiľom paš lende the e daj amenca imar na has.

Na džanav, ko lendar duje dženendar man buter kamelas, či e baba abo o papus, bo so dujdžene manca kerenas baro baripen. Šoha ňigda mange na phende jekh nalačho lavoro, avka man kamenas, hoj mek akana som olestar džiďi. Pregejľa imar but paňi, sar dživav, jon imar so duj, čore, mule, aľe andre miro jilo dživen the den man zor. Te phandav o jakha, šunav le papus, sar bašavel pre lavuta, dikhav les, sar kerel o kašta, sar kerel o pherasa, šunav les duma te del.

SAR DARANĎIĽOM LE PAPUSTAR

Sar cikňi čhajori dživavas paš e baba the o papus. Igen mištes pal mande bajinenas. Moneki man kamenas the kerenas perdal mande savoro, so džanenas. Varekana oda has the pherasuno, bo e baba le papuha na dživelas mištes, halasinenas pen dujdžene. Le papus has invalidno duchodos the mek chudelas o love vaš oda, hoj andro mariben has paš o partizana. O papus mek phirelas pal o gava the cinkerelas le manušendar avri o cipa pal o džvirini. Has maškar o manuša the tiš phenelas le manušenge, kas hin save džvirini, te vareko kamelas te cinel či gurumňa, grajes, abo aver džviros, the te len kamenas te primukhel paš pende. Na kampelas leske te phirel andre buťi. E baba zorales kerelas paš o pozemne stavbi u rakinelas leske, hoj ňič na kerel, ča phirel upre tele. Sar o papus dživelas, na has la babake pre dzeka, bo sar les has love, ta has baro raj, no e baba has pro love sar beng, kim diňa jekh koruna, ta duj ďives pal oda duminelas.

Ačhelas pes, sar le papus na has o love, ta les na kamelas te del pro duhanos, varekana les košelas the vaš o chaben the kerelas leske pre choľi. Narokom džalas andro foros the cinelas mange calo čokoladovo bokeľi.

Paľis užarelas, sar avela o papus khere, the thovelas man te bešel paš leste the čhurelas mange e bokeľi, nukinelas man te chav. Mange pre goďi na avelas ňič, bešavas, chavas, bo na džanavas, hoj e baba le papus košľa, te leske kirňol o vast, te chala. O papus ča asalas, the sar les has love, ta džalas andro foros jov the cinďa mange oda, so e baba rado chalas. Me na džanavas, hoj pen halasinen, na achaľuvavas oleske. Perdal mande oda has baro ďives, bo na has amen sako ďives ajse lačhe chabena.

Sar kampelas vareso mange, ta akor pen šoha na halasinenas, bisterde pre savoro nalačho. So dujdženen igen kamavas, aľe o papus has perdal mande ajso moderno, džanelas te genel the somas leha rado. Jov anelas khere nevipena. Či oda has gramofonos the o kale vinilova platňi, kaj has o paramisa, či ajsi lampica ciknore čitrenca, so bonďaľolas sar labolas. Ada bi e baba šoha andro kher na kamelas. Pre aver sera e baba has tradično. Joj chudelas te del duma, sar has avri šišitno, vakerelas o paramisa, daravelas amen the ajse veci. Sar delas duma, ta manuš latar daralas, bo has igen sugestivno. Tiš me buterval dikhľom, hoj džanelas, so pes ačhela, imar anglal.

Nekbuter ajse dumi delas e baba, sar avelas e rat. Jekhvar, sar mange has efta, abo ochto berš, man e baba vičinďa kija peste. Pašľolas pro haďos, thoďa man šukares paš peste. Imar na leperav, či vareso kerďom, aľe e baba mange vakerelas pal oda, so hin le čhavorenca, so khere na šunen. Phenelas, hoj dikhľa ajse muršes, savo ajse čhavoren kidel andro gono, the ľidžal len het. Chudľa te vakerel, sar dičhol avri, hoj les hin baro gono, pro phiko les hin tover, the sar les manuš dikhel, ta maj džanel, hoj oda hin nalačho manuš.

Me pašľuvavas paš e baba the but daravas. Avri has imar o jesos, rat, the mange imar but na kampelas, kaj te rovav. Lakere lava, te na kerav ňič, kaj man oda manuš te na ľidžal het, mange ačhenas andre goďi. Paľis šunďom vareso andre kuchňa the andro vudar avľa ajso manuš, pal savo mange e baba vakerelas. O papus has andre kuchňa the šunelas la baba, ta kamelas tiš vareso te sikhavel. Iľa gruľi, čhinďa sano koter, kerďa andre o cheva pro danda the thoďa andro muj. Pro muj čhiďa o jaro, pro šero peske cirdľa chevalo gonoro, so has andre o gruľi, urďa baro gerekos, andro vast o tover, the avľa andre.

Duminav, hoj e baba daranďiľa avka sar me. Me avka daravas, hoj chudľom histerija. E baba le papuha na džanenas, so manca te keren, ta vičinde paš mande le doktoris. O doktoris man diňa varesavi inekcija, hoj te zasovav. E baba pes paľis le papuha vaš oda halasinelas the but ďives mange vakerelas ča šukar paramisa. Sar čeporo bariľom avri, ta pale mange vakerelas pal o mule, the aver čudne paramisa.

ĽIMAĽI ČHAJORI SAR RAKĽORI

Kana somas cikňi, e baba kerelas paš ajso podňikos, hoj phirenas andro but fora the budinenas bare betonove kvadrendar o khera. Phirelas čori andre buťi pre stavba, pal o murara pratinelas o blaki, o vudara, e phuv, o gangi. Has la čora phari buťi.

Sar mange kampelas te džal peršo ďives andre škola, ta joj kerelas le podňikoha andre aver foros. Našťi manca džalas pre ochto ori andre škola, ta phenel mange e baba: „Evičko, imar sal bari čhajori. Tosara tut ľidžava angle škola, užareha tuke, sar phundravena e škola, the paľis džaha andre the phučeha, kaj tuke kampel te džal, he?"

Sar man e baba uštavelas upre, dikhav, hoj avri mek šišitno. Has pandž ori tosara. La babake kampelas te džal pre mašina, ta so manca šaj kerelas. Urďa pre mande lole ceplaka, ajse, so has dži upre tel e meň the phandelas pes pro duj gombički pre sako sera the žebi man upre has. Has bares šukar. Na has pre mande urďi vizitka, aľe flanelovo gad sar pro muršoro. E baba pre ma kamibnaha dikhelas: „Joj, miri somnakuňi, tu sal šukarori!" Ta man šunelas, hoj som šukar sar rakľora. Samas čore, na has man šoha ňič nevo, ča oda, so amen vareko delas. La baba has mek ajso paradno štilos, hoj pre mande urelas, so lake avelas tel o vast. Lake has jekh, ča hoj te man nane šil, abo te man hin vareso pro šero, či radiovka abo khosno, oda has jekh.

Paľis andre žeba mange thoďa o maro le žiroha, phenďa: „Dža Devleha, mri čhajori," u man mukhľa te bešel pro gangi angle škola the siďarelas pre mašina. Avri has šil, ta na pregejľa aňi deš minuti, imar mange čuľanas le nakhestar o ľima. Na has man soha o nakh te khosel, ta so šaj keravas, khosavas o nakh andro gad.

Ta sar bešavas korkori pro ola gangi, has šil, šišitno, chudľom odoj te rovel. Paľis mek bareder ľima mange čuľanas, o nakh sar gruľi, bešavas ta bešavas.

Sar chudle te phirel o čhavore le dajenca the le dadenca andre škola, ta ča dikhenas, pre mande. Ľimaľi čhajori andro ceplaka. Varesave daja man prindžarenas, bo phiravas lengere čhavorenca andre školka, ta man ile andre škola. Phende mange, kaj te džav, the imar oda has feder.

Paľis avľa varesavi učiteľka the phenďa savorenge, te džan andre ťelocvičňa, hoj odoj vakerela o rjaďiteľis. Me gejľom lenca the odoj amenge phenenas, so amenge kampel andre škola, so amenge te cinen khere.

Somas cikňi, aľe mištes džanavas, hoj mange e baba kada šoha na cinela. Ta mange has pharo, hoj man oda na ela. Sako odoj mek kerelas baripen peskere čhavorenca, u me maškar lende somas sar nekčoreder ľimaľi čhajori. Ta savorestar pale chudľom te rovel.

Androda dikhľom, hoj paš mande terďol varesavo učo manuš, hazdľom o jakha the dikhľom mire papus. Ča pre mande čhiďa la jakhaha the imar džanavas, hoj ela mištes. O papus man chudľa vastestar the zorales man ľikerelas. Jov amenca akor na dživelas, aľe pre ada baro ďives man kamelas te dikhel, ta avľa pal mande.

Paľis manca gejľa andro foros the savoro, so mange kampelas andre škola, mange cinďa. Mek manca gejľa te cinel parne štremfľi the rokľica. The paľis čačes somas sar rakľori. Oda has miro baro peršo ďives andre škola. Mek mange leperav, hoj e baba sar dikhľa, so mange o papus cinďa, ta mek gejľa the paš oja rokľica mange cinďa o trampki, hoj te avel te dikhel lakero štilos.

O BALIKA

Miri baba has buťakeri romňi. Sako tosara lelas e koča u džalas andro rajonos. Avlas pale khatar o dilos the sig tavelas varesavo chaben. Pal o dilos pale džalas la kočaha het. Pro dilos kerelas ča gruľi purumaha abo zumin gruľenca podmarďi thudeha, bo siďarelas. Sako ďives anelas pherďi koča.

Andro foros la sako prindžarelas, ta sako, ko kamelas vareso purano te čhivel avri, ta vičinelas la baba. Savoro lelas u but lenge paľikerelas. Vaš varekaske oda has haraburďi, aľe e baba sar dikhelas, so čhiven avri, ta imar rachinelas keci love upre kerela avri. Buterval latar šunavas: „Adaďives džav ke jekh rajkaňi džuvľi, dela man varesave renti." Aver ďives oda has o hrački či o lepedi pro haďos.

Sar avelas e Karačoňa abo e Patraďi, ta e baba na birinelas te phirel pal o gadžija. Ňič olestar, so la denas, lake na kampelas, aľe džanelas mištes, so lenca kerela. Pre gadžengero pratišagos e baba kerďa o chulajipen. O džuvľija lake denas savoro avrirajbindo, bigľimen, ta e baba upre ča dikhľa u thoďa savoro andro balikos. Paľis vičinelas man. Oda has perdal late igen angluno, bo na džanelas te irinel či te ginel.

„Evičko, av kadaj, irinaha o ľil la Helenake khere pre Slovensko." Na phenelas mange kavka šukares gadžikanes, bo na vekerelas mišto, phenelas mange romanes. Dikhelas pre mande sar te somas inžinirka, bo džanav te irinel.

Duminav, hoj sar phenelas mange o ľil, ta imar džanelas, hoj chudela o love. Ta irinavas, so mange e baba phenelas:

Miri Heleno.
Irinav tuke me, e Haňa. Bičhavav tuke o balikos. Biken oja želeno rokľa vaš o pandž koruni, oda kalo svedros vaš deš koruni th'o lepedi pro haďos vaš bišthepandž koruni. Bičhavav tuke but šukar renti, ta šukares biken the bičhav mange vaš o balikos trin šel the biš koruni. Pozdravin le phrales the bičhav mange o love andro dešupandžto ďives andre kada čhon.

Charno ľil, savo kerďa la babake avri o love, thovahas andro balikos u e baba balikos la jagaha andro jakha šukares phandľa la doraha. Te has buter balika, lakeri loš barolas. Darekana bičhavahas the pandž balika andro čhon. E baba has bari kšeftarka, pre savi na has. Cinďa mange špecialno fiksos pro atresis the paľis mek brožurka, kaj has irimen poštovna numera, save kampelas te irinel paš o gava. Andre amaro romano gav pre Slovensko džanav oda poštovno numeris the akana.

Feder veci e baba mek kidelas avri the bičhavelas mira bibake. O lovore vaš o balika garuvelas, the sar duminďa, hoj imar hin dosta, vičinelas le bačis la bibaha, kaj len lenge bare baripnaha te del. Vičinelas lenge pre pošta telefoňicko vizvaha. Ajsi telefoňicko vizva oda has akor vareso ekstra. E baba džalas pre pošta u telegramoha vičinelas la biba pal e Slovensko pre pošta, abo le bačis la boraha, save bešenas Bruntaliste. Chudle o telegramos, kaj has irimen, kana te džan pre pošta andro foros. Paľis džanas andre kabina, kaj has o telefonos.

E baba imar tosarastar pre vizva užarelas. Pale the pale peske phenelas, so lenge phenela, pre soste te na bisterel. Perdal late oda has baro technicko čudos, pre savo peske rado trin, štar ori užarelas. Joj pro ori but na dikhelas, ta samas odoj sig pal o dilos the užarahas the užarahas.

Na džanav, či paťalas, hoj la andro telefonos šunen, bo avka zorales vičinelas, hoj la šaj šunde the bijal o technicko čudos. E gadži pre pošta imar anglal savore manušen bičhavelas dureder, phenelas lenge, hoj e baba vičinela. O kabini has kerde avka, kaj te ňiko na šunel so phenel, aľe perdal e baba oda has čepo, bo la šunenas savore manuša dži avri.

Te dikhel la na has, aľe šunelas la sako. Te lake na has vareso pre dzeka, ta paľis e kabina izdralas. O gadže pre pošta šaj mišto šunenas lakero monologos, bo aver sera na has kana te del duma. E baba peske phenelas: „Me poťinav, ta me dav duma!“

Nekbuter vičinelas vaš o balika pre Slovensko. Sar lake na bičhaďa e bibi o love avka, sar kamelas joj, maj džalas te del e vizva. La kabinatar paľis šunenas o manuša lava, so lenge na achaľonas: „Šun kadaj. Bičhavav le phraleske o svedros the tuke e kaľi rokľa. Ola aver renti biken the bičhav mange o love. Užarava dži dešupandžto ďives kada čhon.“

Jekhvar somas paš e vizva pre aver sera, andro Bruntalis. E baba kamelas te vičinel la bibake u me odoj somas pro prazdňini. Duminavas, hoj te e bibi hiňi terňi, ta na bešaha calo ďives pre pošta. Bešahas. E bibi prindžarelas la baba, ta kamelas pre pošta te avel avka, sar e baba kamel. Maj pal o dilos bešahas paš e kabina u užarahas, sar e baba vičinela.

Sar somas načirla pal e bibi, ta vakerahas pal e baba the leperahas o vizvi the o balika. Has amenge pharo, hoj e baba imar čirla nane maškar amende. Me paťav, hoj adaďives bi e baba bikenelas pro internetos!

ZAJDA

E baba hordinelas savoro pro dumo andro pochtan. Savo pochtan lake avelas tel o vast u has zoralo the mek has farbasto, ta paľis oda has čači romaňi zajda.

Phirahas ko bačis u bije zajda ajso drom šoha našťi džahas. E baba savoro, so arakhľa abo chudľa varekastar, garuvelas perdal o bačis the leskere čhavore. Sar kamelas pal lende te džal, thovelas e zajda pre phuv u rakinelas savoro andre. Paľis phandľa e zajda u phirlas pašal, sar te oda has somnakaj.

So bareder has e zajda, avka e baba lošanelas. E taška hordinelas e baba ča pro kleji. Has la ajsi saňori silonovo taška, odoj thoďa o kleji u kerďa upre gombos. O lovore phandelas andro agor pro khosno, jekhvar čhinďa le vastenca, u e zajda has lake pro dumo. Phandľa e zajda pro phike u šaj džahas. Andre mašina džalas la zajdaha pro dumo u sako lake džalas pal o drom, sar la dikhelas.

Me korkori man čudaľinavas, so savoro andre zajda has. Leperav, sar e baba asalas tel o nakh, sar phenďa la bibake, oda has lakeri bori, hoj te phundravel e zajda u lel avri o viganos le jakhorenca, save lake e baba anďa. E bibi o viganos le jakhorenca dikhľa u but lošanďiľa, bo ajso viganos igen kamelas. Polokes lelas avri o viganos, u kana lestar avri pejľa ajso sap, sar džido. E bibi avka daranďiľa u e baba asalas. „Ma dara, oda ča ajsi čačka," phenelas lake, aľe e bibi imar kije zajda na džalas.

E baba gejľa ke zajda u kidelas avri jekh pal aver, so anďa.

„Oda le Josivkoske, kada vaš o Bango, kada vaš e Buchta.“ La biba has ochto čhavore u ta has la baba so te kerel, hoj te sakoneske vareso anel. But e baba chudelas le gadžendar andre amaro foros, abo len arakhelas paš o popelňici, u tiš kerelas bare kšefti oficirengere rusike romňijenca, save bešenas andre amaro foros. Sar kidľa avri e baba o renti, ta paľis chudľa te del o chaben. Anelas le bačiske o konzervi th'o proviantos khatar rusike skladi, igen lačhi šunka, o mačhe, balano the guruvano mas andro konzervi, o rezanki, cukros the aver lačho chaben. Pro agor e baba thoďa e zajda andre taška paš o kleji. Sar phirelas e baba pal amaro foros, ta dikhelas vareso, so šaj varekaske khatar e fameľija kampel, ta lake e zajda furt kampelas.

Jekhvar man andre zajda ľigenďa ko doktoris. Has mange vaj ochto berš u has man bari horučka. Sar bari na džanav, bo teplomeris amen khere na has, aľe e baba duminelas, hoj imar kampel o doktoris. Thoďa e zajda pro haďos, thoďa upre e perňica, phandľa man u čhiďa peske e zajda pro dumo. Bešahas vaj dešthеduj minuti le doktoristar, the avka has e baba zoraľi, hoj man odoj ľigenďa.

Jekhvar, sar pal mande e baba la zajdaha avľa andre špitaľa, ta o gadže duminenas, hoj mange anel e televiza. Has man akor šargo nasvaľipen pro buke u somas pro infekčno kher the has man zoraľi dieta. Calo zajdatar man andre špitaľa dine ča jekh gonoro le mandarinkenca u čori baba ľidžalas e zajda pale khere.

O ČIŽMI

Miri baba has cikňori, aľe sar chudelas te kerel vika, ta manuša denašenas. Duminav, hoj e intonacija, savi den o Roma andro hangos, phenel buter sar o lava. Mištes džanav, so kamelas e baba te phenel akor, sar vičinelas „Jáj! Júj! Ííí! Joj!“ Imar na kampelas te phenel mek ča jekh lavoro.

Andre amari uľica džanenas savore manuša, sar džanel te vičinel. E baba šoha na garuvelas o emociji, phirelas pal o foros upre tele u rakinelas pre oda, pre soste chalas choľi. Varekana, te la has lačhi dzeka, šukares giľavelas, aver ďives dudrinelas tel o nakh u varekana košelas sakoneske, ko džalas pal o drom, la vikaha phenelas: „Raňije, ta me phirav andre buťi, bajinav pal amari cikňi čhajori, oda miro kujdušis man love na del, u te kamav e školka vaš e cikňi, ta mange phenen, hoj len nane kana mange te irinel o papira! Bo oda hin ča Jarmilko kadaj, Jaruško odoj, aľe sikhaďom len. Phenďom lenge: ‚Ta tumen nane kana manca te vakerel! Duškom mange vičinen le šerales, maj leske phenava, sar pijen ča o kaveji, keren tumenge o naja u man, phura romňa, bičhaven het!' Te dikhľanas, sar pašal mande chudľa te chuťkerel, fircimirka jekh. Maj phenďa: ‚Mištes, me odoj tosara vičinava pro telefonos, hoj te tumenge den e školka u la čhajora odoj šaj den.' "

Na užarelas, so phenela o manuš, so leske vakerelas, u džalas peskere dromeha khere. Mek andre aver uľica o manuša šaj šunenas, sar vičinkerel: „Me tut dava, te tut nane kana! Ta me phuri paťivaľi romňi u tu, jaj, fircimirko jekh, tu man čhives avri?!"

Džikim avľa khere, ta la e choľi pregejľa, bo kheldľa avri, ta imar polokes giľavelas u andro vudar avelas le asabnaha u giľavelas lakeri nekfeder giľori Na tarki, na tarki, s košarikom na tarki. Sar preačhelas, ta mek pre lačhi dzeka phenďa: „Me la dava!"

Pro amti pre baba dikhenas sar pro dilino manuš, bo te ginel the te irinel na džanelas, u te laha vakerenas uradňicko čechika dumaha, ta lenge na achaľolas. E baba na džanelas, so te kerel. Te lendar phučelas: „Čo mluvíte?", ta o gadže na džanenas, so lake te phenel pale.

Leperav, hoj o viboris delas le manušenge andro duchodos ajso prispevkos pro topanki. E baba akor imar has andro duchodos u varesavi gadži lake pal o prispevkos phenďa. Te kampelas te džal pro urados abo vareso ajso, peršo lelas e baba andro vast e kangľori pro džuva. E baba thoďa jag andro bov, bešľa pro cikno stolkocis, rozkerďa o balora, has la ajse sanore varkočici phandle farbasto doricaha. Šoha amen khere džuva na has, the avka e baba chanelas len avri. Kerelas oda akor, sar la has varesavo pharipen, te kampelas vareso pro uradi u varekana ča vašoda, hoj te o ritualos na bisterel. Dudrinelas tel o nakh the paľis vakerelas zorale hangoha, so phenela la uradňičkake pro viboris: „Ta me avľom, te man den pro topanki, bo nane man so pro pindre te urel. La gadžake khatar amari uľica diňan, ta me kamav tiš." Korkori peske

phenelas pale. „Jaj, sar man na dela, phagerav lake odoj e kancelarija!“
Tosara gejľa e baba pro viboris. E uradňička lake phenďa, hoj o prispevkos chudela, mi cinel o topanki the te anel o paragonos. E baba has rado, minďar chudľa te špekulinel, sar te kerel, te lake o love ačhen u o topanki te na cinel. „Pre soste mange kamašľi. Sem kala mek lačhe.“
Sar šunďom la baba, maj kamavas topanki me. Has mange vaj dešujekh berš u dikhľom andre sklepa igen šukar čižmi. Sanore, phandenas pen la doricaha dži upre, pro cikno štikľikos. Has čačipen, hoj ajse topanki na has vaš o čhavore, aľe me len but kamavas. Mangavas la baba, te mange o čižmi cinel, te lake topanki na kampel. Angutnes na phenelas ňič, paľis lake avľa pre goďi, hoj man nane so pro pindre, ta na dela o love vaš mire. Gejľam jekhetane andre sklepa.
Sar avľam andre, e baba džal kijo regalos, kaj has avri thode o tuleňki (topanki pre save has morči u telal has ajsi zoraľi guma), u mek dikhelas pre ajse, so has bareder, hoj te len šaj urav the aver berš. „Íií, Evičko, ala tut taťarena!“
Me chudľom te rovel, hoj o tuleňki na kamav, hoj kamav o čižmi, hoj o tuleňki na urava, rovavas, hoj hiňi e baba nalačhi, te mange na kamel te cinel o čižmi. Joj mange phenelas, hoj o čižmi hine sane, šmikinava man andre, avla man andre šil, aľe na šunavas u ča pre late dikhavas rovľarde jakhenca.
E baba gejľa te phučel, keci o čižmi mon u sar avľa pale, ta na paťalas. O tuleňki monas 160 u mire čižmi 699 koruni, aver topanki buter na monas. Vaš e baba oda has ajci love sar luksusno motoris. Joj na cinkerelas perdal peste ňič, the te kampelas vareso te cinel mange, ta ča oda, so molas čepo love u so mange čačes kampelas. Ajci love andre sklepa e baba šoha na mukhľa. Čori, ča odoj terďolas the bonďaľolas le šereha. Paľis phenďa, hoj o viboris o čizmi poťinela, ta len cinďam the ľidžahas len baripnaha khere.
E baba mištes garuďa o paragonos u me urďom pro pindre o čižmi vaš phureder manuša u phiravas lenca pal o kher. Paľis phučľom la babatar, či šaj džav avri, hoj džava pro saňki. Neve topankenca. E baba man but na kamelas te mukhel, aľe mukhľa man u me džavas le foroha u cirdavas o saňki. Avka sar e baba phenelas, o čižmi

mange šmikinenas, has man andre šil, aľe keravas baripen!

Na džanav kecivar gejľom tele le heďoha, sar dikhľom pro jiv loľi farba odoj, kaj thovavas o pindre, sar kamavas te terďol. Sar dikhľom pro čižmi, chudľom te gravčinel sar miri baba. O čižmi has pre paluňi sera sa tele randle u tel e kaľi cipa has te dikhel loľi farba. O čižmi has mosarde u me šaj ča rovavas. Bije dzeka džavas khere, o čižmi čhiďom pre chodba, te na dikhel e baba, u počoral rovavas.

Mek na džanavas, so avela tosara. E baba iľa o paragonos u gejľa pal e uradňička, te sikhavel, keci o topanki monas. E raňi laha delas šukares duma u diňa lake papiris, te džal andre pokladňa, kaj lake dena o prispevkos pro topanki. O prispevkos has 200 koruni.

E baba pes chudľa la uradňičkaha te halasinel. „Ta tumen mange phenďan, hoj man dena pro topanki, u akana man den duj šel koruni?“

„Amen tumenge phenahas, hoj oda hin prispevkos!“

„Sem me diňom vaš o čižmi 699 koruni, so akana kerava?“

„Našťi kerel ňič, amen tumenge buter našťi poťinas.“

„Jaj! Ta me poťinďom ajci love, sem me som čori! Joj, so kerava?“

Bara vikaha džalas e baba khere. Khere mek rakinelas u delas pal oda but duma u paľis iľa andro vast mire čižmi. Sar dikhľa, so lenca kerďom tel jekh ďives, duminavas, hoj lakeri vika ňigda šoha na preačhela.

Mek paru ďives faďinavas the šmikinavas man andro mosarde čižmi u paľis mange e baba gejľa te cinel ola tuleňki, save avka na kamavas. Čačo, bareder, te len šaj urav the aver berš. O čižmi has čhide pre chodba u paľis len e baba bara košaha čhiďa andro bov.

GOING TO THE MOVIES

BY ILONA FERKOVÁ

I may have been eight or nine years old when *Winnetou* came to the movie house in Rokycany. The photos in the display cases alone were enough to drive us kids wild. We didn't know the first thing about Indians, and now we could see them in a movie! The big news spread to every family, and even before it came to town, all the kids were pleading for money to get tickets. But where to scrape it up? Our moms had no money to spare and didn't give a dime away without a solid reason. "We don't even have enough for food," they said. "That's half a loaf of bread, two crowns! And you want me to spend it on crap?" You could cry as much as you wanted, you weren't getting the money.

My cousin Škypár (Chuckles) and I were the same age, we loved the movies, and tried everything we could to scrounge up money for tickets. To go see *Winnetou*, we needed two crowns each.

I said to my dad: "Dad, could you give me thirty hellers for a roll?" There were a hundred hellers in a crown.

"We've already got bread, just cut yourself a slice and eat."

"But I want a roll, I get tired of bread all the time!" I said, standing my ground.

"Just give her the thirty hellers! Let her buy a roll if she wants it so bad," my mom called to my dad.

"Here you go then, Rumpy," my dad said using my family nickname, "and be careful on the way!"

The moment I had the money, I made a beeline for Na bouračce, Demolition Town, where a lot of Roma lived, including Škypár. My own family lived out of the way, and we were the only Roma on our side of town. So I was constantly running away to the neighborhood where my cousin lived, I liked the feel of it there. "Škipi! Škipi!" I called up from underneath the windows. "Come on out, I've got money!" The Roma in Demolition Town lived in these ugly old hovels that were being torn down one after the other, which is why they called it that. There was one tall building where only gadjos lived. Next to it was a house with a garden and a wall about two meters high that ran around the whole house.

Škypár held our hellers and a few small rocks in his hand, rattling them and shouting to the kids to come and play.

Whoever threw their coin closest to the wall got to scoop up all the money lying on the ground. In other words, pitching pennies, but we called it "Whoever's closest." No one beat Škypár. He would secretly spit on the coins so they landed close to the wall. No one could outpitch him. He might rake in a whole crown or as little as fifty hellers. But he never gave up! "Who's playing this time, come on, kids! They're showing *Winnetou* at the movies today, so let's go, look sharp, here's your chance to win enough to buy a ticket!" He shouted his pitch and the kids came running. Some had just a ten-heller coin, some a twenty, either way they got in line and tossed their change at the wall. Sometimes Škypár spat so much, his mouth completely dried up, but he didn't care, he would play from morning until three in the afternoon, as long as it took him to get those four crowns in his pocket.

I squatted down on a rock by the local fountain and waited until he announced: "All right, kids, that's it, my hand is starting to hurt." I knew that meant he'd reached four crowns. Now all the coins had to be cleaned. "Quick, get a move on. We've gotta wash these things fast. The cashier doesn't take sticky change!" he hollered at me. He tossed the coins onto the rock, and one after the other, I rinsed them off. Then Škypár washed himself off too, his hands and face were covered with dirt. He slicked down his hair and we proudly marched off to the theater.

Standing in front of the movie house was a wooden shack where tickets were sold. Two cashiers took turns there. One was scrawny—she fit inside easily—but the other one was fat and could barely squeeze herself in. The fat one was nice to us, even though her husband was a cop. People called the skinny one Whiskers, since she had a moustache under her nose. Her husband was the senior doctor in the local hospital's women's ward and he was a really great guy. He'd helped a bunch of our mothers give birth, so all the Roma women loved him. His wife, though, was an old bat. She refused to take our coins, she was too lazy to count them. "Which one is working today?" Škypár asked the kids already waiting in line.

"It's the fat one, don't worry, she takes small change. How many tots did you fleece today?" laughed the older kids.

"A game's a game!" Škypár laughed back.

We got tickets for two crowns apiece. That was why we had gotten in line so early, to make sure we got the cheap tickets for the chairs they set up in addition to the fixed seats. It was just three rows at the front of the house and the tickets tended to go right away. Gadjos wouldn't sit there, but us Roma didn't care if we were close enough to lick the screen. God, what a gorgeous film! As the Indians whooped and galloped across the plain on their horses, we gave the battle cry along with them, patting our mouths with our hands. The usher came up and screamed at us: "Shut your mouths, and you and you"—she pointed to the guilty parties—"are never getting back in this movie house again!" Škipi and I didn't make a stink, even though we wanted to. Škipi knew the woman wouldn't let us in next time otherwise. But as soon as the doors of the movie house opened, we all screeched at the top of our lungs.

Every Sunday at ten a.m. the movie house showed fairy tales. Tickets were only one crown, but we didn't have even that. "Come on, we'll go by the garbage cans and see if we can find some jars," Škypár said. These were returnable mason jars that people sold goulash in. They didn't bother washing them and just threw them away. If you took the jars to a shop, you could get 50 hellers for a half-size one and a whole crown for a large. They were so dirty, though, it took some work to clean them up. We put them in a net bag and went to the swimming hole, where there was a little stream, and rinsed them in the cold water. In the summer it was fine, but in the fall our hands froze, the water was so icy. It seemed like nothing could get the grease off, but Škypár figured out a way. He tore up some grass and scooped up some mud and cleaned them off using a twig.

"Whenever I wash them, it makes me want to puke."

"Do you wanna go to the movies or not? Then stop running your mouth, come on!" he said, and dragged me into town. That Sunday we got lucky and found three jars, two large, one small.

"What did I tell you? See? We've got enough for the movie *and* candy!" he laughed.

"We do, but look, my hands are all red and I'm soaking wet."

"That's nothing. As soon as the sun comes out, you'll dry off. Don't worry, I'll buy you whatever you want."

We took the jars to a store.

"Well, they aren't exactly clean. You know we only take clean jars," the saleslady said.

"Please, ma'am, they're clean."

"Look at all the smudges."

"But, ma'am, they're clean. You can see there's nothing in them. Please, ma'am, just take them, we're trying to go to the movies."

"All right then, they're gonna wash them out again anyway."

The movie house was in the center of town in a building with a big gate. The gate opened up and you passed through an arcade to a small courtyard, where on one side they sold tickets and on the other there was a lady selling sweets from a window with a wooden shutter on it.

"Pick whatever you want for 50 hellers," said Škypár. My eyes lit up. I didn't know what to get first.

"I'll take two Mejdlíčko bars, the pink ones!" I told the saleslady, pointing through the crack between the sliding glass panes to my favorite candy.

"Take your hand out of there, you animal!" she said, slapping me. "I'll hand it to you."

"All right, and a pack of those Lipo Energit sweets."

"I'll give you the brown ones, those are already open."

"I don't want those! I want pink, the brown ones are gross!" I scream at the saleslady. The pink Mejdlíčko bars were raspberry-flavored and the yellow ones were lemon. Both of them were really good, but no one liked the brown ones. A Mejdlíčko bar with five pieces cost one crown. If you broke off only one bit, it cost twenty hellers.

"Show me you have the money, if you're going to be so picky!"

"Fine, see, I've got fifty hellers." There was a long line of people waiting behind me, so finally she gave me the pink ones.

"There, now get lost. Look at this line of people I have."

Then Škypár put in for good measure: "I hope you have a heart attack, you witch!"

"Look at these little Gypsy whelps! All they have is crumbs, and still they pick and choose!"

I wanted to dig into the Mejdlíčko right away. "You can't eat it now, save it for the theater," Škypár chided me. Once we had settled into our seats, he took the candy out of the bag and said: "Now you can eat." We ate slowly, to make it last as long as we could. The Mejdlíčko was nice and sweet.

Škypár would always come get me when there was a good movie playing. One time he came by and said: "Come on out, there's a great flick at the theater!"

"Where are we going to get the money, though? Who's going to give it to us?"

"Not to worry, I went to look for jars on the garbage heap. I didn't find any, but there were loads of cans. Just bring the baby carriage and you'll see how much we make!"

"Forget that, I'm not going all the way out to the garbage heap!" It really was a long way, past the cemetery and up the hill. In the end, silly me, I took my little brother's baby carriage anyway, and we headed out to the dump. "Škipi, listen, we can't get the carriage dirty, or my mom'll tan my hide to kingdom come and back."

"Don't worry, the cans are burnished like glass."

"Where did you get that from, 'burnished'?"

"My mom says it all the time."

We got to the dump and, seriously, there were so many cans there, they must have been poured out by a dump truck. We filled the whole baby carriage and set out to see the man at the recycling center. As we walked along, I turned to my cousin and said: "We're going to get ten crowns for this, don't you think? Maybe even more!" We pictured all the things we would buy with the money and arrived at the recycling center in high spirits. The pot-bellied man took one look at us and roared with laughter. His stomach bulged like our carriage full of cans.

"So, what have you got for me?"

"Metal, can't you see?"

"You want to sell that to me? How much you want for it?"

"I don't know, ten crowns at least?"

The fat man laughed even harder. "Don't even bother putting it on the scale, it's a kilo, toss it there on the pile. Here's twenty hellers for each of you, now get out of my sight."

We were beside ourselves with rage. "The nerve of that fatso, dikh!, cheating us like that!" Škypár seethed on our way home. He declared a proper curse on the man, but then said: "Good thing we stuck a pebble in every can so it would weigh more on the scale!" and burst out laughing.

I was on the verge of tears that we had gone to all that trouble for a measly twenty hellers, but when I looked over at Škypár, I had to laugh, too. "And here I was, saying we'd get ten crowns! Now let's get to the fountain quick, and give that carriage a good washing-out, or you'll see how bad my mom beats me."

"Don't worry, we'll wash the carriage, then cash in on that forty hellers and go to the movies!" And Škypár was right.

Romani kids all loved playing Indian. We would run around Demolition Town, whooping like them. The older boys would make guns out of matchboxes and rubber bands, then herd us up against the wall and shoot rubber bands at us. That's how we played, the big kids were the cowboys and the little kids were the Indians. That's why all us little kids were so crazy about the movies, from watching them we learned to play at being Indians.

SAR AMEN O ČHAVE PHIRAHAS ANDRE MOZI

ILONA FERKOVÁ

Šaj mange uľahas avka ochto abo eňa berš, kana avľa adej Rokicaňate andre mozi o filmos, so pes vičinlas Vinnetou. Imar pal o fotki, so sas thode avri andro mozakre oblaki, amen diliňaľuvahas. Šoha ňigda na dikhľam indijanen, u akana len šaj dikhas andro filmos! Oda baro hiros džalas andre savore fameľiji u savore čhave imar anglal rovenas, kaj kamena andre mozi love. Aľe khatar te lel love upre! Le dajen na sas a na dinehas aňi deš haľera. Phenenas: „Pro chaben nane dosta, a vaš o duj koruni, oda imar jepaš maro! A pro diliňipena davkeraha love?!“ Šaj rundžal, keci kamľal, na dinehas.

Me the miro strično phral o Škiparis, sas avka phuro sar me, ta amen merahas pal o filmi u stradahas peske love pro ľiski, sar pes delas. U akana pro Vinnetou kampľa mange duj koruni a leske tiš.

Phenav mire dadeske: „Dado, šaj man des tranda haľera pro rohľikos?“

„Kodej hin o maro, ta peske čhin u cha.“

„Joj, me kamav rohľikos, ča mindig maro me imar na kamav!“ terdžuvavas pre miro.

„Ta sem de la imar ole tranda haľera! Mi džal peske te cinel, the avka kamel oda rohľikos,“ zvičindža pro dad e daj.

„No ta le, tu Buľačko,“ — avka man vičinenas — „a merkin pro drom!“

Sar man has o love, ta me imar trispras denašavas Pre buračka, kaj bešenas but Roma the o Škiparis. Amen bešahas dur le Romendar. Pre koja sera na bešenas ňisave Roma, ča amen. Ta vašoda me ča denašavas tele Pre buračka, odoj mange sas mištes. „Škipi! Škipi!“ vičinavas avri paš lengri oblaka, „hin man love, av het!“ Pre buračka, avka pes odej vičinlas, o Roma bešenas andre ajse purane džungale khera, vašoda pes vičinlas Pre buračka, bo po jekh kher imar čhivenas tele. Sas jekh učo kher, kaj bešenas ča o gadže. U khatar kada kher sas dvora the the uči murimen fala, avka duj metri, a bondžarlas pes pašal calo kher.

Le Škipariste sas andre burňik ole haľera the vajkeci barora a čerkinlas lenca the vičinlas le čhavoren te bavinel. Ko čhivlas o haľeris nekpašeder ke fala, oda lelas savore haľera, so sas pre phuv. Sako phenelas pre kada bavišagos „Ko pašeder“. Pro Škiparis na sas ňiko. Počoral

čhungardelas fejs pro haľeris, kaj te doperel dži kije fala. Ňiko les na premarlas. Avka skidelas varekana the jekh koruna, abo tiš ča penda haľera. Aľe na delas pes! „Ko mek kamel te bavinel, aven, čhavale! Adadžives den le Vinnetou andre mozi, aven, šaj vikhelen peske pro ľiskos!“ Kavka vičinlas u o čhavore avenas. Sas len ča deš abo biš haľera u imar terdžonas andro šoros the čhivkernas peskre haľera ke fala. Varekana les imar aňi šľini na sas, aľe bavinlas tosarastar the dži trin ori, kim ola štar koruni kerlas.

Me bešavas pro bar paš e kašňa the užaravas, sar lenge phenla: „No, imar dost, čhavale, dukhal man e musi.“ Oda imar džanavas, kaj les hin ola štar koruni. Akana kampelas savore haľera te premorel. „No! Imar ma beš, kampel het te morel o haľera, džanes? E gadži kajse melale love na lela!“ zvičinďa pre mande. Čhiďa o churde pro bar u jekh pal aver moravas andro paňi. Paľis pes the ov morďas, bo les sas o vasta the o muj žužo melalo la čikatar, cindžarlas o bala u džahas baripnaha kije mozi.

Avri paš e mozi has ajsi kaštuňi buda u odej bikenenas o ľiski andre mozi. Sas odoj duj gorija. Jekh šuki — oj andre mišto rešťolas — the oki sas thuľi, ča hoj avka odej rešťolas. E thuľi sas kij’amende lačhi, choc te lakro rom sas šinguno. La šuka savore vičinahas Bajusato, bo la sas tel o nakh bajusi. Lakro rom sas primaris andal e špitaľa pal o džuvľikano the has igen lačho manuš. Buter amare dajenge šigitinďa, sar ločhonas, vašoda les savore Romňija rado dikhenas. Aľe leskri romňi sas aver, baro bitangos. Na kamelas amare haľera, bo sas leňivo te rachinel. „Savi andre bešel?“ phučelas o Škipis le čhavendar, so imar odej terdžonas.

„Ma dara, e thuľori adej, oj tuke ole churde lela. Keci cikne čhavoren obkheldžal?“ asanas o bareder čhave.

„Hra je hra!“ asalas the o Škiparis.

Cinahas jekh ľiskos vaš o duj koruni. Vašoda odoj terďuvahas imar avka sig, kaj te dochudas kola tune ľiski, so pes vičinenas „pristavki“. Oda sas ča trin šori lavki igen pašes paš o javiskos u o ľiski sas maj het. Odej gadže na džanas te bešel, aľe amenge le Romenge sas jekh, hoj pašes. Jój, savo šukar filmos has! Sar džanas o indijana pro graja u vičinenas, the amen andre mozi marahas le anguštenca pal o vušta u tiš kerahas vika. Avelas ke amende e gadži a zavičinlas: „Držte huby, a tebe a tebe—“ a sikhavlas le vasteha pro čhave, „vás už do kina nepustim!“ Me the o Škipis na kerahas vika, choc tiš kamahas. Jov džanelas, kaj e gadži bi amen masovar na mukhelas. Aľe soča phundravenas o vudar avri, imar savore gravčinahas.

Sako kurko denas andre mozi paramisi, deš orendar tosara. Ľiskos molas ča jekh koruna, aľe tiš amen na sas. „Av, džaha te dikhel savore popeľvarki, so terdžon paš o khera, dikhaha, či na rakhaha varesave cakli,“ phenelas o Škipis. Andre sas the mas the omačka, abo armin maseha, u o gadže na mornas, čhivkernas avri. Kala cakli kidenas andro sklepi, vaš o jepašuno denas penda haľera the vaš o baro imar jekh koruna. O cakli sas ajse melale, hoj sas amen so te kerel, kaj len te žužes moras avri. Thovahas andro gono u džahas paš amaro kupaľiskos, kaj čuľalas e leňori, u odej andro šilalo paňi len morahas. Ňilaje na sas avke phares, aľe jesoste amenge o vasta faďinenas, bo sas o paňi but šilalo. Ňisar na džalas tele o makhľipen, aľe o Škipis avľa pre oda, sar te morel. Čhingerlas čar, lelas čeporo čik, thovlas pro kaštoro u maj vimorelas avri.

„Mindig, sar len morav, ta čhandav.“

„Kames te džal andre mozi? Ta av het!“ cirdelas man andro foros. Akana kurke amen bachtales rakhľam duj bare cakli the jekh cikno.

„So phenavas?! Dikhes! Hin amen andre mozi the pro guľipen!“ asalas.

„No se he, aľe dikh, o vasta žuže lole a caľi som cindži.“

„Oda ňič, ča mi avel avri o kham, maj šučoha. Ma dara, cinava tuke, so kameha.“

Ľigendžam o cakli andre sklepa.

„No moc čistý nejsou, víš, že bereme jenom čistý,“ phenďa mange e gori, so o cakli kidelas.

„Paní, jsou čistý.“

„No, jsou nějaký upatlaný.“

„Ale jo, paní, jsou čistý, vidíte, že v nich nic není. Paní, vemte je, my chceme do kina.“

„A tak jo, voni je stejnak ještě budou mejt.“

Sar džahas andre mozi, ta sas maškar o foros baro kher u les has ajsi bari kapura, oj pes phundravlas the predžalas pes ajso sar gangos, sas odoj kajso pľacos, u pre jekh sera bikenlas o ľiski andre mozi the pre aver sera phundravla e gori ajse duj kaštune oblaki u odej la sas savore guľipena.

„Vaš o penda haľera kide tuke avri, so kames," phenďa mange o Škiparis. Mange o jakha labonas, na džanavas so sigeder.
„Pani, dvě tuty mejdlíčka, ty růžový!" sikhavav lake le angušteha maškar o duj skleňimen oblaki.
„Dáš tu ruku pryč, ty potvoro jedna?!" čhinel man pal o vast, „Já ti to podám."
„No, a ješte jedno lipo energit."
„Dám ti ty hnědý, ty už mám načatý."
„Ty nechci! Chci růžový, ty hnědý jsou hnusný!" kerav vika pre gori. O ružova šunďonas pal o maľini u o šarga pal o citroni. Kale sas igen lačhe. O kavejova ňiko na kamelas. Jekh tabľička, kaj sas pandž cikne sapuňica, molas calo jekh koruna. Te phagelas ola tabľičkatar ča jekh sapuňicis, molas biš haľera.
„Ukaž, jestli vůbec máš peníze, když si tak vybíráš."
„Jo, mám tady padesát halířů." Pal mande sas šoros nipi, ta e gori mange diňa o ružova.
„Tak, a už mazej, vidíš, že tady mám frontu."
O Škiparis mek lake phendža: „Šlak tě trafí, ty bosorko!"
„No vidíte je, Cikáňata, mají samý drobáky, a ješte si vybíraj!"
Kamavas o sapuňicis te chal takoj. Kajča o Škiparis kerďa vika: „Akana ma cha, chaha andre mozi." Sar imar bešľam andre mozi, iľa avri andal o gonoro o cukri u phenďa: „Akana šaj chas." Chahas koda cikno sapuňicis polokes, kaj amenge te ľikerel so mek nekbuter. Sas igen lačho gulo.
O Škiparis avelas vaš mange, te denas šukar filmos andre mozi. Jekhvar avľa pale u phenel: „Av het, davkeren lačho filmos!"
„No o love khatar? Ko amen dela?"
„Ma dara, somas pro šmeciskos, či rakhava cakli. Na sas ňič, aľe pherdo plechovki hin odej. Ča hoj te les e kočija u dikheha, keci zarodaha!"
„Jojš, me na džav avke dur!" Čačes sas dur, až dži pal o cintiris upre pro hedžos. Pro agor me diliňi iľom le cikne phraleskri kočija the denašahas pro šmeciskos. „Hej, Škipi, na tromal les te meľarel, bo man e daj marla ajci, keci andre mande rešťola!"
„Ma dara, oda hine žužore sar somnakaj."
„Oda kaj iľal kada lav somnakaj?"
„Oda šundžom imar kecivar la datar."

Avľam pro šmeciskos u čačes, ajci plechovki, oda mušindža odej te čhivel varesavo motoris. Čhivkerdžam andre kočija pherdo the džas ko goro andre sberňa. Pal o drom leske vakerav: „Škipi, oda chudaha kajse deš koruni, na?! Talam the buter!“ Anglo jakha amenge sas, so savoro vaš kala love peske cinaha, ko goro andre sberňa avľam asabnaha. Sar amen dikhľa o pervačis, chudľa ajci te asal. Kajso per les sas, sar amaro kočikos le plechovkenca.

„Tak copak jste mi přivezli?“

„Železo, ne?“

„Tohle mi chcete prodat?“ A amen phenas he! „A kolik za to chcete?“

„No já nevím, aspoň deset korun?“

O thulačis mek buter asalas: „Ani to nedávejte na váhu, to má kilo, rovnou to vyhoďte na tu hromadu. Tady máte každej dvacet halířů a zmizte.“

Save samas choľamen! „Hej, kajse nervi, dikh, sar amen očorarďa,“ bara rušaha džalas o Škiparis khere. Le gadžes but prekošťa, aľe paľis phendža: „Mištes, kaj thodžam andre ala plechovki bara, kaj te en phareder!“ asandžiľa fejs.

Mange pes kamelas te rovel, hoj pes ajci trapindžam vaš biš haľera, aľe sar dikhľom pro Škipis, ta pes tiš asandžiľom. „Fejs amen diňa deš koruni! U akana kije kašňa te morel poradnones e koča, bo dikheha, sar man marla e daj.“

„Ma dara, the e kočija moraha the mek pre ala saranda haľera kerava love u o filmos dikhaha!“ U sas les čačipen, le Škiparis.

Amen savore Romane čhave pes igen rado bavinahas pro indijana, denaškerahas pal caľi Buračka the kerahas kajsi vika sar o indijana. O bareder čhave kernas peske le šabľikendar the le gumicendar kajse pištoľa u thovnas le ciknen kije fala te terdžol the ole gumici pre amende viľikernas. Avke pes bavinahas, hoj o bare sas „komboja“ u amen o cikne indijana. Vašoda amen savore čhave vaš kala indijanska filmi merahas, hoj šaj paľis bavinďam sar on.

OPEN-SKY FLAT

BY OLGA FEČOVÁ

In summer 1968, I lived at my mother's place on Na Poříčí Street in Prague, with my husband Fečo and my daughter Erika from my first marriage, my sister Květa, and my brother Michal with his wife Věra and their daughter Monika. Three families squeezed into one flat. And me expecting my second child. I spent all summer looking for a place to live. You couldn't just get one through the local government, even if we did have communism. All I ever heard was: "Nothing, not a thing . . ."

I had a job cleaning flats in Prague 1, and one day the head of the District Housing Management Company (OPBH) told me: "There's a building on Truhlářská Street with a flat free on the second floor. I used to clean there myself. Just go ahead and crash in there."

I was shocked: "I can do that?"

"If you want a place to live, you've got no other choice. But don't tell anyone I suggested it."

I thought it over a long time. I'd never had any run-ins with the law, but I couldn't get it out of my head. I confided my plan to Fečo. He didn't want to hear about it. An old childless couple named the Lachmans lived off the courtyard on Truhlářská. They ran hot water for me when I cleaned. I really liked them and called them Grandpa and Grandma. I told them what was going through my mind. Grandma was hesitant, but Grandpa was clear from the get-go: "The flat is nothing great. Two rooms with a coal stove. The water and toilet are out on the gallery that runs around the courtyard. But better a bird in the hand than two in the bush. What can they do to you, Olga? The most they can do is evict you! I'm sure they'll take Erika into consideration and your advanced state of pregnancy."

Grandpa gave me courage and a skeleton key, and I eagerly set out to break into the flat. Grandpa and Grandma helped move in a bed for me, a crib for Erika, and a small table with two chairs.

When Fečo came home from work, he was so upset I thought he'd have a heart attack. "What have you done, wifey?" Grandpa and Grandma Lachman tried to help me calm him down. Finally we succeeded. I put Erika to bed and the two of us went to lie down. But neither of us slept a wink all night. At about seven a.m., we heard a pounding on the door.

I answered the door and said: "What are you doing, scaring my child?" It was four young officers and one of about fifty, of higher rank. They took what little furniture we had and carried it out to the courtyard. I was a week away from my due date, my belly was literally about to burst and so big it looked like I was going to have triplets at least. The older cop politely explained that they had a report of a forced entry into the flat and that was illegal, which meant I could be punished, "but given that you're pregnant," he said, "and you've never been convicted, we'll dismiss the case."

Fečo and I were about to breathe a sigh of relief when one of the younger policemen started calling us Gypsies, saying we get away with everything and he wasn't going to stand for it. He got so mad, he shoved me, hard. I wasn't expecting it and lost my balance, but then I gave him a proper slap in the face. Now he was the one caught off guard. And I said to him: "You're just a half-pint trying to show off! You Slovak piece of shit! Just wait till this gets back to your wife's family. You may live with a Gypsy, but you've got no integrity. Just wait till I tell her how you behaved!"

The older cop didn't say a word. I could tell he was glad I had given that Slovak a piece of my mind and slapped him red in the face. He dismissed his men, asked if I was injured, and said if I had anything wrong to go to the doctor, he would testify that the officer had assaulted me, and handed me his card.

The building had a gallery running around the courtyard, so everyone had seen and heard the whole thing. And they knew me, because I did the cleaning there. They started shouting at the young cop: "Boo, who do you think you are, laying hands on a woman, and a pregnant one at that!"

Grandpa Lachman was fired up too, but he calmed down when he saw the way the older cop treated me. I said to him: "Grandpa, would you mind if we stayed living here in the courtyard?" Both he and his wife agreed. So we moved our bed and Erica's crib underneath their windows and I spread our rug out between them and put the table and chairs on it. There was a sink with water in the courtyard, and Grandpa plugged a lamp in for us through the

window. It was August and the weather was on our side. That evening we changed into our night clothes and slept beneath the open sky. From then on, I cooked in Grandma Lachman's kitchen. The whole building was rooting for us, in the evening our neighbors would come down to the courtyard to visit. Fečo would take out his guitar and everyone had a good time, playing music, singing, and playing cards.

The police always came, peeked in on us, I told them we had nowhere to go, I wasn't going to budge, and so they left again. We lived outside like that all week, and I was just waiting for it to start to rain. Finally they made up their minds and assigned us a flat on the ground floor. The head of the District Housing Management Company came to take a look, and she told me: "Seeing as you're our employee, I can open up a flat for you here on the courtyard." I could hardly say no.

It was only two tiny rooms—a little bedroom and a narrow windowless shoebox with a stove that served as a kitchen—but at least it was housing. The amazing thing was, that whole week we lived in the courtyard it didn't rain. And the moment we moved inside, there was an enormous downpour.

On the twenty-ninth I gave birth to a beautiful four-kilogram baby girl named Lída, and three days later I was home, where I found a surprise waiting for me: a summons from the court. The policeman had filed a complaint against me for calling him a Slovak piece of shit. I dressed up my little Lída and set out for the court on Fruit Market Square. When I walked into the courtroom, it was packed—it looked like three judges, some lawyers, I don't even know who all was there. I said hello and looked around, I had never been in a space like that before.

I laid my little one on the table in a swaddling blanket. Liduška was a gorgeous baby, brown-skinned and wide-eyed, and kept everyone in the courtroom delighted up until the proceedings began. The officer testified first, saying I'd called him a Slovak piece of shit and started hitting him. The judges heard him out, then asked: "And what reason did Mrs. Fečová have for doing this?" He didn't have an answer for that.

Then it was my turn. I truthfully recounted everything that had taken place, and as proof I showed the judges the older cop's calling card. The judges consulted together and the verdict came to light. The officer got a suspended sentence, I was acquitted. The woman judge told me: "If you take back calling him a Slovak piece of shit, I'll waive the two hundred crowns' fine." I replied that I would happily pay the fine, I stood by what I'd said. The judges shook their heads, but banged their gavels to approve.

We lived on Truhlářská Street for twenty years. I did laundry in the courtyard, ironed in the courtyard, in short lived in the courtyard, and they were the most beautiful years of our life. All you had to do was shout: "Marčo, av tele"—the Harang family also lived up there—"Džal e čhaj andre škola, kames vareso?"[1] We looked after each other's children, handing off the keys to our flats, even with the gadjos, for instance the Mušáleks, who lived upstairs.

I'd ask my neighbor: "Maruš, have you got any milk?"

"Sure."

"I have to go to work tomorrow. Could you look in on the kids for me?"

"You bet."

We lived like that for twenty years. After those twenty years, we moved to Jižní Město, in the south of Prague, and I couldn't imagine having to close the door behind me. How do you live inside all the time? I had lived in the courtyard so many years.

1 "Marča, come downstairs, my daughter's going to school, do you need anything?"

MY WONDERFUL FAMILY

BY MARKÉTA ŠESTÁKOVÁ

THE STOVE

It's wintertime, snow falls thickly from the sky. I sit at the table, dipping a piece of marikľi in sauce. Memories of my husband's grandma replay in my head—of her cozy room and old stove. Through the broken door, barely hanging on one hinge, you could see the fire crackle.

My grandpa-in-law stoked the fire with wood while my grandma-in-law laid sheets of dough as thick as her thumb onto the hot stove plates. Meat fried in a large pan. She brewed a pot of Melta chicory coffee, poured it out into tin cups, and set them on the table. In the middle she placed the pan of meat and the hot, delicious-smelling marikľa. We dipped them in fat and ate them with chunks of meat. To help it slide into our stomachs, we washed it down with hot black Melta.

Then my grandpa-in-law sat down by the stove, lit up a cigarette, and stoked the fire. Outside it was already dark. The light from the forty-watt bulb was so weak, we could see the stove plates glowing red. After a while, my grandma-in-law lit up too, and proceeded to tell a story about the war and how people in those days worked in the homes of Jews. I burrowed into a huge duvet and listened, even though I knew some of her stories practically by heart by then.

The logs crackled in the stove, and I slowly fell asleep. I felt like I was in paradise. Looking back on it today, it gives me such a beautiful feeling in my soul, I can't even put it into words.

ALL SOULS' DAY

For me, All Souls' Day evokes the atmosphere before Christmas. When I light the candles for my grandma-in-law, I remember the first Christmas I spent with her. I knew only the classic version: carp, potato salad, cookies. But this was totally different.

It was about two weeks before Christmas. We were moving from the rural outskirts into the city. It was so cold, our nostrils froze shut. We had already moved all the furniture. We wouldn't be able to keep our poultry in the city—hens, ducks, and a goose we fattened with cracked corn—so my grandpa-in-law slaughtered them all and hung the meat in the shed to freeze. There were no freezers in those days. The day before Christmas, he screwed a hook into the ceiling and hung a little Christmas tree over the dining table. My grandma-in-law took some chocolates out of a classic holiday assortment wrapped in colored cellophane, which she called "vizolanki," and decorated the tree with them. Meanwhile she kneaded dough for pásky and sweet rolls, which only she knew how to do and I learned from her. We had those instead of the traditional Christmas cookies. And whenever she got to kneading, she never made less than a fifty-liter tub. She baked so many trays, she was toiling till nightfall.

On Christmas morning, my husband's grandpa brought in some straw and scattered it under the table, to keep us in bread all year, he said. Then the boiling, frying, and baking began. Forget carp and potato salad! My grandma-in-law made soup out of the hen, and homemade noodles to go in it. Then she roasted the goose and ducks with sauerkraut and dumplings. The aroma of fresh marikľa wafted from the stovetop. Plus a pot of plňimen armin, and bobaľki sprinkled with poppyseeds, which she threw into the oven to bake. She didn't give us anything to eat all day, just a little coffee and a slice of bread in the morning. We couldn't wait for evening to come.

Once it got dark, she lit a candle, said a prayer, and served up a bowl of bobaľki. We each got a little bit on our plate, and a few of them were set outside the window for the dead. My grandpa-in-law poured everyone a shot, then put one out on the windowsill too, a drink for the souls of the dead, he said. After the ceremony, my grandma-in-law carried the goodies she had made to the table. Once she had set it down, nothing could be cleared away—it had to stay till morning. We didn't give presents back then. People told all sorts of stories, eventually someone picked up a guitar, and my grandma-in-law began to sing sad songs from Eastern Slovakia, so sad she cried as she sang. The fire in the stove crackled, the vodka in the bottle dwindled, and everyone slowly got in the mood. At that point, the neighbor showed up with her husband and they joined in the merriment. The party lasted long into the night, but I crawled under the covers exhausted and slept the sleep of the dead, even despite all the whooping and dancing around me. We enjoyed Christmases like that with my husband's grandma for years. Today she is no longer alive, and the Christmas holidays aren't what they used to be, when neighbors were closer, people appreciated one another, and family meant everything.

CAKES

My grandma-in-law loved to bake. Whenever it was getting close to Easter or Christmas, she would bake an enormous quantity of pásky. So one time, before Easter, she was once again kneading dough into a fifty-liter wash basin and letting it rise, when she realized she had forgotten to buy raisins. So she assigned my husband's grandpa to pop out to the shop for two packs of raisins, and gave him ten crowns. That was a mistake! My grandpa-in-law, who had a fondness for beer and liked rum even more, took one look at the ten crowns and his eyes lit up. He slipped the bill in his pocket and no one had to ask him to leave twice. Before you could turn around, he was out the door and headed straight for the pub. Ten crowns bought him a large rum and three beers. Meanwhile the dough in the bowl rose and rose under the duvet. My husband's grandma ground the poppyseeds and walnuts while she waited for her spouse. After a good two hours had passed, and the dough in the bowl didn't know which way to overflow, my grandma-in-law decided she'd had enough and went to see if something had happened to my grandpa-in-law.

Far from it! He sat in the pub, sucking down beer, having forgotten all about his wife and the raisins. As the drink went to his head, he got happier by the minute. He was in high spirits when the door burst open and there stood his wife. My grandpa-in-law froze. His wife sternly sized him up, turned around, and went home. My grandpa-in-law quickly paid his bill and scurried after her—he knew it was bad. Drunk and no raisins to boot, oh boy, there's going to be shouting now, he thought with a sinking feeling. And so there was.

No sooner had the door to the flat clapped shut behind him than my grandma-in-law let loose: she swore, scolding her husband and calling him every name under the sun, and as she did so, she pulled the duvet off the dough. When she saw how it had overflowed into the bed in those three hours, she snapped. She started scooping up the dough with her hands and flinging it at my grandpa-in-law with all her might. He tried to duck, but most of her shots were on target. I tried to save the dough, saying it was a waste and she would have to do it over, but my efforts were in vain. She was in such a rage, there was no stopping her, she just went right on flinging dough, so sticky it barely came off her hands. One piece stuck to my grandpa-in-law's head, another to his arm, in short it stuck wherever it landed. The dough was soft and pliable, so it stretched nicely over his body. My grandma-in-law was also plastered with dough from head to toe, but she didn't stop until the bowl was empty.

My husband and I just watched. We didn't dare intervene, we knew what his grandma was like. She wouldn't have spared us, and the dough would have rained down on us too. When we saw the way the two of them looked, though, we couldn't help but laugh. Softly at first, but then out loud, till the tears ran down our cheeks. My husband's grandma suddenly noticed. "What's so funny?" My husband and I couldn't hold back and began roaring with laughter. She stared at us a moment, then looked at my grandpa-in-law, standing there with dough over his eye. She turned to the dressing table mirror, and beholding herself in all her beauty, she began to laugh with us. We split our sides as we wiped the dough off of them. My husband's grandma refused to speak to her husband, though.

Early the next morning, my grandpa-in-law took the pushcart and left. He didn't come home again till evening. He laid a full shopping bag on the table and glanced at my grandma-in-law out of the corner of his eye to see what her reaction was. She sat by the stove without a word, paying him no attention. The bag sat on the table for hours. My husband's grandma walked past several times, pretending not to see it. I knew she was curious, but pride wouldn't allow her to peek inside, and my husband and I didn't dare in front of her. So we went to bed not even knowing what was in the bag. In the morning I was woken by the delicious smell of pásky. My husband's grandma was baking, sliding one tray into the oven after another. She always baked at least eight to ten trays: poppyseed, cocoa, cheese curds, walnut, and plum jam, or she would mix the fillings. Immediately it dawned on me what was in the bag. My husband's grandpa had bought flour and other baking ingredients, to make it up to her.

The next time she spoke to him, he got itchy feet again. So he secretly popped out for a beer. My grandma-in-law baked and cooked, not even noticing that he kept disappearing and coming back again. First he brought wood and stoked the fire, so the cakes would come out nice and golden, then water, then whoop, out for a beer, and then he ran right back again, before my grandma-in-law could notice anything suspicious. But then he started to get frisky. She gave him a stern look and said: "Jouža, you better not be drinking! You promised me this morning!"

"What makes you think that, Marienka?" my husband's grandpa replied. But my grandma-in-law still didn't believe him. Then he popped back out for a beer, then rushed back for lunch, then back out for a beer, and the next thing you know, he was lost in the pub again.

Afternoon rolled around and we womenfolk were the only ones left at home. My grandma-in-law was glad she was done baking. I helped her tidy everything up, and she went to lie down on the couch and fell asleep, exhausted. We tiptoed around her, so as not to wake her up. She slept until nightfall.

Meanwhile my sister-in-law showed up. My husband's grandma woke up and her first words were: "Where's Grandpa?" We kept our mouths shut. "You all know as well as I do that he's sitting in the pub, pouring liquor down his throat. The old geezer, but he better not mess with me, I'll teach him, he's going to sleep in the shed tonight. I won't have a drunk in my home!" She took the keys, locked the flat, and went to make some coffee. She cut up the delicious-smelling pásky on a plate for us.

It was already dark out when someone knocked on the door. We all fell quiet. After a moment, the knock came again, this time harder. "You're not sleeping in this house! Go back to where you got sozzled, you sonuvabitch sot!" my husband's grandma yelled. "You aren't coming in here, go sleep in the shed!" and she called him a few dirty names for good measure. At that point, the person on the other side of the door started pounding even harder and shouting: "Open up, open up!"

"So you won't leave me alone? I'll show you!" My grandma-in-law took a bucket and filled it with cold water. The loud banging came again. "So he won't stop, eh? Well, I'll show him! Come on, unlock the door," my husband's grandma ordered me, and she readied the bucket. I unlocked and opened the door. My grandma-in-law took the bucket of water and doused the person in the hallway, from head to toe.

"What are you doing? Are you out of your mind?" We recognized from the voice that it wasn't my husband's grandpa, but my sister-in-law's husband, who had come to pick her up. My husband's grandma stood glued to the floor. As soon as she came to her senses, she apologized to my brother-in-law and helped him dry off. She made him a cup of hot coffee and pushed the plate of cakes toward him in a gesture of peace. My brother-in-law grumbled that it was dangerous to a person's health to go on visits and he should have stayed at home. My grandma-in-law felt terrible about it. On the other hand, it made her even angrier at her husband and she swore that she would punish him. And so she did. For the next two days he slept in the shed, and I carried meals out to him in a pot. And my husband's grandpa stuck to the straight and narrow for some time after that.

FILM SHOOT

One day my grandpa-in-law's pal Miško came over and asked if he wanted to make some money. My husband's grandpa said he'd love to and how much? Miško explained that they were shooting a historical film at the castle in Hluboká nad Vltavou and they needed extras to shout "Long live the king!" That's it, he said.

And for doing nothing they'd get a hundred and fifty crowns. When my grandma-in-law heard how much money my grandpa-in-law could make, she gave him her unconditional approval.

"Go ahead, tu hercona, just make sure to bring some money back!" My grandpa-in-law was delighted that she gave him permission.

Early Saturday morning, Miško picked him up and off they went. My grandma-in-law was expecting him to come home that evening, but my grandpa-in-law was nowhere to be found. He didn't show up until the next morning. We almost didn't recognize him! Clothing in tatters, barefoot, covered in dirt, scratched and bruised from head to toe.

"Jesus, Jouža, what happened? Who did that to you?"

"They did!" he said.

"Who they?" she asked.

"You know, during the shoot. We had to take off our clothes and they gave us these tattered old rags instead, so we would look like beggars, they said. When we shouted 'Long live the king!' someone started throwing rocks at us and then the brawling began. I tried to defend myself. I mean, I don't let anyone slap me around for nothing! When it was all over, some fellow walked up to me, stuck a hundred and fifty crowns in my hand, I signed three x's on a sheet of paper, and that was the end of the shoot. We didn't have any place to wash up, I couldn't find my shoes or any of my things, and when I asked where they were, they told me, 'Sorry, gramps, you must have lost them somewhere drinking.' I couldn't find Miško either, they must have taken him away in an ambulance, there were a few of them there after the battle. So I left like this, half-naked and by myself. And since I was too embarrassed to get on the bus, I walked along the train tracks all night. I'm freezing cold and dying for something to eat. My feet are covered in blisters," my grandpa-in-law lamented.

My grandma-in-law washed him off, tended his wounds, fed him a meal, and put him to bed. She didn't even dare to ask if he had the money. Once he was asleep, she searched through the rags he was wearing when he came home. And to her surprise she found the promised one hundred and fifty crowns. My grandma-in-law had a pension of four hundred and forty crowns a month, so that was a lot of money. She didn't even mind that my grandpa-in-law walked around all week with bruises that changed color every day.

GOJA

It was a lovely summer evening. We were sitting in front of the TV, sipping hot coffee, absorbed in the story of the beautiful Angélique and her love for the Comte de Peyrac, when my grandma-in-law said: "Chaľomas goja!" We all turned and gave her a look, wondering what had spurred her to crave a dish like that out of nowhere, but then went back to watching the film. My husband and his grandpa, though, along with our neighbor Ďula, got an idea. They whispered back and forth a while, gave each other a wink, and then one by one disappeared.

As soon as the film was over, my husband's grandma noticed the men were gone. "Back at the pub again. A person can't even watch TV without them taking advantage of it!" Little did she suspect, though, that it would be worse than usual. My husband loves goja, so the moment my grandma mentioned it, he began to drool, and from then on, there was no stopping him. They teamed up and set out to the slaughterhouse to get intestines for goja. It was pretty far, but that didn't bother them. First they went for a beer, to fuel up for the trip. At the slaughterhouse, my grandpa-in-law stood watch—he was supposed to whistle if he saw anything. My husband and Ďula scaled the wall and each of them grabbed a bundle of intestines, uncleaned—in those days they threw the large intestines out in the trash. My husband found a sack, they put the intestines inside, threw the sack over the wall, climbed back out, and hurried home.

They were a short way from home when my grandpa-in-law got the bright idea to go for one more beer, knowing that my grandma-in-law wouldn't allow him anymore after that. Ďula and my husband tried to talk him out of it, but he insisted, so they went to have a beer at the pub standing outside. As they stood there drinking, a police car pulled up. The cops had come to buy cigarettes and something to drink. One stayed in the car, the other went inside. And of course intestines stink like crazy if they haven't been cleaned of feces. Even more so when it's hot, so the cop comes out of the pub, stops next to them and says: "Jesus, that stinks! What have you got in the sack there, fellas?" My grandpa-in-law, my husband and Ďula didn't know what to say, so they just stared at him. They knew they were in trouble. "Well, come on, fellas, cat got your tongue?" and the cop took a step closer. "Jesus, that reeks! Show me what you've got in there!" Ďula untied the sack and the cop said: "Those are intestines. You fellas robbed the slaughterhouse!" The men nodded, what else could they do? "All right, gentlemen," said the cop, "you're bringing back those intestines and we're taking you to the station." My husband took the sack, threw it over his shoulder, and they had to make the long trip to the slaughterhouse on foot. The cops drove slowly behind them. Then, on the way back to the police station, the three of them had to walk again, since the intestines had burst and whatever was inside them had run down my husband's back. When they made it to the station, his shirt stank so badly he had to take it off and throw it away.

We meanwhile sat at home, chatting unsuspectingly. Just then someone banged on the window. "Hey, a cop! Go ask what he wants." I went to the window and he launched in right away:

"Are you Mrs. Šestáková?"

"I am," I said.

"We have your husband and his grandpa."

"Lord, what have they done?"

"They can tell you that themselves. Bring two hundred crowns with you and a shirt for your husband."

Dark thoughts ran through my head, why of all things a shirt?! They must have beaten him so badly his shirt was torn to shreds. I grabbed the money and a shirt and walked with the officer to the station, just across the park from us. My husband stood outside, chatting with a cop. My grandpa-in-law stood off to the side, puffing on a smoke. Ďula was nowhere in sight. My husband put on his shirt and gave the cop two hundred crowns. "Get out of here, but don't let it happen again," the officer hollered at him.

On the way home, my husband told me everything.

"Where's Ďula?" I asked.

"They kept him there, since he was sassing them."

I ran off to let Ďula's wife know what had happened. She took some money and headed off to the station to fetch him. My grandma-in-law was watching for us from the window. The first thing she did was chew the men out. "What were you thinking, walking into a pub with goja? You didn't bring home a thing, and on top of that we had to pay a fine!" She turned to my husband: "Did they beat you up? Did they do anything to you?" Then she turned to my grandpa-in-law and cursed him out for letting their son get locked up over a pint of beer. Just then the door opened and there stood Ďula, with a black eye and a swollen lip.

"They let you have it, huh?" said my husband.

"Yeah," said Ďula. "I told them to take the money and shove it, and they beat the crap out of me." Ďula was so angry that he and my husband decided to go and get the intestines back, in exchange for the fine and the ass-kicking they got from the cops. My grandma-in-law and Ďula's wife tried to talk them out of it, but it was no use. The men took their plastic bags and went. Lord, was I scared! I prayed the whole time, walking back and forth around the flat until they finally returned. Intestines and all. So the next day we had goja.

THE MOVIES

One Sunday, after lunch, my grandma-in-law made up her mind that we should go to the movies. They were showing a movie about the war and some Russian soldiers who were so hungry they ate their own horse, and she insisted on seeing it. So we went to the afternoon show. We bought tickets and potato chips and settled into the back row of the theater. There were a total of ten people there, including the four of us: my grandma-in-law, my grandpa-in-law, me and my husband. The usher looked at us like we were crazy.

After the newsreel, the movie began. That was the signal for my grandma-in-law to open the chips. The bag rustled and everyone turned to look at us. The lady who was ushering ran up to us and gave my grandma-in-law a warning. It was quiet for a while. Then my grandma-in-law started to offer us the chips again.

"Gramma," I said, "we have to be quiet!"

"OK, from now on, I'll be quiet as a mouse," my husband's grandma promised. But she had no idea how deeply moved she would be. First she shouted at the soldiers onscreen in a mix of Slovak and Romani, at times loudly and with lots of swear words. The usher came running up and once again had a word with her. "I'll keep quiet from now on," my grandma-in-law swore.

But of course the whole way through the film she kept interrupting, and the ticket lady kept running over and scolding her like a little girl. At the end, my grandma-in-law added the crowning touch. When the scene came where the poor starving soldiers killed and ate the horse, she began sniffling and blowing her nose. Finally she burst out in tears so loudly that the other six people in the theater turned to us, annoyed, and the usher had to escort her out of the theater. She cried and cursed the whole way home.

After that experience, my husband and I vowed never to go to the movies with his grandma again. In the end we went with her three more times, but she wasn't the only one who carried on, unfortunately, since they were showing *Planet of the Apes*, *Jaws*, and the classic, sentimental Romani love story *Gypsies Go to Heaven.*

THE WAY WE USED TO LIVE

BY MICHAL ŠAMKO

Believe it or not, in a little village by the name of Radkyně, not far from Nová Paka, where in winter it often snowed so much that the bus didn't come and the children had to make it to school on foot, there was a house. My parents—Michal, known as Béla, and Helena, named after her father Belaňa—got the place in exchange for the home they owned in Slovakia. It wasn't big, just three rooms and a kitchen. In front of the house we had a sloping meadow, with apple trees and nice grass that my dad cut for his rabbits. Behind the house, where there used to be a school, led a path, and beyond that an enormous linden tree grew, the oldest tree in the village. In spring it was always covered in flowers and the whole yard was filled with its intoxicating scent. A huge meadow also extended behind the house. We had trees there too. The cherry plums tasted the best. We loved them as kids. Sometimes we would pick them even before they were ripe. Our dad would give us a good chewing out, since our mom made jam out of them, but there were times when we didn't leave her a single one.

We lived in the middle of the village and had a lot of gadjos living around us. On one side, behind our house, was an old-timer named Pavel. He lived alone and was a real dirty old man. Our dad used to make fun of him, since he, begging your pardon, went poop on the manure pile and wasn't the least embarrassed that people could see his naked behind. One day our dad took a handful of nettles, snuck up on him, and lashed him across the rear end. You should have seen how Pavel carried on! He quickly pulled up his pants and yelled at our dad: "Come on, Míša! What're you doing? You son of a gun! Just wait till the next time you need something. I'll smack you one right back!" My dad and I laughed so hard we practically fell down.

At the top of the meadow, behind our house, was a small wooden home with a red porch where old Mrs. Raisová lived. She was a kindhearted old lady. My dad bought goat milk from her for his pigs. As a little boy, I used to go and help her out sometimes, then afterwards she would feed me some of her yummy sweet rolls. Her son Franta lived at home with her. I was afraid of him—he was just as mad as his black dog Alan. I didn't like going there when he was home.

My parents were excellent household managers. Even though we were the only Roma in the village, the gadjos treated us like we were one of them. My mom and dad knew how to do everything around the house themselves, including masonry work, absolutely everything. More than once the gadjos themselves came to help us. It was always a lot of fun when they came.

I'm the youngest of six children. We were three boys and three girls. My oldest siblings were named Láďa and Božena, and people called me Mižu. My mom and dad were employed down at the brickyard. So every now and then, my oldest brother or sister had to stay home with me, since I didn't go to school yet.

One day my father said to me: "Mižu, son, no one can stay home with you tomorrow, since Láďa and Božena have to go to school. But you're a big boy now, so listen, here's what you'll do tomorrow! Get up, take your scooter, and come straight in to see us at work. Is that clear, kiddo?"

"Uh-huh," I said, and since it was nighttime, I went off to bed.

The next morning I woke up, looked around, and no one was home. Just me, all by myself! I was so proud! I hastily put on my tracksuit and shoes, and shot out the door like a bullet. We had a bench in the courtyard, underneath the window, so I sat down and looked around at the beauty surrounding me. Some little ducklings, ducks, hens, geese, and my little doggy Fuňa all came by to see me. The upper part of the courtyard was closed off by a wooden gate. On the other side, our rams were grazing out in the meadow. Janku, Ferko, and I don't remember the name of the third one anymore. The hens promenaded around the meadow, and since some of the gadjos didn't have a fence, every so often our hens and geese would wander into their meadow and their hens would come into ours.

Hurry, hurry! Time to get going! I should have been at the brickyard ages ago, my mom and dad were definitely expecting me by now. I quick slammed the door, grabbed my wooden scooter, and went barreling off downhill to find my dad. There was one gadjo who lived and worked at the brickyard, his name was Groha, and he bred huge geese. I was scared of them, since when I tried to walk past them through the gate, they started chasing me. The gadjos, who were just arriving for the start of their shift, practically split their sides laughing. They thought it was funny I was scared. I stood at the gate, too terrified to go inside, and every time the geese came near, I chased them off with a stick. Just then I spotted my father. Saved! I thought.

"Come on now, Josef," my dad said to Groha. "Can't you see the boy's afraid? Those geese of yours are worse than a dog, even grown-ups are scared of them. Would you please lock them up?"

The gadjo laughed out loud, but then said, "OK, OK, Mišu, I'm shooing them away!"

My dad took my hand and asked, "What took you so long? You were supposed to be here ages ago, we were expecting you at ten. Anyway, it doesn't matter now. Run along to the canteen and buy yourself something to eat, just tell the lady at the window what you want and she'll give it to you. Then come find me at the conveyor belt. Got it, kiddo? And get a move on, it'll be lunchtime soon and the canteen will be packed."

"Sure, Dad, don't worry. I know my way around. I'll come find you after." My dad went back to his work and I headed to the canteen.

"Hello, Mrs. Vonzová! I'd like to order something."

"Of course, and how is my clever little boy today? What'll it be?" Mrs. Vonzová asked.

Just then I noticed the chlebíčky! Those little oval slices of bread topped with ham and cheese and eggs, yum! "I'll take a chlebíček! I can pay for it as soon as I get my paycheck, OK? Just put it on my tab for now."

The lady at the window started laughing like crazy. "Why, certainly, here, take two, I'll put it in my book. Don't forget to bring the cash as soon as you get paid!"

I had no idea what she was laughing about, but I didn't really care. I was just glad to have those excellent chlebíčky. Everyone here knew who I was. They knew who I belonged to. Sometimes they would give me a ride in the forklift, other times they would take me to see the kilns. Groha, the gadjo with the geese, had a soft spot for me. The moment he saw me he'd start in with the shenanigans.

Throwing me up on his shoulders and charging back and forth. Lighting a pipe of tobacco for me. Fool that I was, I thought I was some kind of bigshot. When the gadjos saw me they just laughed. My dad gave Groha a talking-to, especially about the pipe, but also the other things. He was afraid something might happen to me. But even he laughed sometimes—it made him feel good that his workmates liked me and kidded around with me.

I hadn't even finished the first chlebíček when I saw my mom and dad, with the foreman and a bunch of other people, walk into the canteen. I got up, wiped off my mouth, then I saw the lady come out from behind the window and laugh: "Excuse me, Mr. Foreman, I just wanted to ask, when will our little Michal here be getting his paycheck? He put two chlebíčky on his tab today, and he said he'd pay me back once he got paid."

The foreman and the others burst out laughing. "Well, Mrs. Vonzová, our little Michal will be getting paid just as soon as his dad does," my father said. He and my mom had a good laugh, too.

Ever since then, whenever the foreman or anyone else from the brickyard wanted something from the canteen, they would send me, saying, "Tell them to put it on your tab and you'll settle up on payday!" And I went, knowing I would get a piece of candy out of it.

When I was still a little boy and didn't go to school yet, I thought everything around me was perfect. I played with my dad a lot. He made me all sorts of things—a toy gun, whistles—whatever, just as long as I had something to play with. I liked helping him while he worked. When he built walls, I handed him bricks; if he was making a hutch, I'd pass him the nails and whatever other tools he needed.

He taught me to mow the grass, forge metal on an anvil, raise animals, everything. I liked watching my father, I was constantly at his heels. Sometimes he would yell at me to leave him alone and stop going wherever he went. I even followed him into the pub. My mom used to send me to bring him home, because when he ran into the guys from the village, he would stay out late drinking. I was the only one he would listen to when he was drunk.

Every so often, my dad played some pretty good pranks on me, too. For instance, this one time he took a big knife, went out in the meadow under a tree, and made it look like he'd killed himself. My mom, playing along, came running after me, screaming: "Look, your dad stabbed himself!" Me being a little boy, I fell for it, and went racing out right away to see what had happened. I sobbed so hard I couldn't stop.

When my dad realized it had gone too far, he stood up and said: "You would cry like that for me, kiddo? You love me that much?" I hugged him out of sheer happiness he was still alive, as he covered my face in kisses and said: "My precious little boy, I love you so much!" Then he lifted me up on his shoulders and played with me.

Some people who got a flat on a former farmstead moved to our village. They worked in the cowhouse. They were Roma too, but different than us. At home they didn't speak Romani, but an Eastern Slovak dialect. Because Štefan, the father, was a Slovak. To be fair, though, he did know Romani well. His wife, Květa, was a Romňi. They had three children: Štefan junior, the oldest, and two girls: Květa, named after her mom, and Milka. I quickly made friends with them. My mom and dad went to visit them too. Sometimes they had parties and stayed up all night making merry.

I really loved life in our village. The gadjos were nice and whenever I went to visit them I always felt at home. Sometimes they'd give me a bite to eat, other times I would lend a hand with something or other. It never even crossed my mind that I was different from them because I was a Rom.

I wasn't going to school yet. But soon I was supposed to enter first grade. I was a little bit scared, but more than that, I was proud that I too would learn to read and write, and everything else my older brothers knew how to do. They wouldn't be able to make fun of me anymore. I too would be a schoolboy, as my dad used to say. I just felt a little sad that I wouldn't be able to spend as much time with the animals anymore.

One Saturday, my uncle Vasil and my aunt and Štefan and his wife came to visit us. Early the next morning, my dad and Štefan killed a pig, so there was lots of cooking: brawn, tripe sausage—in short, everything you make when you slaughter a pig. "We could do with a drop of something to wash it down with," said my dad. So people drank, had a good time, laughing and dancing a little too. Then suddenly, out of nowhere, my dad, who'd had a fair amount to drink, came up and told me to quick put on my red running shorts and a T-shirt, the people from the TV were coming to film me running a race with our ram Ferko. It was true, I couldn't go anywhere without that little ram of mine chasing after me.

We were going to be on TV! I was thrilled, because everyone told me a lot of gadjos had heard about me and my Ferko. And whoever won would get a medal. I quickly changed clothes, ran off to fetch Ferko, and we waited out on the road in front of our house for the start of the race. My mom and dad and uncle, everyone stood out in front of the house, watching us.

"Where are the people from the TV, Dad?"

"Don't worry, they're hidden," my dad said, reassuring me. "Quick, run as fast as you can, so you'll come in first!"

The neighbors came out to watch the spectacle too. "You see, son, even the gadjos came to watch, so don't embarrass us!" After that, all I heard was "Go!" I went racing off as fast as I could, with Ferko behind me. He almost overtook me, but I shifted into higher gear, and Štefan was waiting down at the finish line with the flag. I came in first! I won! My chest swelled with pride. Ferko stood next to me, waiting. "I won, Feri. I'm better than you!" I laughed.

The Roma hooted with laughter so hard they got the hiccups. And the gadjos laughed as well. Then our neighbor came to me and said: "You deserve a medal for winning." And she presented me with an enormous chocolate plaque. I was proud, but I didn't see any cameras anywhere. By that point, though, I didn't even care. I had my medal and that was enough.

A month later, my dad sneakily sent me to my aunt Raisová's to get milk for our pigs. By the time I got back, my best friend Ferko was history. I couldn't stop crying and refused to speak to my dad. But time heals all, even the pain of death. Days and months went by, and the day came when I was supposed to go to school for the first time. My older brother Dušan walked me there. He himself was in fifth grade, so we were both schoolboys now. My other siblings went to the special school.

So this was going to be my class, room 1B. I opened the door and saw a roomful of gadjo boys and girls sitting at the desks. The teacher walked in right behind me. "You must be Michal!" she said. "We've been expecting you. Have a seat there by the girl in the second row, Monika. You can take off your bag and soon you'll find out what we're going to do today." I thanked her and went to take a seat. The teacher was a tall lady with long blond hair who wore nice perfume. She looked like she would be friendly enough.

I took off my satchel and hung it on the hook attached to the desk. I peeked over at the girl next to me, she was pretty, with long light hair and a beautiful red dress. "Hi, I'm Míša," I said, introducing myself. She took one look at me and moved away.

"Ew!" she blurted. I looked around the room, inhaling through my nose.

"I don't smell anything in here, do you?" I couldn't figure out what she thought smelled so bad. I knew I didn't stink! My parents had bought me a new outfit, so how could I stink, you silly girl! I decided it would be best if I didn't talk to her. The teacher went over the basics with us, and then we were each supposed to introduce ourselves, so we could get to know one another. When my turn came, I stood up and turned to the class: "I'm Michal. I live in Radkyně. I'm seven years old and I really look forward to learning something here. That's what my dad told me." And I sat back down. Everybody laughed at me, I couldn't figure out why. It wasn't as if I'd said anything funny. The teacher quieted them:

"What is the matter with you kids, is that any way to behave? It's Michal's first day here, just like you, and I'm sure he's looking forward to school as much as all the rest of you!"

Just then a small boy named Martin got to his feet and said: "But he's a Gypsy! I refuse to talk to him, I don't want to get fleas. Plus my dad said they steal." I sat glued to my seat. Everything I had previously imagined about school flashed through my mind. I wanted nothing more than to disappear and run straight home, but the teacher came up to me, took my hand, and said:

"I'm sure Michal is nothing like that. His parents have jobs and I know his brother who comes to school with us, and we've never had any problems with him. So listen up, children. If I hear the word 'Gypsy' in my classroom again, I'll have to tell your parents."

I was just starting to think that everything was all right when Monika stood up and said: "But Miss, if I sit next to him, the other kids won't play with me. Why should I have to sit next to the Gypsy?" She was right. All day long, none of the other children talked to her. "Ew, you stink," they said. "Keep your hands off of us!"

The teachers were well aware of this. After I'd been going to school for a while, it became a regular thing that whenever a boy did something wrong, as punishment they put him in the last row next to me, where I normally sat by myself. They knew that putting the children next to me was a worse punishment than if they marked them down for it. But not all of the teachers did that.

It's hard to express how I felt that first day. When I was little, the Czechs in our village never talked to me that way, let alone called me a Gypsy. I was happy when Dušan came to pick me up after school. On the way home, he asked me how my day had been, but I didn't want to talk about it. I was ashamed they had written me off like that on my first day. I acted like nothing had happened. "It was great," I mumbled. I kept my thoughts to myself.

My dad came home that evening. I had my bag all ready and waiting to go for the next day. "So, kiddo, how did it go at school?" he asked. I didn't want to tell him, or my mom, but I couldn't keep the tears from springing to my eyes. My dad saw right away and took me on his knee. "You can tell me, son, what did they do to you?"

"Nothing, daddy."

"The kids called you names, didn't they? And what about the teacher, did she say anything to them?"

"She did. She told them they shouldn't talk like that and call someone names when they don't know anything about them. But then she left the room and they called me names anyway. I beat up one of the boys for it, Martin was his name. The teacher ran over and yelled at me, saying, 'What do you think you're doing, we don't act like that here.'"

My dad was furious. "Tomorrow I'm going with you and wait till you see what I tell them!"

I burst into tears like a little boy. I didn't want my first day at school to be ruined like that! My dad could see how upset I was. "Come on, little fella, I'll put you to bed and tell you a nice story." We lay down in my bed together, my dad wrapped an arm around me and ran his other hand through my hair. "Now listen, son, and I'll tell you a story about a Rom who everyone made fun of." He told me the tale of Šargo the cripple with blond bangs who went and lived with a hermit to get away from everyone mocking him. He learned from him how to identify herbs and it ended up changing his life.

"You see, son, there you have it. A boy who everyone made fun of and took for an idiot became a doctor and married a princess. Now his mom doesn't have to work anymore and his sister, Maruška, also married a doctor, a man who worked in the hospital with Šargo. And you can do it too, kiddo! As long as you don't give up and fall apart because people call you a Gypsy and whatnot. If you study hard, you'll be smart. If you're smart, then everyone will treat you with respect. You'll do well for yourself, and someday you'll look back and remember this story."

Everything was just as my dad said, may the earth rest lightly on my parents. I kept going to school and studied diligently. The kids in school called me names, but I just kept on thinking about that story. Once we'd grown up a little and had gotten a little smarter, the gadjo kids saw that I may have been a Rom, but I went to school regularly and got good grades. They stopped calling me a Gypsy and started coming to me asking me to tutor them in math, Russian, and other subjects. When I was older still, I trained to be a mason, and after the revolution I passed my A-levels. Why not until after the revolution? My dad refused to join the Party, so they wouldn't let me into the school.

The years flew by and the boys who used to call me names in my childhood are now my best friends. It isn't easy for a Rom to go to school. You have to be twice as smart to be acknowledged and accepted.

Today I'm older and I know that if you want to achieve something in life, you can't lower your head but have to hold your head high and overcome the obstacles. Ultimately, it's up to you to fight for a better life for yourself here in this world.

I'll never forget my mom, and my dad, who told me this story. Today I tell it to my own children, and to anyone else who's afraid to go to school because the children there call them names. Someday all of us Roma will have an education and there won't be anyone left to make fun of us. May God be with you all, Roma!

ČIRLATUNO DŽIVIPEN

MICHAL ŠAMKO

Has na has, andre jekh cikno gavoro, so pes vičinelas Radkiňa, paš o bareder foros Nova Paka, has jekh kheroro. Najekhvar sar cikne čhavore, te na džalas o autobusis, džahas ada drom andre škola pal peskere. Oda kheroro Radkiňate chudňa miro dad o Michal mira daha Heľenkaha vaš o kher, so len has pre Slovensko. Le dades vičinenas Bela the e daj has pal o dad Belaňa. Na has igen baro, ča trin kherora the e kuchňa. Pašal o kher amen has anglal cikňi luka. Saľigori tele plajiha odej baronas phabaľina the šukar čarori, so miro dad košinelas le zajacenge. Ke amaro kher pal e čirlatuňi škola pes cirdelas cikno dromoro, paš leskero agor barolas bari ľipa. Nekhphureder stromos andro gav. Sako ňilaj, te obbarolas le kvitkenca, šukares pachinelas pal calo dvora. Palal pal o kher amen has bari luka, odoj amen has tiš o stromi. Jekhfeder has ola šarge khiľava, so amenge baronas. Igen rado len sar čhave chahas. Varekana mek na dogele u imar len čhingerahas pal o stromos. Amaro dad pre amende vašoda kerelas vika, bo e daj lendar kerelas o gulo makhľipen, aľe amen lake na mukhahas varekana choc ča jekhori.

Bešahas maškar andro gav, pašal amende dživenas but gadže. Pre jekh sera pal amaro kher dživelas phuro manuš o Pavel. Has korkoro u ajso džungalo. O dad peske lestar kerelas pherasa, bo phirelas, sar te phenel pre paťiv, te chinel pro ganajos u ňisar pes na ladžalas, hoj leske dičhol e nangi bul. Jekhvar o dad iľa e labarďi čar, počoral les obgeľa u ola čaraha les čhinďa pal e nangi bul. Ta bi dikhenas, so o Pavel kerelas! Sig pre peste cirdľa e cholov u thovelas pro dad vika: „No Mišo! Cos to udělal?! Ty jeden! Počkej, až zas budeš něco potřebovat, taky tě přetáhnu!“ Le dadeha asahas, maj na perahas tele.

Opral amende pal bari luka has cikno kaštuno kheroro loľa veranďicaha u odej bešelas e phuri Raisovo. Joj has lačhi babkica. Mro dad latar cinkerelas koziko thud le baľičeske. Varekana ke late sar ciknoro phiravas, pomožinavas lake u joj man delas igen lačhe bokeľa. Laha odej bešelas lakero čhavo o Franta. Lestar man daravas, bo has ajso choľamen sar leskero kalo rikono o Alan. Sar has khere jov, narado odej phiravas.

Kampel te phenel, hoj miro dad la daha has lačhe chulaja. Choc samas ča korkore Roma andro gavoro maškar o gadže, savore amen ľikerenas avka, sar te Roma na avahas. Mro dad la daha peske sa khatar o kher džanenas te kerel korkore. The murinenas, savoro sa džanenas. Najekhvar pes ačhiľa, hoj amenge o gadže korkore avile te šegitinel. Joj, ta has pherasa!

Me somas jekhterneder maškar šov čhave. Samas trin phrala the trin pheňa. Jekhphureder has mro phral o Laďis the e pheň e Božena, man vičinenas Mižu. Miro dad la daha phirenas andre buťi, kerenas tele andro gav andre cihelňa. Vašoda e pheň či o phral sar jekhphureder mušinenas manca varekana te ačhol khere, bo me mek na phiravas andre škola.

Jekhvar mange o dad phenel: „Mižku, tajsa tuha ňiko khere na ačhola, bo lenge kampel te džal andre škola. Tu imar sal baro čhavoro, ta šun, so tajsa kereha! Ušťeha, leha tuke tiri kolobežka the sig aveha pal amende andre buťi. Šunes, Mižku?!"

„Ha, ha," phenďom u imar has rat, ta geľom mange te sovel.

Has tosara u me ušťiľom. Dikhľom pašal mande u ňiko khere nane. Ča me korkoro! Joj, sar somas barikano! Sig pre ma urďom e ceplakica, bogančici, u sig prastavas avri. Pre dvora tel e blakica amen has lavkica, pre late mange bešľom u ča dikhavas khatar mande pr'oda šukariben, so amen has pašal o kher. O cikne kačkici, o kachňora, o papiňa the miro rikonoro o Fuňa avenas dži kija mande. Opre pre luka o dad zakerďa e dvora kaštuňa kapuraha. U odej pasinenas pen amare trin bakre. Jekh pes vičinelas Janku, aver Feris u oda trito nav imar na leperav. O kachňa phirenas pal calo amari luka, bo varekana na has le gadžen o bara, ačholas pes, hoj amare kachňa the o papiňa džanas ko gadže u lengere ke amende.

Sig, sig! Imar kampel te džal! Sem imar mange kampľa čirla te džal andre cihelňa. Bizo pre ma imar o dad la daha užaren. Sig phandľom o vudar, iľom mange miri kaštuňi kolobežka u imar tradavas tele plajiha pal o dad. Andre odi cihelňa dživelas the kerelas jekh gadžo, o Groha. Les has bare papiňa. Me man lendar daravas, bo sar kamavas te predžal khatar lende andre kapura, prastanas pal ma. O gadže andal e buťi, so has pre dešatka, maj asabnastar na pukinenas. Has lenge pherasuno, kaj man darav. Terďuvavas pro agor, u te avenas o papiňa pašeder kija ma, la raňikaha len zatradavas. Sar dikhľom le dades, duminďom mange, „imar mištes!“

„No tak, Josef,“ phenďa o dad le Grohaske, „copak nevidíš, že má ten kluk strach? Vždyť ty tvoje husy jsou horší než pes, bojí se jich i dospělí. Zavři je, prosím tě!“

„Haha!“ bares asalas o gadžo, „ale neboj, Mišu, už je zaženu.“

O dad man iľa vastestar u phučľa: „Kaj salas avka but? Imar čirla adej kampľal te avel, užarahas tut pre dešatka. Ta imar jekh, vareso tuke cineha. Akana tu džaha andre kantina u odej tuke vareso chaha, ča la gadžake phen, so kames, u joj tuke dela. Paľis aveha pal mande ko pasos. Ha, Mižku? U siďar, bo maj hela dilos u pherďi kantina.“

„Ha, dado, ma dara, sem me imar adej savoro džanav, kaj so hin, paľis avava pal tute.“ O dad geľa pale te kerel u me mange geľom andre kantina.

„Dobrý den, paní Vonzová! Já bych si něco dal.“

„Jistě, a jakpak se máš, ty malej šikulko? Co to bude?“ phučel e Vonzovo.

Androda dikhľom ola chlebički! „Paní, dejte mi chlebíček! Až dostanu výplatu, tak vám to dám, jo? Zatím mi to napište.“

E gadži sar te diliňaľiľa, chudňa mandar te asal. „No jistě, na, tady máš dva a napíšu ti to do knihy. Tak až dostaneš výplatu, nezapomeň mi to přinýst!“

Na džanavas, soske asal, aľe has mange calkom jekh. Me somas rado vaš ola lačhe chlebički. Sako man adej imar mištes džanelas. Džanenas, hoj som le dadeskero the la dakero čhavoro. Varekana man tradenas la ješťerkaha, abo lenas man paš o bova. O Grohas, oda gadžo, so les has ola papiňa, pre ma na domukhelas. Sarča man dikhľa, imar manca kerelas pherasa. Lelas man pro phike u prastavkerelas manca okle arde. Varekana mange labarďa e pipa le dohanoha. Me sar dilino mange duminavas, savo som ternochar. O gadže oda dikhenas, ta avka mandar asanas. O dad pre leste thovelas vika vaš odi pipa the savoro, bo daralas, hoj pes mange vareso šaj ačhol. Aľe varekana tiš mandar asalas. Has leske mištes, bo džanelas, kaj man o gadže rado dikhen u keren manca pherasa.

Mek na chaľom jekh chlebičkos, ta dikhav le dades la daha, le majstros the but manušen, sar aven andre kantina. Ušťiľom, khosľom mange o muj u dikhav, sar avri aviľa odi prodavačka le asabnaha: „Pane mistr, chtěla jsem se jen zeptat, kdy tady náš malej Michálek dostane výplatu? Dnes si ode mě vzal dva chlebíčky na dluh, prý je po výplatě zaplatí.“

Sar ada šunďa o majstros, ta the jov, the ola aver gadže, pukinenas asabnastar. „To víte, paní Vonzová, náš Michálek bude mít výplatu tehdy, až bude brát jeho tatínek,“ phenďa miro dad. Asanas sar diline the miro dad la daha.

Akorestar, te o majstros, abo aver džene andre buťi vareso kamenas, bičhavenas man andre kantina u phenenas: „A řekni, ať ti to napíšou, že to o výplatě srovnáš!“ U me geľom, bo džanavas, hoj chudava cukrikos.

Sar somas cikno u na phiravas mek andre škola, has khatar ma sa šukar. Me man but bavinavas le dadeha. Jov mange sa, so džanelas, kerelas — pišťalki, pištoľa. Sa, ča kaj man te hel soha pes te bavinel. Rado leha keravas buťi. Te murinelas, davas leske o cehli, te kerelas le zajacenge kaštendar o than, podavas leske karfinora u sa, so leske kampelas.

Sa man sikhavelas te kerel. E čar te košinel, pre kovinca, la džvirinaha, savoro sa. Rado les dikhavas, kaj jov džalas, me pal leste. Varekana pre ma rakinelas, kaj les imar te mukhav, hoj našťi všadzik phirav leha. Me pal leste džavas the andre karčma. E daj man pal leste bičhavelas, bo te odej zgeľa pes le gadženca, but pijelas u na avelas sig khere. Ňikas na šunelas, ča man, te has matoro.

O dad peske varekana kerelas mandar ajse pherasa. Jekhvar iľa e bari čhuri, geľa pre luka tel o stromos u kerelas oda, hoj pes murdarďa. E daj pal ma sig kamukeri aviľa u zvičinďa: „Dikh, o dad pes demaďa la čhuraha!“ A me, sar cikno čhavoro, pal leste sig prastavas u paťavas oleske. But rovavas.

O dad te dikhelas, hoj imar but, ušťiľa u phenďa: „Tu bi pal ma rovehas, Mižku? Avka man rado dikhes?!“ Me lošatar, hoj dživel, les obchudavas. Jov man čumidelas u phenelas: „Tu sal miro cikno, Mižku, me tut igen rado dikhav!“ Iľa man pro phike u bavinelas pes manca.

Jekh berš andre amaro gavoro chudle te bešel varesave manuša, so chudle o kher odoj, kaj has varekana o JZD — o statkos. Kerenas andro kravinos. Tiš has Roma, aľe aver sar amen. Na denas khere duma romanes, aľe hutorinenas. O Štefan has Slovakos. Čačes kampel te phenel, hoj džanelas lačhes romaňi duma. E Květa, leskeri romňi, has romaňi. Has len trin čhavore. Jekhphureder o Štefankus, paľis duj čhajora, e Květka pal e daj u e Milka. Nabut olestar, so pen zabešle, somas ole čhavorenca baro kamaratos. The amare ke lende phirenas, varekana pijenas, mulatinenas dži tosara.

Rado dikhavas ada dživipen andro gavoro. O gadže has adej igen lačhe u me mange phiravas ke lende sar khere. Varekana man the vareso lačho dine, varekana lenge the šegitinavas. Na avelas mange andro šero oda, hoj me som romano čhavoro.

Andre škola me mek na phiravas, aľe vaš o duj čhon imar šaj geľom andre perši trjeda. Saľig man the daravas, aľe buter somas barikano, hoj the me man sikhľuvava te irinel, te genel u sa oda, so džanenas mire phureder phrala. Imar mandar na asana, imar the me avava školakos, sar phenelas mro dad. Ča has mange čeporo pharo oda, hoj imar na avava ajci mira džvirinaha.

Has sombat u ke amende aviľa o ujcus o Vasil, e bibi th'o Štefan la romňaha. O dad idž nebo oka ďives sig tosara murdarďa le Štefanoha le baľičes u tavelas pes, kerenas o tlačenki, sa so paš e zabijačka hin. „Kija oda kampel saľig te popijel," phenďa o dad. O manuša pijenas, bavinenas pen, asanas the saľig khelenas. Androda pal ma aviľa miro dad, imar matoro, kaj pre ma sig te uravav loľi cholov th'o tričkos, bo kamel te avel e televiza te cirdel oda tele, sar me the miro bakroro Feris dujdžene prastaha u ko khelela avri. Oda čačipen, miro bakroro pal ma prastalas všadzik, kaj ča džavas.

E televiza aviľa kij'amende! Me somas igen rado, bo mange sako phenelas, hoj but gadže imar šunde pal ma the pal miro Feris. U ko khelela avri, chudela medajla. Sig man preurďom, geľom pal o Feris u imar užarahas pro startos pro drom anglal amaro kher. O dad la daha, o bačis, savore has paš o kher avri u dikhenas pre amende, hoj ko khelela avri.

„Dado, u kaj e televiza?" phučľom lestar.

„Joj hiňi garuďi. Ma dara, sig prasta, kaj te kheles avri!" phenďa o dad.

Th'o susedi avile te dikhel, so pes avri kerel. „Dikhes,

Mižku, th'o gadže avile pre tute dikhel! Ta ma ker amenge ladž!" Paľis ča šunďom: „Start!" Me denašavas, sar ča džanavas, u Feris pal mande. Imar bi man preprastalas, ta sig mek buter chudľom te denašel. Odoj tele imar andro agor užarelas o Štefan la fanaha. Somas peršo! Khelďom avri! Somas igen barikano. O Feris terďiľa paš mande u užarelas. „Me khelďom avri, Feri, som feder sar tu!"

Savore Roma, so paš amende has, savore avka asanas, hoj hojkinenas. Th'o gadže asanas. Paľis aviľa e suseda u phenďa mange: „Za to, žes vyhrál, zasloužíš medaili!" U diňa man ajsi bari čokoladovo medajla. Me somas barikano, ča ňikhaj na dikhľom ola kameri. Imar mange has savoro jekh, has man medajla.

Pre aver čhon man o dad bičhaďa ke Raisovo, ke odi babka, ča avka kamukeri vaš o thud le baľičeske. Sar aviľom khere, imar has miro kamaratos bakroro Feris murdardo. Igen rovavas u na davas duma le dadeha. Savoro pregeľa, the e dukh, th'o ďivesa, th'o čhona denašenas u anglal mande has oda ďives, kana somas te džal perširaz andre škola. Andre škola man ľigenďa miro phureder phral o Dušan. Jov imar phirelas andre pandžto trjeda u so dujdžene phirahas andre zakladno škola. Ola aver phirenas andre zvlaštno škola.

Oda miri trjeda, 1. B. Phundraďom o vudar u dikhľom pherdo rakloren. Imar bešenas andro lavki. Sig pal ma aviľa e sikhľarďi. „Ty jsi ten Michálek! Už na tebe čekáme. Sedni si tam k té dívence do druhé lavice, k Monice, odlož si tašku a za chvíli se dozvíš, co budeme dneska dělat." Paľikerďom lake u geľom mange te bešel andre lavka. Miri sikhľarďi has uči gadži bare šargone balenca u šukares pachinelas. Na has te dikhel, hoj bi helas nalačhi.

Iľom mange e taška pal o dumo tele u figinďom la pre lavica. Dikhľom pre odi rakľori. Has la šukar bare bala, tiš ajse sar šarge the šukar lole rentici pre late has. „Ahoj, já jsem Míša," phenďom lake. Joj pre ma dikhľa, saľig pes odcirdňa.

„Fuj!" zvičinďa. Dikhavas pašal peste, pocirdavas le nakheha.

„Já tady nic necítím, ty jo?" čudaľinavas man, so lake khandel. Sem me na khandav! O amare mange cinde sa neve rentici, ta sar šaj khandav, diliňi! Feder hela, te laha na dava duma. E sikhľarďi amenge sa phenďa, so u sar keraha andre škola. Paľis sakoneske kampelas te phenel amaro nav, kaj amen savore te prindžaras. Te aviľa miro časos, ušťiľom upre u visarďom man kija lende: „Já jsem Michal. Bydlím v Radkyni. Je mi sedm roků a moc se těším, že se tady něco naučím. To mi říkal můj táta." U pale bešťom tele. Savore mandar asanas, na džanavas soske. Sem ňič ajso na phenďom, kaj te asan. E sikhľarďi pre lende zvičinďa.

„Tak copak to je, děti, to se sluší takhle se chovat? Michálek je tu první den jako vy a jistě se těší na školu jako každý z vás!"

Jekhvareste ušťiľa jekh rakloro, o Martin, u phenel: „Ale on je Cikán! Já se s ním bavit nebudu, nechci dostat blechy. A táta říkal, že kradou." Somas sar primardo andre odi lavka. Sa, so mange duminavas pal e škola, man pregeľa u kamelas pes mange te denašel, te džal sig khere. Ča e sikhľarďi pal ma aviľa, chudňa man vastestar u phenďa:

„Michálek takový jistě není, jeho rodiče pracují a znám jeho brášku, který chodí sem k nám do školy a nejsou s ním žádné problémy. Takže, děti, už tady slovo Cikán nechci slyšet, jinak to budu muset říct vašim rodičům."

Imar duminďom, hoj hela savoro lačho, te ušťiľa odi Monika, so bešelas manca andre lavka u phenel: „Paní učitelko, já s ním sedět nechci, ony by si pak se mnou ostatní děti nehrály. Proč zrovna já musím sedět s Cikánem?" Ada has čačipen. Calo ďives laha ňiko le raklorendar na denas duma u phenenas lake: „Fuj, ty smrdíš, nešahej na nás!"

Ada mištes džanenas savore sikhľarde. Sar me phiravas buter andre škola, te varesavo čhavoro kerelas nalačhipena, thoďa ajse čhavores paš ma te bešel andre paluňi lavka, kaj bešavas korkoro. O sikhľarde džanenas, hoj ada trestos hin goreder, sar te chudenas poznamka. No, na savore sikhľarde oda kerenas.

Na džanav, sar tumenge te phenel oda, so andre ma has. Ňigda sar cikno andre miro gav ada le gadžendar na šunďom, aňi oda lav Cikán. Somas igen rado, sar pal ma aviľa o Dušan. Sa mandar phučelas pal o drom, aľe na kamavas leske te phenel. Ladžavas man, hoj peršo ďives andre škola u imar mange čhinde e paťiv. Keravas sar ňič. „Sa has lačhes," phenďom le Dušanoske. Aľe duminavas mange peskero.

O dad raťi aviľa khere. Me mange sa sthoďom andre taška, so has man aver ďives andre škola. „Ta sar, Mižku, sar has andre škola?“ phučelas o dad. Na kamavas leske ňič te phenel, aňi la dake, aľe o apsa mange andal o jakha korkore džanas avri. Sar o dad dikhľa, iľa man ke peste pro khoča. „Ta s'oda, Mižku, vaker, so tuke kerde andre odi škola?“

„Ňič, dado.“

„Rakinenas tuke o raklore, so? U so oja sikhľarďi, ňič lenge na phenďa?!“

„Phenďa, dado. Phenďa, hoj našťi avka vakeren u te rakinen varekaske, pal kaste ňič na džanen. Aľe paľis geľa het u jon mange rakinenas. Jekhe raklores, le Martinos, marďom. Aviľa e sikhľarďi u phenelas mange, hoj sar mange oda duminav, hoj adej na som maškar peskere.“

O dad but choľisaľiľa. „Me tajsa džava tuha andre odi škola u dikheha, so me lenge odej phenava!“

Me sar ciknoro chudňom te rovel. Na kamavas oda, kaj miro peršo ďives andre škola te avel ajso džungalo. O dad dikhelas pre ma, hoj mange phujes. „Av, mro čho, thovava tut te pašľol. Vakerava tuke šukar paramisi.“ Pašľiľam amenge so dujdžene pro miro haďocis, o dad man jekhe vasteha obchudňa, u aver vasteha mange pipinelas andro bala. „Šun, mro čho, vakerava tuke šukar paramisi pal jekh romano čhavoro, so lestar sako ča asalas.“ Delas mange duma pal o Šargo, šargone balenca so leske perenas andro jakha, savo pes garuďa paš vešengero manuš. Sikhľiľa lestar sa pal o draba u oda leske visarďa o dživipen.

„Dikhes, Mižku, avka has u hin. Ole čhavorestar, so lestar sako asalas u phenenas pal leste, hoj hino dilino, akana hin doktoris. Iľa peske la princezna romňake. Leskera dajorake imar na kampel ňič te kerel, u e pheň e Maruška peske tiš rakhľa le doktoris, so kerelas le Šargoneha andre špitaľa. „The tu oda šaj džanes avka te kerel, Mižku! Te tut na deha u na banďuveha o dumo, te tuke vareko phenel, hoj sal Cikán či vareso aver. Te mištes sikhľoha, aveha goďaver. Te aveha goďaver, sako pre tu dikhela, sar te avehas raj. Paľis tuke mištes dživeha u lepereha tuke pre adi paramisi.“

Avka sar mro dadoro phenďa, mi del leske the la dajorake o Del loki phuv, avka sa has. Andre škola phiravas. Sikhľuvavas, but sikhľuvavas. O raklore mange rakinenas.

Me duminavas ča pal odi paramisi. Pal paru berš imar samas bareder čhavore u tiš goďaveder. Ola gadžikane raklore dikhenas, hoj som Rom, aľe tiš dikhenas, kaj phirav lačhes andre škola, u dikhenas, kaj man has lačhe znamki. Imar mange na phenenas Cikán. Korkore pal ma phirenas, kaj me len te sikhavav e matematika, e rušťina the aver so na džanenas. Sar bareder čhavoro sikhľiľom avri murariske u pal e revolucija mange kerďom e maturita. Soske ča pal e revolucija? Mro dadoro na kamelas te irinel tele papira, kaj te avel paš o komunisti. Vašoda man na mukhle te kerel odi škola.

O berša džanas u ola raklore, so mange rakinenas, hine akana mire jekhfeder kamarata. Nane lokes le Romeske te phirel andre škola. O Rom kampel te avel duvar feder sar o gadžo, kaj les te dičhol.

Akana imar som phureder u mištes džanav, hoj te o manuš vareso kamel te kerel, našťi thovel o šero tele. Mušinel oda šero te hazdel u la zoraha pes te marel savore nalačhipenenca. Pro agor hela jov, so khelela avri peskero feder dživipen pre adi luma.

But berš oleske hin, aľe pre mri dajori th'o dadoro, so mange vakerelas adi paramisi, šoha na bisterava. Adi paramisi me akana vakerav mire čhavorenge u savorenge, so pen daran te phirel andre škola, vašoda hoj lenge odej rakinena, kaj hine Cikáni. Jekhvar amen o Roma avaha savore sikhade avri u imar na hela oda manuš, so amenga rakinela. O Del tumenca savorenca, Romale!

GOING TO GRANDPA'S

BY EMIL CINA

I've decided to reminisce about the days when the word romipen, meaning "Romaniness," was still a living concept among us Roma. It's a real shame it's disappearing now. But let me just tell the story.

In the nineteen eighties, I was still living in Prague with my first wife and two children: Lucka and Marek. They both went to school in the district of Karlín. I don't know how many times my daughter begged for us to go see her grandpa, my father-in-law, in Slovakia. The kids' holiday had just begun, I had just bought a Škoda 105, and all of a sudden I decided: We're going. My wife loaded everything into the car and off we sped.

By early morning, we were outside of Prague. Our dog rode with us, too, barking and barking while the kids made a racket, and in the midst of all that, my wife was talking into my ear, but I couldn't even hear myself think. Then, when we stopped at a parking area, she said to me: "I'd also like to visit my brother in Vsetín along the way." So she got her wish. My brother-in-law's face completely lit up when he saw us. My sister-in-law loaded up our plates with food and egged us on: "Eat, eat!"

We talked about all sorts of things, and then I told my brother-in-law: "We're going to see Grandpa."

He thought we had come to see him. And out of the blue he says: "All right, we'll come with you!"

My eyes popped out of my head, and in my mind I thought: How're we going to do that? My brother-in-law, his wife, and their two children to boot?

When my sister-in-law, dainty and light as a fawn, climbed into the car, everything tipped to one side. I wanted to tell them we couldn't all fit, but I couldn't refuse them or they might have been offended. So what could I do? We squeezed eight people into the car, the kids sitting on the laps of the people in back.

So I drove and drove. It was blazing hot that day. Just outside of Poprad, in northern Slovakia, a cop pulled us over. He came walking up, and the moment he saw how many people there were in the car, he rubbed his eyes and yelled: "For God's sake, how many of you are there in that vehicle?"

My sister-in-law, the hefty one, stepped out of the car, breasts bouncing, and angrily told the cop: "This is our vehicle and it's none of your business!"

She started to argue with him, so I shouted: "Pavla, stop!"

The cop was all red in the face and didn't want to hear it. She got him so worked up that suddenly he screamed: "Go fu-- yourselves!"

To which my brother-in-law replied, leaning out the window: "Thank you!"

My sister-in-law, satisfied, climbed back in the car, a stick of salami in one hand, and proceeded to gorge herself. "You want some bread?" my wife asked, and she just said, "What for?"

We drove and drove. The children couldn't take sitting anymore; they wanted to go to sleep. We arrived after dark, exhausted, in the Košice suburb of Krásna nad Hornádom, in Romani known as Siplaka.

We knocked on the door, but nobody answered. We stood there for what seemed like half an hour. Finally, when my mother-in-law heard us speaking Romani, she came and opened the door. Suddenly the whole household was up and on its feet.

My father-in-law was delighted to see the kids again after so many years. He dug up a bottle of spirits from somewhere, and a few other Roma came by who also lived in the neighborhood. The conversation was never-ending.

Sometime around three a.m., my mother-in-law offered to put us to bed, but when I saw how many people were sleeping in the house, I said: "We'll sleep out in the car!" And so we did.

The next morning, we heard music coming in the windows. My father-in-law was standing next to our car, playing the fiddle. I'd never been woken up like that before.

I found out that the next day the local musicians were playing a gadjo wedding. The group had about seven people and one was a woman named Puci. She dressed like a man, though, with a brimmed hat on her head. As they were rehearsing, the first violinist kept telling her: "Puci, you're playing it wrong," and knocking her on the head with his bow. To which Puci replied: "That's because I was up all night shagging Helka." Helka was her girlfriend.

I went to the store with my wife to buy some groceries and also picked up a liter of spirits. But what good is one bottle? You have to pour a shot for everyone. There was a woman who didn't get any, and you should have seen the stink she made! Her husband got a drink and she didn't. So she went over to the house where they lived and started busting everything up. She tore the pillows and duvets off the bed and threw them out the window, cursing her husband the whole time. As soon as I saw that, I ran straight out to buy more booze.

On my way back, I poured her a cup, the woman downed it, and instantly turned into an angel. She and her husband got drunk, wrapped their arms around each other, then lay down in the duvets beneath the window and talked about how beautiful it is to live in this world.

We stayed with my father-in-law for ten days. The money I had for holiday, and there had been a lot of it, was all gone. My wife had loaned some to my sister, who promised to send it back to us just as soon as her husband earned enough. I had forgotten about that. I asked my wife how much we had left. "None," she replied. What could you do? As soon as my wife's father found out we didn't have money to make the trip home, he got a loan from someone and gave it to us.

We made it back home just fine, apart from the dog being covered with fleas and bringing three puppies into the world a little ways from Brno, right there in the car.

I'm in line at the post office in Prague, sending the money back. It's more than my father-in-law gave us. The children plead: "Daddy, can we go see Grandpa again?" I didn't know what to say, so I reassured them: "Sure, kids, sure, how could we not?"

DŽAS KO PAPUS

EMIL CINA

Phenďom mange, hoj kampel te leperel ajse berša, kana o lav romipen mek dživelas amenca le Romenca. Baro zijand, kana sa imar našľol. Ta imar chudav te vakerel.

Andro ochtovarde berša oka šelberš, dživavas mek perša romňaha the duje čhavenca — la Luckaha the le Markoha. So duj imar phirenas andre škola Prahate andre Karľina. E čhaj mange kecivar phenelas, hoj kamel te dikhel le papus pre Slovensko. Le čhavenge aviľa ňilaj, cinďom o motoris Škoda 105 the phenďom jekhvarestar: džaha. E perši romňi sa kisitinďa andro motoris the imar džahas.

Sig tosara samas imar pal e Praha, e rikoňi amenca, bašol the bašol, o čhave gravčinen, e romňi manca vakerel the me na šunav ňič. Sar zaačhiľam pre jekh parkoviskos, ta e romňi mange phenel: „Kamav tiš te dikhel dromeha peskere phrales, so bešel Vsetinate.“ Avka esas pal lakero. O šogoris, sar amen dikhľa, esas igen rado. E šogorkiňa thoďa chaben pro skamind the phenel: „Ča chan, ča chan!“

Vakerelas pal savoreste the paľis leske phenav: „Džas ko papus pre Slovensko.“

O šogoris duminďa, hoj aviľam ke leste. Jov ňisostar ňič phenel: „Amen džas tumenca!“

Me ča poraďom o jakha the peske phenďom: ta sar džaha? Jov la romňaha the mek lengere duj čhave?

E šogorkiňa esas ajsi šukori, hoj sar bešľa andro motoris, ta sa banďiľa pre jekh sera. Kamav lenge te phenel, hoj savore na rešťuvaha andr’oda motoris. Našťi lenge te odphenel, bo bi rušenas. So te kerel? Ochto džene, o čhave palal lenge bešen pro khoča.

Džav, džav, oda ďives esas but tato avri. Paš e Popradna amen zaačhiľa pro drom o šinguno. Aviľa ke mande, the sar dikhľa keci manuša džan andro motoris, le vasteha peske rozkerďa o jakha the imar zorales phenel: „Ta pre Boha, keľo vás idze v tom motoru?“

E šogorkiňa, derešno manušňi, ušťiľa andal o motoris, o koľina lake ča chuťkerenas the choľaha le šinguneske phenel: „Šak toto je náš motor!“

Chudňa pes leha te dokerel, me pre late: „Pavlo, preačh!“

O šinguno, lolo andro čhama, na kamel la te šunel. Oda manuš latar esas dilino, jekhvarestar gravčinďa: „Icťe do pi...!“

O šogoris andal e oblakica leske phenel: „Ďakujem!“

E šogorkiňa smiroha bešľa andro motoris, e salama andro vast the imar chal. E romňi latar phučel: „Kames maro?“ Joj lake odphenel: „Pre soste?“

Džas the džas. O čhave na džanen, sar te bešel, kamen te sovel. Raťaha savore zmožimen avľam andre Siplaka, oda hin pro agor paš o foros e Kaša, inakšeder Krásna nad Hornádom.

Durkinas pro vudar, ňiko amenge na phundravel, vaj jepaš ori terďuvahas paš o vudar. Te le papuskeri romňi šunďa romane lava, paľis phundraďa. Sa ušťile.

La romňakero dad esas igen rado, hoj pal o berša dikhel le čhaven. O phuro takoj varekhatar stradňa paľenkica, avile tiš aver Roma, so odoj bešenas, vakeriben baro.

Vaj trin orendar kijo tosara amenge e phuri kerďa o than andro kheroro, sar me dikhľom keci manuša odoj soven, phenďom: „Sovaha andro motoris!“ The avka esas.

Tosara šunas bašaviben paš amaro motoris. O phuro la lavutaha paš e oblakica. Ajso uštaviben me mek na predžiďiľom.

Dodžanľom pes, hoj pre aver ďives bašavena o lavutara pro bijav le gadženge. Vaj efta džene, so bašavenas, esas maškar lende jekh romňi, so lake phenenas Puci. Romňi urďi andro muršikane gada, staďi pro šero. O primašis, kana bašavenas, lake phenel: „Puci, bašaves namišto,“ the pekľa la le henoveha pal o šero. E Puci phenďa: „Del man buľe e Heľk a.“ Oda lakeri piraňi.

Geľom la romňaha vareso te cinel andre sklepa sar chaben, the tiš cinďom ľitra paľenka. S'oda jekh caklos? Sakoneske mušines te čhivel. Predal jekh romňi odarig imar e paľenka andro caklos na sas, ta na dikhľan odi choľi! Lakero rom piľa, joj na. Geľa andre peskero kher the sa andre choľi rozmarelas, the o zahlavki the e perňica andal o vaďos čhiďa tel e oblaka. Rakinelas le romeske. Me, sar dikhľom, takoj geľom te cinel aver paľenka.

Dromeha lake čhivav paľenka andre kučori, e romňi takoj piľa avri the maj latar jekhvarestar esas anďelos. O rom la romňaha maťile, paľis pen obchudle the pašľile andro perňici, so joj čhiďa tel e oblaka paš peskero kher the duminenas peske, sar o dživipen pre adi luma hino šukar.

Samas odoj deš ďives. Love amen esas pre adi dovolenka pherdo, sa gele. E romňi požičinďa varesave love la pheňake, joj lake phenďa, hoj o love amenge bičhavela pale, kana lakero rom varesave love zarodela. Pre ada bisterďom. Phučľom la romňatar, keci amenge ačhile love. E romňi phenel: „Ňisave." So te kerel? O phuro pes dodžanľa, hoj amen nane o love pro drom, takoj požičinďa o love varekhatar the amenge diňa.

Dogeľam mištes, ča e rikoňi samo pušuma, the mek paš e Berna amenge andro motoris uľile trin rikonore.

Sam Prahate pre pošta u bičhavav o love pale. Mek buter, sar amenge o phuro diňa. O čhave man mangen: „Dado, džaha mek jekhvar ko papus?" Na džanavas, so te phenel, ta phenďom lenge: „Ha, ha, mre čhave, sar te na."

ČUKČA'S GREAT MISFORTUN

BY GEJZA DEMETER

Čukča came to our little town in 1979. He and his wife and three children moved in with his relatives and he took a job in the local factory. As long as he lived with his family, he got on well with everyone, envied no one, and would have shared his last crust of bread with anyone. His children went not only to school, but also to after-school day care. Everything changed, though, once Čukča got a flat.

Suddenly he became the master of his own home and everyone had to do what he ordered them to do. His children still went to school, but they couldn't even dream of after-school care anymore. When they got home from school, they had to do chores around the house. He sent his wife to work, and he himself started moonlighting so they would have more money. He turned stingy. Gone were the good qualities that he used to abound in, replaced by envy, greed, and inflated pride. In less than a year, he had fixed up the flat so nicely that his friends' eyes practically fell out of their heads when he showed them around.

About a year before Čukča died, I broke my leg, so I was stuck at home. My wife and daughter left town for a festival out by Náchod, and probably because it was free, Čukča's wife Buda and their children went with them. They were supposed to be back home by six or seven p.m. I couldn't do anything, and I suddenly remembered that Čukča was home alone, so I could go visit and see for myself whether or not what the other Roma said about him was true. I had heard he was so stingy that he didn't even give his own children enough to eat. But how could I investigate without offending him? I had never been to his place before and he knew I never went anywhere. Well, might as well give it a try. I would ask if he could pop down to the pub and bring me back a beer, since my leg was in a cast, and then take it from there, depending how it went. He lived just a floor down from us, so I figured if he got offended, I would just go back home. I put on some clothes, took the elevator down, and rang at Čukča's door.

When he answered, he was very surprised to see me: "By God, it's a miracle! Are you here to see me? Is it really you?"

"Yes, it's really me. I came to ask if you'd go and get me a beer. With this leg of mine here," I said, pointing to my cast, "I'd never make it."

"You bet I'll go. But don't just stand there, come on in and have a seat! God, I still can't believe it. You sitting here at my place! You, who never go anywhere, and you come to see me of all people!"

"Please, knock it off, don't rub it in. Here's the money," I said, handing him thirty crowns. "Now go already."

"Keep your money, the beer is on me, my treat."

"All right then, but let me go get some klobásas, I brought them all the way from France."

"Bring them down. They'll be good with the beer." He took the jug and left. Meanwhile I went back upstairs to our flat.

At home I grabbed about a kilo of klobásas, a few bell peppers, and a jar of spicy pickles. The pub where he went for the beer wasn't far, so we both got back to his place at about the same time. I flopped down in the armchair and Čukča got everything ready. He set the table, poured the beer into glasses, and sat down with me.

"Eat and drink for now. Then I'll show you the whole flat. You haven't seen it before."

"Excellent, I'm really curious to see it."

After three beers or so, he showed me around the flat, making a point to emphasize, as he did to everyone, how much it had cost him. When, with great pride, he gave me a demonstration of his new computer, I couldn't hold back any longer and had to ask: "So, what are you going to eat, now that you've spent almost all of your money on a computer?"

"You want to know what we're going to eat? If you were anyone else, I'd throw you out the door, but since it's you, I'll show you."

"That's OK, you really don't have to," I said, afraid he was going to belt me one. "I just wondered, since you spent twelve thousand on a computer, and you yourself said that you and your wife make only fourteen thousand a month. Two thousand leftover seems pretty low for a family of eight. There's only three of us, and we spend six thousand a month on food."

"True—now don't get mad at me—but you make so much money and spend it all on food. You and your family take an expensive holiday every year, and you've been living in the same one-room flat with old furniture for fifteen years now."

"I don't want new furniture."

"If I had as much money as you, I'd show the Roma what suckers they are. Take Pipin, for instance, just the other day! I showed him my computer and he asked why I'd bought another TV. Then he made me so angry I tossed him out."

"Why, what did he do?"

"You know what that twit told me?"

"How would I? I wasn't there."

"He told me if I didn't want to end up in prison, I'd better stop robbing folks! He said people aren't dumb and they could turn me in."

"For real? He actually said that? So what did you say?"

"Nothing! I threw him out. But not to change the subject, here, come and see for yourself."

He took me under the arm and led me into the pantry. He pulled a key from his pocket, unlocked the door, and walked straight to the freezer. He opened it up and showed me what he had inside.

"Look at that! I've got twenty-five chickens, ten kilos of fatback, and forty frozen meals. Those are my snacks, lunches, and dinners at work. And besides that, every week I take food out of my own mouth and give one or two chickens to my kids. And here," he opened the fridge, "here's ten kilos of sauerkraut for halušky, twenty cubes of lard, ten bottles of oil, cottage cheese, some pâtés and odds and ends, and two kilos of ground meat for Sunday."

The pantry shelves were loaded with onions, garlic, carrots, parsley, all kinds of soups, five kilos of sugar, twenty kilos of flour, and five sacks of potatoes were sitting on the ground.

"So, what do you say? Have we got plenty of food or what? And I still had five hundred crowns leftover, and my kids chipped in about fifteen hundred for meat, bread, and other household stuff."

"What kids?"

"My kids. Pušum, Ľeľus, and Kandro."

"They have jobs already? How old are they?"

"Pušum and Ľeľus are eighteen now, and Kandro recently turned sixteen. They all work at the factory."

"Jeez, time flies! It wasn't that long ago they were still little runts, and now they're bringing home paychecks. You must be proud of them, huh?"

"You've seen what you wanted to see," Čukča said, acting like he didn't hear. "We can go sit back in the living room now." We returned to the other room, each of us drank a glass of beer, and that was all we had left.

"Čukča, go and get more beer. But this time it's on me."

"Fine, I'll go, but aren't we going to get drunk then?"

"What are you worried about? Neither one of us has to go to work."

"You're right. You're a smart guy, not like those other stupid Roma. I could buy some hard stuff too, what do you say?"

"You know I don't drink liquor, and as far as I know, neither do you, so who would you be buying it for?"

Čukča said nothing, just picked up his jug and left. As I waited for him to return, I considered asking him why he kept the pantry locked. He was sloshed enough by now that maybe he would spill his secrets to me. He came back with the beer, we sat down at the table and started to drink again.

"So, Čukča, why do you keep your pantry locked, anyway? From what I saw, you've got enough food in there to last our family at least a year."

"Not that they would steal it, but if I didn't lock the pantry, the kids would eat me out of house and home in two or three days, and the first thing to go would be the meat. This way it stays right where it should. Every morning I give Pušum the ingredients she needs to cook lunch, and tell her what to make. On Saturdays and Sundays, Buda cooks. I always give her everything she needs, too. Today, for instance, she cooked two chickens with a whole potato and boiled noodles to put in the broth. Tonight she's going to make pierogies filled half and half with potatoes and sauerkraut."

"Then why do all the Roma say you don't feed your kids properly? From what I see and hear, they're not exactly starving."

"The Roma can say whatever they want, I don't give a damn. All I can say is this: I don't go to them when I need a loan, they come to me, and believe me, it isn't just money but also food."

Then we went on drinking and talking about everything under the sun. Including his dad, who he inherited the nickname Čukča from. His father came from the Čukči tribe, out in eastern Siberia. He herded reindeer and ended up in Slovakia with the Red Army during the war. He was seriously wounded in the woods outside of Svidník. The Roma found him there and saved his life. He was the one who taught Čukča to work hard and save. Now he was doing exactly what his father had taught him to do all those years. If the Roma didn't like it, that was their problem. He had to eat meat every day to be strong enough to work. His kids only needed meat once a week, as far as he was concerned. The other days, they had to make do with broth.

Čukča by now had drunk six or seven beers and was pretty loaded. All of a sudden he got to his feet, walked to the cupboard, dug around inside it a while, and finally came out with a bankbook.

"Look how much money I have!" He had a balance of sixty-eight thousand crowns. "No one knows about it but you. Come Christmas, I'm going to buy a new car." If he'd had any inkling what misfortune that car would bring, he never would have bought it.

In January 1990, his daughter, Pušum, and his sons, Ľeľus and Kandro, left the country for Belgium. Buda, his wife, wept when they left, but she begged the Lord to help them find a better life than they'd had with their dad. For his part, Čukča cursed them out and argued with her bitterly. In February he and Buda got fired from their jobs, and right after that he got into a serious car accident. The car was totaled, and Buda, poor thing, was dead on the spot. He still hadn't recovered from the accident yet when his youngest daughter, Churďori, born after the first three children, passed away. Then, in June, his son Pervalo died, and in November, another of his new daughters, Kašuki. Čukča himself died in December that same year, right on Christmas Eve. The Roma weren't the only ones surprised that God would allow such a thing. They didn't feel sorry for Čukča. He was a miser and a mean person, but his wife and children were very nice people, so why did they have to suffer for his sins? Some said it was their destiny, others insisted that Buda had taken their children to heaven and sent him to hell, so he could starve there, serving the devils, just as she and her children had served him all their lives.

LE ČUKČUSKERI BARI BIBACHT

GEJZA DEMETER

O Čukčus aviľa andre amaro forocis andro berš 1979. La romňaha the le čhavenca gejľa te bešen ke peskeri fameľija a chudňa buťi andre tovarňa. Dokľaj bešelas paš e fameľija, sas sakoneha baro kamaratos, ňikaske ňič na zavidzinelas a sakones bo delas te chan, kaj bo leske korkoreske te na ačholas. O čhave phirenas na ča andre škola, aľe the andre družina. Sa pes zmeňinďa, sar chudňa peskero bitos.

Prejekhvar ačhiľa chulaj le khereske a sako mušinelas te keren oda, so ov phenelas. O čhave dureder phirenas andre škola, aľe e družina lenge na džalas aňi suneste. Sar avenas andal e škola, mušinenas khere te keren sa, so kampelas. La romňa thoďa andre buťi a korkoro, kaj len te jel buter love, chudňa te keren brigadi. Chudňa te chulajinen. Akana sa, so sas andre leste lačho, les omukľa. Ačhiľa lestar zavisľivo, pažerno the baro barikano Rom. Aňi na vaš jekh berš zarjadziňďa o bitos avka, že o Roma ča poravenas o jakha, sar lenge sa sikavkerelas.

Jekhvar, berš angl'oda, sar o Čukčus muľa, phagľom o pindro, ta somas khere. E romňi la čhaha gejle pro romano festivalos varekaj až dži ko Nachodos a može vašoda, že o festivalos the o autobusis sas hjaba, gejľa le čhavenca the e Buda, le Čukčuskeri romňi. Pal o festivalos majinde te aven až šov abo efta orendar raťi. Me ačhiľom khere korkoro a može vašoda, že našťi ňič kerás, avľa mange pre goďi, že o Čukčus hino khere tiš korkoro. Ta šaj bo džavas ke leste te pobešen a te dodžanen pes, so hin čačipen pre oda, so pal leste o Roma vakeren. Šunďom, že hino ajso skupo, že na del le čhaven aňi te chan. Aľe sar te keren, kaj pre ma te na rušel? Šoha mek ke leste na somas a ov džanel, že me ke ňikaste na phirav. No, probaľinava les te bičhaven lovinake a paľik dikhava, so jela dureder. Bešelas ča jekh patros tel mande a te choľasaľola, ta avava pale khere. Skidňom man, gejľom tele le vitahoha a zabrenkiňďom pro brenkos.

Phuterďa o udar a sar man dikhľa, chudňa pes te čudaľinen: „Devla, baro čudos, tu aves ke mande? Čačes sal tu?"

„Čačes som me a avav tut te mangen, či bo mange na džahas te cinen lovina. Me kala sadraha," sikaďom pro pindro, „darav, že bo na dodžavas."

„Džanes, že džava, aľe so terďos maškar o udar, av

dureder a beš andro kreslos. Devla, me oleske furt na paťav, tu a bešes ke ma andro kher. Tu, kaj ke ňikaste na phires, avľal ke ma."

„Imar dost, som adaj, ta so mek buter? Le o love," dav les tranda koruni „a dža imar."

„O love garuv, e lovina ciná me, sal miro hojscos."

„Ta mišto, aľe me aná kolbasa, anďom la až dži andal e Francija."

„Ča an, ke lovina jela lačhi." Iľa e kuči the gejľa. Me gejľom tiš.

Khere iľom vaj kilos kolbasa, lole the šarge paprigi a jekh caklos kherutne uhorki feferonkenca. E karčma na sas dur, ta avľam ko Čukčus so dujdžene maj prejekhvar. Me bešás andro kreslos a ov sa porichtinďa, thoďa pro skamind, čhiďa andro pohara lovina a bešľa paš mande.

„Akana cha the pij a paľik tuke sikavá o bitos, mek les na dikhľal."

„Mišto, imar pes našťi doužarav."

Jekhbač pal trito lovina sikaďa mange o bitos. Avka sar sakoneske, ta the mange na bisterďa te phenen, so keci molas. Sar mange, bare baripnaha, sikaďa o počitačis, na avriľikerďom a phučľom lestar: „So akana chana, te maj savore love diňal vaš o počitačis?"

„Tu kames te džanen, so amen chaha? Te bo kada phučľa vareko aver, ta leha avrilemav o udar, aľe tuke sa sikava."

„Na, na mušines!" darandňom, te man jekh na čhinel pal o muj. „Me ča avka gondoľinav, že te diňal dešuduj ezera vaš o počitačis a sar korkoro phenďal, la romňaha chudňan ča dešuštar, ta mange phenďom, že duj ezera čuno pro ochto nipos. Amen sam ča trin džene a pro chaben kelteľinas šov ezera."

„Ča tu — tu ma ruš pre mande — aľe tu chudes ajci love, a sa ča prechan. Sako berš džan pre kuč dovoľenka a bešes imar dešupandž berš andre garsonka, kaj tut hin purano nabitkos."

„Me nevo na kamav."

„Man te elas ajci love sar tut, ta sikavás le Romenge ajsi kocka, že bo ča poravenas o jakha, sar varekana o Pipin. Sikaďom leske o počitačis a ov phučľa, soske cinďom mek jekh televizija. A paľik man avka choľarďa, že les čhiďom avri andal o kher."

„Ma vaker, a soske?"

„Džanes, so mange phenďa koda dilino?“
„Sar šaj džanav, na somas adaj.“
„Phenďa mange, že te na kamav te jen zarimen andre bertena, ta kaj imar te preačhav te čorkeren, bo o Roma nane diline, ta šaj man uden le šingunenge.“
„Ma kochav! Čačes kada phenďa? A tu, so kerďal?“
„Ňič, čhiďom les avri. No, aľe imar dost vakeriben, av, sa tuke sikavá.“
Iľa man tel e khak a gejľam ko špajzos. Andal e žeba iľa e kľeja, phuterďa a gejľa prosto ko mrazakos. Phuterďa les a chudňa sa te sikavkerel.
„No le, dikh, kadaj hin bišupandž kachňa, deš kila bučkos, saranda mikroteni — andro gonoro zamražimen dilos. Kada sa mire svačini, dili the večeri andre buťi. No a mek the alestar mange lav andal o muj a dav sako kurko jekh abo duj kachňa, kaj te jel le čhaven buter. No a kadaj,“ phuterďa e ledňička, „hin deš kila šutľi armin pro haluški, biš kotora žiros, deš cakli olejis, ciral, pašťiki a mek vareso churďipen the duj kila erňimen mas pro kurko.“
Andro špajzos mek sas purum, sir, marchva, petruška, všeľijaka zumina, pandž kila cukros, biš kila aro the pandž gone bandurki.
„No, so akana pheneha? Hin amen so te chan abo na? A mek mange ačhile pandž šel koruni mire a o čhave man tiš dine pro chaben ezeros the jepaš, kaj te jel pro mas, pro maro a mek pre vareso, so kampel andro kher.“
„Save čhave?“
„Mire. E Pušum, o Ľeľus the o Kandro.“
„On imar phiren andre buťi? Keci lenge?“
„La Pušumake le Ľeľuha imar dešuochto a le Kandreske sas načirla dešušov. So trin džene keren andre tovarňa.“
„Devla, sar sa denašel, načirla sas mek cikne čhavore a akana imar tuke zaroden lovore. Sal the barikano, čačes vakerav?“
„Akana imar dikhľal sa, so kamehas,“ na kamelas buter te vakeren, „ta džas peske pale te bešen.“ Gejľam pale andro obivakos, pijľam po jekh poharis lovina a imar amen na sas.
„Čukču, dža pale, cin lovina, bo imar nane. Aľe akana poťinav me.“
„Džava, aľe na avaha mate?“

„So daras, šak andre buťi na džas, aňi tu aňi me."

„Čačes vakeres, tu sal goďaver manuš, na sar akala diline Roma. Činá the thardi?"

„Džanes, že me thardi na pijav, a so džanav, ta tu tiš na, ta kaske la cineha?"

Na phenďa ňič, iľa e kuči the gejľa andre karčma. Sar pre leste užaravas, ta gondoľinás, či lestar te phučen, soske zarinel o špajzos. Hino imar jekhnaj matoro, ta šaj bo phenelas sa, pre soste phučava. Aviľa la lovinaha, bešľam pal o skamind the chudňam te pijen.

„Čukču, soske zarines o špajzos? Sar dikhľom, tak koda savoro chaben bo amen na chahas aňi vaš jekh berš."

„Na že bo čorenas, aľe te bo na zarinás, ta bo sa chanas vaš duj trin ďives a jekhsigeder o mas. Avka te hino zarimen, ačhol sa pro than. Sako tosara dav la Pušumake — bo kerel o dilos — sa, so kampel, a phenav lake, so te taven. Sombatone the kurke tavel e Buda. The lake dav sa, so kampel. Adaďives imar taďa duje kachňen cale bandurkenca a andre zumin čhiďa rezanki. Raťi tavela pišot bandurkenca the arminaha. Avka jepaš pre jepaš."

„Ta akor so kola Roma vakeren, že na des le čhaven te chan? Sar šunav the dikhav, ta tire čhave našťi bokhaľon."

„Me pro Roma čhandav, mi vakeren, so kamen. Me tuke phenava ča jekh: na me ke lende, aľe on ke mande phiren, te mangen kejčen, a paťa mange abo na, na ča o love, aľe the o chaben."

Pijahas the vakerahas pal savoreste. The pal leskero dad, pal savo chudňa aver nav. Ov sas andal jekh bari fajta, kaj la vičinenas Čukču. Bešenas andro jurti až andre vichodno Siberija a pasinenas odoj le soben. Pre Slovensko aviľa andro mariben le Rusenca a andro veša paš o Svidnikos sas phares raňimen. O Roma les andro veš arakhle a avrisasťarde. Oda ov sikaďa le Čukčus te keren buťi the te chulajinen. Adaďives kerel ča oda, so les sikaďa. A že pes kada le Romenge na ľubinel? Oda lengeri veca. Ov mušinel te chan sako ďives mas, kaj les te jel zor te keren buťi. Le čhavenge dost, te chana mas jekhvar kurkeste. Pres kurko šaj chan e zumin, andre savi taďolas o mas.

Imar pijľa vaj šov abo efta lovini, ta sas dost mato. Prejekhvar ušťiľa, gejľa ko šifoneris, vareso rodelas a paľik mange sikaďa e šporkňižka.

„Dikh, keci man hin love," sas les odoj šovardeš the ochto ezera, „mek ňikaske na phenďom, až akana tuke. Pre Karačoňa cinava nevo motoris." Te bo džanľahas, savi bibacht leske koda motoris anela, šoha bo les na cinďahas.

Takoj januariste andro eňavardešto berš leske denašle e Pušum le Ľeľuha the le Kandreha andre Belgija. E Buda pal lende rovelas a mangelas le Devles, kaj lenge te del feder dživipen, sar len sas paš o Čukčus, aľe ov len ča koškerelas a macharinelas la daha. Andro februaris les the la Buda čhide avri andal e buťi a takoj duj kurke pal oda kerďa le motoriha bari buračka. O motoris dočista rozmarďa a e čori Buda takoj pro than muľa. Mek pes o Rom na zbatorinďa a imar leske muľa e jekhcikneder čhajori, e Churďori. Takoj andro junos muľa o čhavo, o Pervalo, a andro novembros e čhaj, e Kašuki. Ov korkoro muľa andro decembros, pre holo Viľija. Savore Roma, a na ča o Roma, pes čudaľinenas, sar šaj o Del kada domukľa. Le Romenge na sas phares, že muľa ov, bo sas igen hamižno the pažerno, aľe o čhavore the e Buda sas igen lačhe manuša, ta soske the len o Del zmarňinďa? Pojekh vakerelas, že oda sas le Čukčuskero the leskera fameľijakero osudos, no aver phenelas, že e Buda iľa le čhavoren ke peste andro ňebocis a les bičhaďa andro peklos, kaj odoj te solgaľinel le bengenge bokhate, avka sar oj the lakere čhave solgaľinenas leske.

ŽIŽKOVITE

BY PATRIK BANGA

I'm a Žižkovite. That isn't just someone who lives in Žižkov or comes from there. It's someone who understands Žižkov as a place with its own rules, a place where everybody belongs and always feels at home, even if they haven't lived there in thirty years.

I grew up on Bořivoj Street, right on the corner of Bořivoj and Ježek, in a giant tenement house, back when Žižkov was a neighborhood of musicians, unappreciated intellectuals, workers, and Roma. Loads of Roma. Our building had only cold water, we kept warm using stoves fueled by coal fetched from the cellar, the toilets were in the hallway, and we could only dream of bathrooms like the ones that we have now. From today's point of view, we were down-and-out. Back then, though, almost everybody in Žižkov lived that way.

When the coal ran out, we had to go down to the cellar to get it, which meant four flights down, then four flights up again with a full bucket. You might say that's no big deal, but try doing it when you're four! The cellar was crawling with catsized rats, so we would go down to the cellar in twos, sometimes even in fours. There were enough kids in our family that we could do that. Plus the whole building was dark. The only place where there was even a little bit of light was the hallway to the stairs, where the sun shone in through a purple-and-blue art deco stained-glass window, casting colorful spots of light on the floor. I thought it was kind of scary, but it was the only light there was, since the lightbulbs never worked.

Outside the building's front door was where the world began. Our world, where it didn't matter whose kids were in our flat or whether I was over at some other family's place. We lived like true Roma: everyone together. In almost every building in the neighborhood, we had an aunt who would feed us if we were hungry, or let us stay at her place and play with her kids. Old Mrs. Cínová baked bobaľki, Aunt Siváková cooked hot meals. We were friends with her daughters, Martina and Helena, who gave me my first kiss. A few hundred yards away lived Aunt Olina, and on Olšany Square was our grandmother's place, where the whole Banga family got together for frequent gatherings. In short, Žižkov was our home.

One great thing about Žižkov was the buildings were arranged in enclosed blocks, with little gardens or courtyards hidden away on the inside, where we could spend our time. When that wasn't enough, we would go play on the field by the FK Viktoria Žižkov soccer stadium, where I smoked my first cigarette, a Femina. My mom beat me so badly, I still remember it even now, thirty-five years later. Other times, we would go and scare the girls at the old Jewish cemetery, where they built the TV tower that stands there now. Then, in summer, we would head to Jiří z Poděbrad Square, where we spent hours splashing around in the fountain called United Europe, while the older kids went off to Rieger Gardens—our mom wouldn't let us younger kids go unless we were with her, which was mostly in the winter, when all of Žižkov went sledding there. To this day, I still vividly remember riding downhill on my greased-up sled, heading straight for a hardboard figure of Krteček, the cartoon mole, then the unavoidable crash, leaving the sled a total wreck.

The ultimate experience was when one of the grown-ups took us kids to the now defunct Obzor movie theater. I saw more fairy tales there than I can count, and my mom took me to every single one of the *Winnetou* movies. And Vítkov! The hill with the national monument to Jan Žižka, the fifteenth-century Hussite warrior who gave the neighborhood its name. Our nursery-school teachers walked us over there every day. Plus, Vítkov had tennis courts, and on weekends my whole family would go and play tennis there. In short, we had all we needed right there in Žižkov: parks, gardens, fountains, monuments, culture, sports. Maybe that's why people call Žižkov a state within a state. If it had its own government, it could be a functioning republic, no problem.

When I was little, I didn't see the divisions between Roma and gadjos. It was probably because we didn't have much contact with gadjos, apart from the musicians and intellectuals who visited my father, who was a musician too. One of those intellectuals was Radoslav Dubanský, the actor and theater director, who made the "mistake" of attacking the Communist regime in one of his plays. The authorities thanked him by assigning him to a job in a boiler room where some of my relatives worked. It was only later I came to realize that from Bořivoj Street down to Kostnice Square it was mostly Roma, and up toward Jiří z Poděbrad Square it was mostly gadjos.

It wasn't until I got to primary school that I experienced Czech reality for the first time. Only one other student in my class was allowed to be friends with me. He was Romani too. The other kids would talk with us in school, but outside, they kept their distance. Their parents at home would give them warnings like, "Don't make friends with that Gypsy boy, it isn't appropriate." That lasted basically the whole time I was in school.

As the times and the regime changed, people changed too. In 1990, white people saw us as partners together in the revolution, but a few months later, our parents wouldn't let us go out alone anymore, for fear we'd be killed by skinheads. And we were just as scared as our parents. Wherever we went, we heard about—and more than once also witnessed—how "the skins" were capable of absolutely anything, even when it came to children. In Žižkov, where up until then we'd always felt at home, all of a sudden the guards and the salespeople in grocery stores started checking our coats and bags, assuming we'd stolen something. The police started following us into parks and harassing us, and many of us suffered ugly beatings at the hands of the police. Žižkov began to divide along color lines. Every gadjo knew it was dangerous to go out alone on Kostnice Square after ten at night, and the same was also true for our crew. So the Roma would get together outside the church on Vlkova Street, and the gadjos would sit on the red metal benches at the foot of the TV tower, where three houndred years ago there used to be graves. To this day, I still wonder who had the gall to make that decision, humiliating the Jews who had buried their loved ones there. How many people realize when they walk along Wenceslas Square they're walking on pavement made from Jewish gravestones? The Communists began their liquidation of the cemetery in 1960, then completed their barbaric act over the course of my childhood. So now, instead of it being a place of respect and reverence, TV shows are beamed from there. Honor labor! as they used to say in Communist times.

To each their own—only I didn't belong to the Roma or the gadjos. For one side, I was too dark-skinned; for the other, I was too light. With Roma I played guitar; with gadjos I played soccer. My closest buddies were Martin Sartori and especially Tonda Novák. The Nováks' was like home to me. Even when I was a little boy, I called Tonda's parents by their first names. I could go into their fridge whenever I wanted, they took me along with them when they went to their house in the countryside, and Tonda and I were constantly getting up to mischief together. I actually got into conflicts with my own community for defending gadjos when Roma wanted to beat them up. Like the Stojka brothers, who were notorious in Žižkov. My brother once ill-advisedly loaned my guitar to the oldest one, and that was the last we saw of it. The middle brother liked to pick fights, and whenever he had a run-in with one of my gadjo buddies, I would have to fight on their behalf, since the gadjos were lacking in the Žižkov street education that I got growing up. The youngest Stojka brother was a junkie, who didn't give a damn about anything, so he assaulted any- and everyone, until one day my older brother had to teach him a lesson.

But it wasn't only that. The Roma in the Karlín district thought they were better than the Roma in Žižkov. And the Roma in the Nusle district, who were mostly Vlax Roma, were the worst of all. Whenever we had to go to Bratří Synků Square, it was practically guaranteed someone would step to us. And it always ended in a brawl—even a knife to the kidneys, in my cousin's case. Not only that, but the perpetrator had the nerve to come threaten him again in the hospital. As if we didn't already have our hands full with the gadjos, we also had friction among ourselves. To be honest, I can do without the Nusle Roma. I still get a weird feeling every time I go to that square that something's about to go down.

On the other hand, where else but from Roma could I have gotten such a solid musical "education"? I mean, one of the first questions we'd ask each other whenever we got together was, "What instruments do your kids play?" And you don't even want to imagine the disgrace if you answered "None." The first time the band Khamoro performed on TV, with a young Jarmila Balážová hosting the show, back in the days before she became a famous journalist, it was as huge for us as it would have been if the hockey star Jaromír Jágr had turned out to be Romani. I spent years learning to play with Filip Surmaj, the keyboardist. We both did our best to emulate Stevie Wonder. Later on, when the Romani groups Kale and Bengas had a boom in popularity, I saw Bingáč, Miguel Horvát, and the rest of the musicians from our community on TV. But the highlight was the singer Věra Bílá, she was a phenomenon. She inspired all of us to go full steam ahead, and eventually a lot of Žižkov Roma became respected musicians. They were all part of the crew who used to hang out outside the church.

Each ethnic group had its own thing. From gadjos, I learned about computers and the basics of programming, discovering my ambition; from Roma, I learned to play the piano and guitar, and came to realize being a Rom isn't just about skin color. It's about your thinking and way of life. I made it my life's task to search for a balance between those worlds—a task made all the harder when the principals of Žižkov's primary schools got together and decided to separate off most of the Romani students into the school on Havlíček Square, leaving only two of us in the school on Vlkova Street: Monika Slivková and me.

It was clear I wasn't going to have it easy as soon as I tried to apply to secondary school. I wanted desperately to be equal to the gadjos, and insisted on taking the entry exams for gymnasium, which prepared students to go to university. The school's guidance counselor laughed in my face. She tried to convince me Roma didn't belong in gymnasium, and even if I did manage to graduate, I'd never get a job, since Roma never lasted in any job and most of the time they ended up in prison. She convinced me so well, I lost all my ambition and instead went to vocational school, where I studied to be a mechanic.

But the ways of the Lord are inscrutable. At age fifteen I met my first girl, and her mom, who was a journalist, showed me a different world, where I could fully realize my potential. She brought me into all kinds of newsrooms, and I got my first whiff of what journalism was all about. Thanks to her, I got involved in a humanitarian project in Yugoslavia. From there, it was just a small step to a job at the Ministry of the Interior, where I worked with refugees, and an even smaller step from there into media. I came to iDNES.cz a naïve young man and left a respected journalist for a job with Czech Television, then came back again to iDNES.cz in a senior position—maybe because there was no more guidance counselor telling me I didn't have what it took. She was wrong. Ultimately, I did go to secondary school, and successfully completed it with a specialization in computer networks, graphic design, and the Web. And God knows, once my daughter grows up and I've got a little more time on my hands, I might give law school a try. It's never too late for education—you just have to want it.

Many years have passed since then. I've lost contact with my buddies. Most of them I haven't seen in over twenty years, and most of them aren't in Žižkov either. When apartments in Žižkov were privatized, Roma couldn't afford them, and property developers, the first traffickers in poverty in this country, took full advantage, buying out leases for peanuts, then selling the flats to foreigners and more affluent Czechs at a huge profit. As a result of these "transactions," Roma were evicted and moved to North Bohemia. The smarter ones emigrated to Canada, then to England, and live their lives now in conditions totally different from the ones they left behind. So whenever people ask how the ghettos came into being in northern cities like Litvínov and Most, they should stop and think whether it was worth it. A few individuals made enormous amounts of money, but a whole generation of Roma, and not only the ones in Žižkov, lost their homes and along with them the chance at a twenty-first-century standard of living. Ghettos, after all, aren't the place where doctors and lawyers usually come from.

Žižkov has changed. I can no longer walk in the door of any family and act like I'm at home. When I walk the streets of my old neighborhood, I don't recognize a soul. All that remains are the buildings, the tobacconists and the butcher's shop on Olšany Square. Gone is the cinder pitch next to the FK Viktoria Žižkov stadium, where every local soccer player got his start. Now all that's there is buildings, new, modern, and ugly. Nothing at all like our old neighborhood, where every building had its own set of stairs, beautiful, decorative handrails, frescoes on the ceilings, and those gorgeous purple and blue mosaic windows. I no longer hear musicians anymore, playing outside the church at night, or our Roma girls singing so gorgeously, in three-, four-, and five-part harmonies. The magic is gone. No more harsh environment, no more territorial battles, everything that made Žižkov Žižkov has disappeared. Kids don't go to the Viktoria match with their dads on Sundays anymore. They stay home and play soccer on PlayStation instead.

But we, the true Žižkovites, carry the old Žižkov with us wherever we go. The place where we learned to share everything, where we learned that everyone has their place. We know how to hit hard when that's what it takes. And though everything disappears in time, just like the old Jewish cemetery, we will always remember our state within a state. Our home.

INSIDE THE BUBBLE

BY STANISLAVA ONDOVÁ

I was sitting with my son at the dining room table, helping him with his homework, the same way I did every evening. With the help of a few favors, he had gotten into one of the best primary schools in our city, outside of our district.

"Mommy, what's a revolution?"

"Well, that's when people are really unhappy with the way things work in their country. Ours was called the velvet revolution."

"Velvet?"

"How can I . . . they call it that because velvet is a fabric that's soft and silky. Cat fur is velvety," I say, trying to explain this unusual word to my son. "So it's the velvet revolution because there wasn't any fighting here, do you see what I mean? It was a smooth handover of power. Usually when there's a revolution, people die, but here it was different."

"So what were you all doing on November seventeenth?" my son asked later as I was putting him to sleep. The question caught me a little off guard.

"Well, the day started off normal, like any other. We got up in the morning, my dad had the day shift, so he was already out on the tracks, and my mom, your grandma, walked me to school and then went to work. She used to clean at the school you go to now, but you knew that, right?"

My son nodded yes.

"Then, when we came home, it was Friday, so we were looking forward to spending the weekend together. But that night in Prague the students got attacked, you see, the ones who go to university. They were having a protest against communism on Národní třída, but we didn't know that yet, they didn't show it on TV until the weekend." My son slowly drifted off to sleep as I sank into my memories.

We sat glued to the TV, me and my mom and dad, we couldn't believe our eyes. We were lucky we could follow what was going on in Prague on ORF, the Austrian public TV channel. We were able to catch the station with an ordinary antenna that my dad had fixed up with a fork and some wires. It was a few more days still before the events appeared on Czechoslovak TV. I didn't understand any of what I saw on the Western station, and I couldn't tell if my parents understood either. People here didn't talk about communism, how there should be more than one party to vote for, or democracy at all. The first time I heard the word *democracy* was on TV. For me it was totally normal that my parents said not to tell anyone what I heard at home. Or that they sent me to my room and shut the door when they talked. I just thought it was "grown-up rules." It never dawned on me that my parents might have problems if I accidentally said something at school that I had heard at home.

On Monday, the twentieth, we had class as usual and the teachers acted like nothing out of the ordinary was going on. At home that night my mom and dad were talking about how there was a revolution brewing in Prague.

"One of the teachers came in today and told us it's going to blow. Her son is at university in Prague and he said they want to overthrow the Communists. I'm worried about how it'll turn out, I hope there isn't a civil war," my mom said anxiously. I knew what civil war was. When we talked about it in school, it was always connected with capitalism, something that we, as children living under socialism, didn't have to worry about, since in our country we had peace and prosperity.

My parents got nervous, and the next day they didn't let me go to school. "You're staying at home, alone. Don't go anywhere, not even out in front of the house. You've got food to eat right here." I remember I stayed home the whole rest of the week. Over the weekend, there was a live broadcast from the demonstration in the park on Letná Hill. I sat in front of the screen, baffled by what all those people were doing there. I wanted to see my friends, but it was really cold and the area in front of our building was totally deserted.

"Mommy, can I go out?"

"But there's nobody out there."

"I want to go over to Hanka's house and ask her to play catch." Hanka, a blond little girl with four siblings, was our neighbors' daughter. We were the only Roma in our building, but that didn't strike me as odd at the time. One of my dad's cousins lived in the building across the street from us, and another cousin lived in the next street over. In those days there probably wasn't a single building in the north of the country that was exclusively Roma or gadjos.

"All right, go ahead, but just in front of the house," my mom agreed.

"I have to stay in front of the house," I told my friend Hanka, who was a year older than me, when she opened the door.

"Hm, as usual. I don't see what harm it would do your parents for you to go in the back of the house for a change."

The two of us walked out to the road.

"Weird how quiet it is, isn't it?" I nodded, observing the uncommonly empty street. Not a soul. There wasn't a sound anywhere, except for a few overly loud TVs coming out of the windows.

We threw a ball back and forth for a while, but it wasn't much fun with just us two. "I'm going home to play with my sisters," Hanka announced. I was left outside all by myself, and after a while I got anxious. I quickly ran back home.

I opened the door just as the telephone rang. My parents waited three years before they got a landline. My uncle, who lived in the village, had his hooked up a year after moving in. My mom said it was favoritism and my uncle, her brother, had "slipped something" to someone. She hurried over to pick up the phone and spoke in such a soft voice I couldn't hear who she was talking to or what about. A little while later, my aunt and uncle stopped by. They sat down in the kitchen and sent me into the next room, but I left the door propped open.

"Luděk called," said my uncle softly.

"What?" My mom practically screamed and my uncle put a finger to his lips. I didn't get why they were practically whispering.

"He's coming. He says he wants to see it with his own eyes." My uncle shrugged. I pretended to be playing but I was listening. When my mom put me to bed that night, I asked: "Mom, is Uncle Luděk coming?" She looked at me with her big brown eyes and smiled.

"I think so."

"Do you think he'll bring me something?" I started imagining a Mickey Mouse T-shirt or some special treat, like a twelve-color ballpoint pen.

"I don't know about that, but tomorrow we can give him a call and you can ask," said my mom to my surprise. On Monday my parents let me go to school again. We hardly even had class, though, since the teachers spent the whole time talking among themselves, and some of them didn't even come to class at all. Except for our physics teacher. Mr. Jelínek was the strict, gloomy type, the type who wouldn't hesitate to give you a D on an exam for two mistakes and didn't have any favorites. He seemed constantly angry, and all my classmates, including me, were afraid of him. On that day, though, he walked into class with a smile on his face. He was wearing jeans and a collared shirt, and in general seemed different, more relaxed. He sat down on the corner of his desk, one foot on the ground, the other in the air, and started asking us questions:

"So, children, do you know what's going on?" We were all speechless. None of us said a word. "Do you know who Havel is, or Dubček?" The strict expression he always used to have on his face was gone. I shot up my hand and he nodded at me to speak.

"I heard," I said, intentionally not saying where or who told me, just as I'd been taught, "that Dubček was living by the seaside the whole time and just turned up out of nowhere, but originally he ran away." I sat down, not daring to raise my eyes.

"I'm glad you started with that," said Mr. Jelínek, and then, the strictest teacher in the whole school, who everyone either hated or feared, told us the story of what took place in August 1968 and how Dubček was forced to agree to the invasion and had to work the next twenty years for the forestry service and wasn't allowed to appear in public. He also talked about the crimes of communism and what democracy means. It was so interesting, I didn't want class to end. I couldn't wait to go home and tell my parents about it. At the end of his lesson, Mr. Jelínek praised me in front of everyone, saying my questions were good and I wasn't afraid to ask, because democracy means we don't have to be afraid of asking about anything anymore.

At dinner I excitedly told my parents about what our teacher had said and who Havel was and that Dubček wasn't a traitor, like people had told my dad at work. Then we talked about how great it was going to be when Uncle Luděk came with his Italian wife, Gina, and all the things we were going to do with them. That night, as my mom put me to bed, I felt content. I gave her a hug and whispered: "Everything we have to look forward to is so beautiful,

Mom. We can go to the seaside and you don't have to be scared to talk to Uncle Luděk anymore." To this day I still remember the hope and the childlike joy at the thought of the unknown. Democracy to me meant something like a holiday. I couldn't imagine what it actually meant, but I definitely knew that it was great. And that I could hardly wait, even if I didn't know what to expect. What could go wrong, after all, given that democracy was something people fought for, but in our country it had come to pass without any violence.

At breakfast, my son looked a little lost in thought.

"Mom, did you like school? There are times I don't want to go, when we have a test or English class, but I look forward to seeing my friends and I like the lady who teaches us." I was glad he had such a great teacher and had made so many friends he enjoyed spending time with, even outside of class. And I was happy that it wasn't just other Roma, but non-Romani kids too. Personally, I would just as soon have erased my school days from my memory.

"You bet I liked school, a lot. I learned so much there." After I saw my son and husband out the door, I couldn't resist and pulled out an old photo album from the box under the bed. Glued to the first page was a picture of my first-grade class. Thirty children and one teacher on the front steps of the school. I was in the back row, tucked away in the corner. A short, dark-skinned girl, black hair in a ponytail and no smile on her face.

"Rise and shine, baby, time for you to go to school," my mother said, waking me up for my first day of school in September 1984. The moment I sat up in bed, I got a nervous stomachache. I was scared. I'd gone to kindergarten, but there I had friends—Dáša from next door and her little brother Kal. The two of them were going to a different school, though. A special school, my mom explained. My dad had to tell off the doctor who gave me a check-up to make her assign me to a normal primary school. He said no daughter of his was going to a special school, and if the doctor didn't do what he said he would break every one of her windows. Since the parents' signatures were required for enrollment, they had no choice but to place me in a normal school. Without any friends, though.

I remember that September day was almost as warm as summer, and I had on a white T-shirt with a wide-shouldered blue polka-dot dress pulled over it. I wore white stockings and denim sandals, which were a pretty big deal in those days. My dad stood in line for three hours to get them, and they were the last ones left in my size. The whole way home he prayed they would fit me. I had my hair neatly combed back into a ponytail and a square-edged red satchel bag over my shoulder. I was not looking forward to it. On the first day, parents were allowed to stay with us in the classroom for a while. My mom sat me down in the second row, there were nothing but white kids all around me. I gave my mom a look and she smiled back at me happily. I couldn't figure out why. The teacher delivered a welcome speech, but I didn't pay much attention. I was fascinated by her enormous glasses, wondering whether or not they hurt her nose. I also remember the voice of a man crackling over the school intercom, talking about building socialism and saying we were the country's future. It made me feel important.

I had my books, notebooks, pencils, crayons, and paints all ready to go on my desk. At the end of the day, I packed it all in my satchel and set out for home again with my mom. We lived in a village near Chomutov, a little less than two kilometers from the school. When my dad came home from work, my mom excitedly told him about my day at school, but I just sat there speechless.

I ran into my first problem the very next day, when the parents were no longer there with us. For our morning snack, the teachers gave us milk, bread, and some disgusting-smelling spread, all for free. I had brought my own bread from home, spread with butter, plus an apple and a piece of koláč. I didn't drink plain milk when I was little, I would only drink it with cocoa. I didn't eat any spreads either, and at kindergarten they didn't make me, all I had to do was say "I don't eat that." Now when they put the little sack down in front of me, with the milk and the bread and the spread in a little plastic cup, I felt sick just looking at it. I sat silently at my desk, unable to make myself eat.

"Aren't you going to eat that?" the teacher blurted at me. I shook my head no. "Go on, just try it," she urged. I broke off a piece of bread, dipped it in the spread, and stuck it in my mouth. My stomach lurched. "Oh, come on, you must be kidding," said the teacher, raising her voice. "Children, who here wants some spread?" Everyone's hands went up in the air. I was glad not to have to eat it. Still, for the teacher the fact that I didn't eat the snack was an indicator of my low intelligence, and she concluded there was no need to pay any attention to me.

The next day my teacher decided to show me what would happen if I turned up my nose at the school snacks and refused to eat them, despite their being provided for me by the working class free of charge. This time the snack came with garlic spread.

"Take out your napkin." I obediently spread in front of me the flowered cloth napkin my mom had sewn for me. The teacher unpacked my snack. "Eat!" Her tone of voice was extremely hostile and tears rushed to my eyes. "Stop bawling and eat," the teacher insisted. As I inserted a piece of bread with spread on it into my mouth, my stomach lurched again. I looked at the teacher, but she wouldn't budge. All the other children fell silent. "You're going to sit here for as long as it takes you to eat it! Even if that means all night." The bell reminded her she also had to teach. I sat there like I was chained to my seat, tears falling into my lap, slowly pushing the garlic-spread bread into my mouth. The warm milk made me nauseated. My classmates sat watching me without a sound. I sat there two hours like that, no one else was allowed to speak to me until I finished my snack. I ate the whole thing. And ever since then I've had a revulsion to school food, cafeterias, and to that Communist teacher.

Some of my classmates felt sorry for me and came up to me at break. "You see," they said, "that wasn't so bad." I had a lump in my throat and was counting the minutes till I could go home. That experience turned school into a torture for me. Even twenty years later, when I worked as a kindergarten assistant, I never forced the children to eat anything they didn't like. I just told them to at least try a taste. My colleagues' practice of feeding children even when they didn't want to eat was something I couldn't understand.

Another culture shock at primary school came at gym class. At age seven I wasn't used to getting undressed in front of other people and exercising in clothes that looked like underwear. The blue gym shorts kept digging into me and the white tank top also didn't cover much. I may have been only seven, but I didn't feel good being so exposed. I had already started to sprout little breasts, so I kept hunching to try to hide them. One day the teacher called me over. "Show me your shirt," she said. I obediently walked up to her and all of a sudden she tore off my shirt, pulling it over my head. She examined it closely and put it back on me again. I was confused. I didn't know what was going on or why she was doing it. At home, I told my parents what had happened. The next morning my dad came to school with me instead of my mom. He went straight to the principal and had him call in my teacher.

"You four-eyed cow, who do you think you are? Checking my girl to see if she's clean? What about you, you Peeping Tom, are you clean? Who's checking you?" My dad was furious. The traffic in the hallways had come to a stop, everyone staring at what was going on. The principal threatened my dad with the police. In the end he didn't call, but he did have to report it. As a representative of the working class, my dad was a big disappointment to the Communists and had to go to disciplinary proceedings. As a result of the incident, they posted a picture of my dad on the bulletin board at the office of the National Committee with the caption "Disgrace of the Socialist Village." I have to say, we couldn't have cared less, and my dad's fiercely religious mom was actually very proud of him.

My parents decided I wouldn't join the Sparks or Pioneers, the Communist versions of the Brownies and Girl Scouts. I didn't attend propaganda meetings, mandatory Saturday clean-ups, or any of the other activities that were a standard part of a child's life back then. One day I was paging through a book of fairy tales at the kitchen table, where my mom was peeling potatoes for soup and my dad was doing a crossword puzzle, when suddenly out of the blue I asked: "Mom, what are Gypsies?" My parents looked at each other; my dad laid down his pencil and my mom her knife.

"Where did you hear that word?"

"The kids in school said it, they said that we're Gypsies."

"Well, they were right about that, we are Gypsies, but you see, Gypsy is an insult. We're Roma." That word I knew, Roma, that was us, we had a different color skin.

"But mommy, they said we steal and we're dirty, even though we're not. Why do they say that?"

"Baby, people in life are going to tell you all kinds of things, that doesn't mean they're true."

"I told them how many books you have at home and how you read and you know how to speak French, but they didn't believe me, they said Gypsies don't know that stuff." My dad looked at my mom.

"Listen to me, never tell anyone your mom knows French or they might ask where she learned it. And don't talk about the books your mom has at home either."

"Why not, Daddy?"

"Remember Uncle Luděk, who used to come visit? You know why he doesn't come to visit anymore? Do you know where he is?"

"Yeah, I know. He's in Italy."

"And do we talk about where your uncle is?"

"No, Daddy, it's a secret."

"Right, so from now on, whatever we talk about at home is also a secret, do you understand?" I nodded, even though it wasn't clear to me at all why I shouldn't brag about what my mom knows and why it was a secret that my uncle Luděk didn't live here anymore. But if my dad said so, then that's the way it had to be.

That night I couldn't fall asleep, lying there listening to my parents' conversation. The door to the bedroom was never closed all the way—my parents wanted to keep a steady watch on their only child.

"Feri, we have to get out of here. What about that flat in Chomutov? You think we should take it? Didn't you say they offered you a panelák?"

"Well, it's not exactly a panelák, but it's in a good neighborhood and it isn't far from school either. Tibi and his kids live nearby, so she wouldn't be all by herself."

"We have to move," my mom decided.

My reminiscing was interrupted by the ringing of a mobile phone. "What is wrong with you, girl? I've been waiting for you at the bakery for fifteen minutes already," my mom fumed. It had totally slipped my mind that I was supposed to meet her to order a birthday cake for my dad.

"Sorry, Mom, I forgot. Yesterday they gave the little one an assignment about the revolution and it kind of threw me off." I apologized to her again as we sat over our pastries. I told her about my memories of first grade and the revolution. Back then I was so excited about democracy.

"Well, of course, you were a child, and we were all naïve. No one had any idea it was going to be like the Wild West. There's no reason to torture yourself over it. And as for that school, we moved into the city after that, and there you had friends and things were better, right?"

"They were, for a while, till the revolution came along. Everyone had their own idea of what democracy looked like. Remember how they treated us in the restaurant? Or that stationer's, where they refused to wait on us?"

"I do, I do. Everyone was talking about democracy all the time, but no one actually knew what it meant. We hadn't been to a restaurant or pub in years, because of how they ignored us, and I refused to be humiliated like that. I also remember when your father lost his job and not a single place would take him on permanently. After that he worked in construction and it was a regular thing for him not to get paid. Then we didn't have enough for rent, and sometimes even proper meals."

"But you knew how to take care of us with hardly anything. The food you cooked was always excellent." I reminded my mom that even when we were poor, I had never gone hungry.

"Yeah, I learned that from your grandma, in Eastern Slovakia we had to make do with whatever the house provided, it always came in handy to know how to do that. Maybe we should've stayed there, baby."

"No, Mom. You left in search of better things, Dad left for work and you went with him. That's how it was meant to be and that's the way it was. Who knows if I would have gone to school if we'd stayed in Slovakia." My mom nodded her head in agreement.

"I still remember the way their jaws dropped at school when you passed the entrance exam for the business academy. I was so proud!"

"Yeah, what I remember is when you and Dad came to my school-leaving exam. I thought I'd have a heart attack. I was already nervous enough I wouldn't pass, then the two of you walked in, the only parents there." I smiled at the memory and so did my mom. My mood instantly lifted. "Then when they handed out the diplomas, Dad walked around taking pictures, shoving the camera in my face. 'Smile!' he kept telling me. But just like in primary school, you were the only parents there I remember, even though anyone who wanted to could come."

"Do you remember the time the skinheads marched down our street?" My mom suddenly turned serious.

"No one could forget that. That was an awful time for us all." We both stared into our mugs. Neither of us wanted to talk about those memories. Details of events from early 1992 started coming back to me.

"Pack your things." My mom handed me a bag.

"Should I take my pyjamas too?"

"I don't know. Franta, how long are we going to be gone?"

"Pack enough for a couple of days, after that we'll see."

My mom walked around our flat, filling her handbag with documents, IDs, and money. I sat on the ground in my room, looking out the window at the street. I was picturing what might happen if we stayed at home and someone threw a rock or a Molotov cocktail through the window. Right into my room. On the inside I shuddered, but in front of my parents I acted like I was managing fine. A little while later, we were ready to leave.

"Are we going?" asked my mom, looking at my dad. He shook his head.

"We have to wait for the other guys. They went to escort Deži's family. And Jano's still waiting at home, the rest of them are together already. You'll stay with Tibi and I'll come get you later. Once it's all over."

From the expression on my mom's face, it was obvious she could no longer pretend she wasn't afraid. She looked at my dad in terror. My parents had never hugged or kissed in front of me before, but now they took each other's hand and my mom gave my dad a kiss on the lips. My dad held her close for a while, then pulled me too into his arms.

"What's going on, Feri? We had a good life here. Remember? Gadjos and Roma together. No one attacked anyone, we never had any fistfights, except for the guys in the pub. What happened? It's the city's fault for moving us all into one street, like sheep to the slaughter." We were interrupted by a knock at the window. My dad looked out through the curtain and gave us the nod.

"They're here." It was dark outside now, and six strapping

men formed a circle around me and my mom, protecting us from all sides, as we set out for my uncle Tibi's. Each of the men carried a homemade weapon. Some had a baseball bat, others a piece of wood or a shovel handle. Tibi's family lived on the fourth floor of a block of flats, about half a kilometer from us on foot, and we would be safe there, according to my dad. There were a lot of Romani men out on the street, all holding something in their hands. My dad took us up to the flat, while the others waited out in the courtyard. Then he gave me a kiss, hugged my mom, and she gave him another kiss.

"Don't go outside, don't even look out the window." Those were his last instructions to us before the door closed behind him. Aunt Věra secured it with a steel bar, so it couldn't be easily kicked down. Inside it was just children and women. Uncle Tibi wasn't there, or any other man. I knew my dad would be out all night standing guard with the others. They were going to walk the streets, protecting our homes.

My uncle lived in a large flat with my aunt, their granddaughter, my grandmother, and one of their sons with his wife and daughter. My aunt had a place to sleep ready for us, and a warm bowl of soup waiting. She wanted to ask us a question while we were eating, but my mom had instructed her not to say anything in front of me. Once I was done with my soup, I went with their granddaughter, who was the same age as I was, into her bedroom.

"Do you know why they're doing this?" Týna asked me.

"I think so, it's the skinheads. They want to kill us and they're going to come down our street is why."

"Yeah well, these aren't just any skinheads, girl," said Týna, shaking her head. "These are German skinheads. From what I heard, they already killed some people, and they want to kill us too."

I didn't say anything back, I knew very well what was going on. I could feel it all around me—from the teachers in school, my classmates, from our neighbors whose little girl Hanka I used to play with. I could feel it in the store, on the bus, wherever I went. I could feel the hatred.

"You know Pepa? That cute boy that used to live across the street from you? Last week at the train station, they got ahold of him and beat him up. Then they took his shoes, so he had to walk home barefoot in the snow. Now he's in the hospital, I heard it's not looking good. And they attacked my uncle too. He stood his ground, though. There were two skinheads and he beat them both up, but one of them hit my uncle in the head with a rock, so now his skull is cracked."

I listened, unable to shake the image of my dad lying in the snow, bleeding from his head. I tried to focus on something else, but it was impossible. All night long I kept getting up and peeking through the curtain at the street in case I saw him. Finally, I was overcome by sleep. In the morning I was woken by men's voices from the kitchen.

"I saw that bastard riding by on a motorcycle, so I waited in the bushes and took him out with the bat."

"Fuckin A, and did you see that old Gypsy beat up that other one?"

"Packy got it bad, though, right in the head."

"Yeah, but he'll be fine. That'll teach those baldheaded scum not to come round here anymore."

From these scraps of conversation, I pieced together that the Romani men of our neighborhood had safely tucked the women and children away, taken whatever they had at home, and gone out into the street to defend their families and their community. The skinheads from Germany, who had joined forces with the Czech skinheads at the border, had come down the main street toward us. Into the neighborhood where a lot of Romani families had moved over the past two years, while the white people left for a better part of town.

We came home to find that the balcony window in my room had been broken, so my father repaired it, at least temporarily, by boarding it up with plywood. I had a strange feeling all day long. There were all sorts of thoughts running through my mind.

"You need to do your homework," my mom said as if nothing at all had happened. But I just kept sitting there on the bed, staring blankly into space. Then my parents came and sat down with me and I blurted out: "This must be what it was like when people ran away during the war, right?"

"Don't worry, we're not running away. Your daddy requested a change of flat, we're going to move to a safer part of town, where you won't have to be afraid of skinheads."

"I'm not afraid of them, Mommy, they're just boneheads."

Then I did my homework and the next day I went to school. The atmosphere there was so tense you could have cut it with a knife. During gym class, I overheard a conversation between two of my teachers.

"Poor boys. If you can imagine, one of them they beat so bad they say he's got a concussion, he even had to be hospitalized," one woman huffed. It suddenly dawned on me that he was a relative of hers.

"Fucking Gypsies, spreading all over town, as if they owned the place. Black bastards," the other woman said.

"I tell you, there's gonna be payback for this. His buddies said they won't rest till they burn down a houseful of Gypsies."

"Well, I for one am cheering them on. Those boys are bringing some order back. The government isn't doing a thing about the darkies."

"What're you staring at?" one of the teachers snapped at me. "Did you see that? She was listening to us."

When I got home, I didn't mention a word about what I'd heard my teachers say. I knew my parents would go to the school and then it would be even worse and nothing would change anyway.

"You didn't have it easy in primary school. I can imagine that, all right," my mom said, turning the topic back to school. "I worked as a cleaning lady at the school where our little Matyáš goes now, and I know what our kids went through there back in the day."

"But those days are over. Plus there were some nice things that happened, too," I said, trying to spark more cheerful memories. My mother looked so sad. "Remember coupon privatization? Two hours you stood in line with Dad, waiting to sell your coupon books so we could buy our first satellite."

"Yeah, that satellite was the beginning of our telenovela phase. But I also remember those new Roma that moved in threw rocks at our dish. By then there were hardly any of the old Roma or gadjos left. They had all moved away."

"The Pogoč family, who lived above us, they were the first ones who left. They had a son and a daughter."

"I remember them really well. Their son was named Mirek and all the girls were in love with him." My mom broke out laughing, remembering the way we used to fawn over him.

"But he was so cute, blue eyes, light brown hair." I laughed too.

"Their daughter Jana was gorgeous too. There was hardly

a white girl around who could hold a candle to her. And she was so nice. She always played with you, even though she was older."

"Did you know she was my idol? I wanted to be like her. I also remember Mr. Pogoč was our bank. Dad went to him when he needed to borrow money."

"Yeah, he was strict, but otherwise he was a good man."

"I got so angry at Mirek once when I got my hair cut and he said I looked like a Cuban!" I burst out laughing.

"He also got a good dressing-down from his dad for making you cry that time. You may've been maybe thirteen? Then afterwards, to make it up to you, he lowered a paper bag of cherries down from the balcony on a rope."

"Yeah, and then none of the girls on the street would talk to me. They were jealous," I said, recalling that long-ago feeling of malicious joy.

"Poor boy. You know how he turned out, right? He moved to Prague and got into drugs. Who knows where he's at now. He never did manage to get it together. His mom told me once, when I ran into her in town, that he only came home to get money and he was constantly out of it. The whole family was upset and didn't know what to do."

My mom fell silent.

"Back then we didn't care if someone was white or black. Isn't that odd?"

"You know what, girl, that's because your dad and I tried to keep you in sort of a bubble. We shielded you so you wouldn't run into people who made you feel bad for having a different color skin than them. But it's true, back in those days, people didn't dare show it so much. The intolerance was always there, but it wasn't until after the revolution, when freedom came along and people started thinking anything was allowed, that it showed full force."

Hearing her words, I realized that whatever I experienced in my childhood and adolescence had definitely left its mark on me, but thanks to the way my parents raised me, it hadn't broken me. And that the life we have now is a good one. We can go to the pastry shop and no one chases us out the door. My child is happy in school, my husband and I have good jobs. We can't let the past take our future away from us. Our son has his whole life ahead of him.

THAT'S CAPITALISM FOR YOU

AVIA

BY MARIA SIVÁKOVÁ

"That's capitalism for you, there you have it! Uch, I'm going to have a smoke," my dad says from the living room. He always gets worked up like that during the news. He sits at the table and turns on the portable speaker he got for Christmas. An Eastern Slovak folk song drifts through the kitchen. He sinks into his memories. Neither of us says a word, but we're both a little uneasy.

"So, how bout a drink, huh?" We both like to reminisce about old times.

"I could make some good halušky, Dad."

"All right, get cooking." He smiles.

I remember as a little girl standing out at the corner of our panelák every afternoon at three, trying to spot my mom and dad in the crowd coming home from the Avia car factory, where they worked on the assembly line. In return for their signatures pledging loyalty to the company, they got a deed to a three-bedroom 72-square-meter flat in the Prague district of Letňany. That was where they raised me, my two-year-older brother Pepík, and Martin, the oldest, who my dad fixed up with an after-school job in the rubber factory.

My mom and dad came to the Czech lands from Eastern Slovakia in the 1970s. They were driven to move by a longing for "better tomorrows," as the Communist slogan said. Having a job guaranteed for ten years, and a flat in Prague to boot, was a dream. Ten years turned into twenty-five. I can't imagine working a quarter-century for the same factory. For me it would be more like a nightmare, but for them it meant security, validation, and a peace of mind that they no longer have today.

"Džanes s'oda sas? Dine amenge bitos ča vaš o jekh podpisos! Dža akana te phučel, či tuke les dena! Dža, cin tuke les! Hin tut ajci love!? Nane!"[1] my dad gripes, peeking over my shoulder to check if I'm doing it right, the way he used to do to my mom.

1 "Do you have any idea what that meant? They gave us a flat for nothing but signing our name! Go ask if they'll give you that nowadays! Go on, buy one yourself! You don't have the money? Too bad!"

"No, kajse sanore haluškici me rado,"[2] he teases me. My song comes on the speaker. The one my mom taught me to dance to.

"I never dreamed I would hear my baby say . . ." I turn up the volume and, wooden spoon in hand, let myself be carried away by the Eastern country czardas.

"Sa lakeri daj,"[3] my dad whispers to himself.

"Hey, Mom, when are we going home?" I'd been pestering her with that question ever since early spring, and at long last, it was almost time to go on holiday. Prague, where I was born, was my home, but we regularly spent the whole summer in Slovakia, where I always felt so good. We would be making the trip along with my mom's other siblings.

"Milko, ada berš me khere na džav. Mi džal tumenca o Michal,"[4] my aunt said, making arrangements with my mom about who would travel east with us that year. I started to get a nice feeling of butterflies in my stomach. It was always a big event that everyone really looked forward to. Anyone who couldn't go at least sent a big package. And a package just as big came back—filled with genuine Slovak bread, raspberries, the mushrooms known in Romani as kozara, and other goodies. My mom's parents lived in Radoma, while my dad's mom, his three brothers, and a bunch of uncles and aunts lived in Stročín. My grandpa had been a partisan in World War II, he lost his leg when he stepped on a mine, and died shortly after, so I never got to know him. There was no shortage of cousins, boys and girls alike. Courtyards with animals running around, nightly sausage roasts, trips into town over the half-collapsed wooden bridge, which I was afraid to cross. Sunday masses, soccer tournaments, horror movies in the clubhouse, cherry preserves from Uncle Pali. Both villages had their charm—what one lacked, the other one had. My Radoma grandma with the big pleated skirt and a scarf on her head, my grandpa with the brimmed hat, a vest, and creased trousers. They lived in a little house in the middle of a big garden where they

2 "Mm, I love skinny little halušky like that."

3 "Just like her mom."

4 "Milka, I'm not going home. Have Michal go with you this year."

grew fruits and vegetables. In front of the house stood a tall old apple tree, which we used to lie under on a little sofa to hide from the sun. Next to it was the outhouse and behind that the woodshed, where my grandpa kept the wood neatly stacked for winter. Behind the woodshed flowed a little stream, a jarkos in the local Romani dialect, and spread out a little ways above that was a magnificent countryside framed with a dense forest, where we went to gather kozara, which my grandma made into the best mushroom scramble you ever had. I spent most of my time with my cousin Zdeněk, who was the same age as I was. We went for swims in the jarkos, catching tiny little fish in a washbasin we found in the attic, which we climbed up to on a wooden ladder. Then we'd make three wishes and put the fish back in the water. On our adventurous outings, we followed the stream all the way to the end and feasted our eyes on the beauty of untouched nature.

"Jesus Christ be praised," our neighbor called to us.

"For all eternity," my cousin said, elbowing me to answer too.

"You Prague folk!" she said, laughing at my shyness, which faded away after a few days and I began again to fully understand the Eastern Slovak dialect and Romani, and used it abundantly, too. It was a beautiful feeling.

Returning from Slovakia to the sídliště in Prague was always a terrible shock. I sulked about it for some time, resenting my parents for bringing me back. "Nechcem bivac tu! Včom sce ma nezochabili tam?!"[5] I loudly complained in the Eastern Slovak dialect. It was hard for them too, and I didn't make it any easier on them. But I wanted to live with a houseful of cats and lead a cow to pasture. The last week of holiday, my mom did her best to get me to speak fluent Czech again. She had already tried her luck once before with my older brother Martin's teacher, who tried to put him in a special school.

"Na sas berš, te bi na samas pre prazdňini khere. Akanakes džav ča varekaske pro pohrebos,"[6] my dad explodes.

5 "I don't want to be here! You should have just left me there!"

6 "There wasn't a year we didn't do go home on holiday. Now I only go there when someone has a funeral."

"Everything was better under communism, čhaje. It was totally different. We could afford things. Try going to Slovakia for two months with three children now! You have to buy groceries to bring, you can't just show up empty-handed. Pherdo čhave. Kaj tut hin o chaben, cigaretľi a všelijake iné veci? Našťi aves pre ladž . . . ha,"[7] he smiles sarcastically in that own special way of his, making peace with the fact that our family trips "home" are now a thing of the past.

My grandpa built the house in Radoma, and he was with the partisans too. At first they lived in a wooden chiža out by the woods, where my grandma and her two children, who later died, hid from the Nazis. After the war, anyone could pick a piece of land and build on it. Anyone who could, lent a helping hand. My mom is one of nine children, their house had only two rooms and got too small for all of them, so one by one they began moving away from the picturesque little village in Eastern Slovakia to the growing city of Prague, where their father had been commuting to work for years, and started to see each other again. They all had jobs in the same car factory. They all had steady work and new flats they could move into along with their children, so they didn't have to stay in the company lodgings. They were there for one another. They kept their paťiv, their honor, and passed it on to their children.

When one of my classmates invited me to her eighth birthday party and I showed up at the door with my gift, she surprised me with the words, "Go away, you aren't allowed here." I guess her parents told her she wasn't allowed to be friends with a "Gypsy girl." I didn't really get it. It made me sad, but I quickly shook it off, since I had my whole big family around me. Having two older brothers and all those cousins made me feel safe and secure that I belonged somewhere.

"Dad, were you there jingling your keys?" This provocative question came to me one day when I dropped my spoon and it jingled against the ground. "So sal?" my dad

7 "There are kids everywhere. Where do you get food, cigarettes, all that other stuff? It all costs something. You can't go empty-handed—that would be a disgrace."

frowned at me. He never wanted to talk about November 1989. For him it was a turning point, the time when the dream he was living had been stolen away from him. "Sa pes zachinďa. Tu na dikhes, so pes ačhiľal, so pes ačhol?"[8] he said dejectedly, puffing on his cigarette.

I remember the old wooden phone booths, with the receiver too high for me to reach. They were across the street from a small department store that we called One Two Three because of the giant numbers on the walls of the building sticking up right in the middle of our housing estate. That might have even been what it was actually called. On the ground floor was a supermarket where I would go and spend my hard-saved five crowns on Pedro chewing gum and Zoretky, the best cookies in the world. Later, as teenagers, we used to meet up "at the shop." There was a small fountain with a circle of benches around it, and we would sit there, the boys playing guitar, the girls singing, having a great time. We didn't have a care in the world, we lived for the present and had no idea what the new era of capitalism would bring. We didn't realize that our parents were starting to dread the new tomorrows that they had moved to the capital for. Eventually I started to notice that the area we lived in was divided into upper Letňany, where only a few Roma lived, and lower Letňany, which part of the majority population had started to call a ghetto. The fact of the matter was that it wasn't a ghetto, we were just more visible there. The housing estate was home to several families from all corners of Slovakia, but everyone lived a peaceful, orderly life, as dictated by communism, and we grew into the new generation of Prague Roma. A large part of our crew were non-Roma. We grew up together and remain close friends to this day. Our parents knew each other from Avia, so it was never a problem. For the "uppers," though, we were different. Our crew was really big, and we stuck together, in that sense maybe we really were different. Time ticked along and our parents still had jobs, but they started to be worried they would lose them. There were rumors of privatization.

8 "Are you out of your mind? ... The whole thing's gone to hell. Haven't you been paying attention?"

Before long, our parents were afraid to let us go outside, forbidding us from meeting on the benches "at the shop," or at the gardens in the neighborhood of Kolonky, where we played volleyball. For the first time in my life, I worried about my brother, when he and some other guys in our crew got in a fight with skinheads. The "upper-suckers" probably sicced them on us, but as far as I know, they only came once. They saw the strength we had in unity.

Things went downhill soon after people began wearing wide jeans and moccasins. My dad got more and more worked up about the TV news. Avia changed its name to Daewoo Avia, and the Czech car factory became South Korean. Wages went down, rents went up. My parents began to quarrel, family get-togethers were no longer as frequent or joyful. People started to think about themselves more. Some of the older guys in our crew began using drugs, racism kicked up a notch. Up until then, I never would have believed that a bus ride to Prosek could turn into a horror film.

"Hoho, looks like someone here's having a dark day!" said a voice from behind us.

"Was that directed at us?" my younger brother Pepa asked. I was petrified with fear.

"Don't worry," Martin whispered, trying to reassure us. We stood up and walked to the door. As the gang of skinheads started chanting the hackneyed slogan "Gypsies to the gas," our fellow passengers acted like they didn't see or hear a thing.

"Open the door!" Pepa pleaded with the driver, but just then a Nazi in black army boots decided to give Martin a couple punches with brass knuckles. We jumped out at the last second.

At some point, Daewoo Avia was bought by an Indian company, and the layoffs got under way. Little by little, friends and family disappeared. Some moved to another town, some went to England or Canada. My mom wouldn't even hear of moving. They were used to working their whole lives and didn't intend to give up. But looking for a new job after so many years of steady work in the same factory wasn't easy. There was much less money, and I cried my way through the start of holiday—we didn't go anywhere.

"No, čhaje, lačhe haluškici,"[9] my dad praises me, but I know he would like the ones my mom made more.

9 "All right, girl, good halušky."

THE NINETIES

BY VĚRA HORVÁTHOVÁ DUŽDOVÁ

We always had scads of people coming over to visit. Our aunt's aunt, our aunt's grandaunt, our grandma's cousin twice removed, and other family from this or that town either passing through, or by, or coming straight over to see us. It was great; so great my dad decided to hang a sign on the front door that he brought home from his construction job: "Due to infectious illness, order of quarantine in effect until further notice."

So one day I looked out the window and I saw Uncle Bandy standing in front of our house. With his tall strapping frame, the only thing that marred his polished appearance was his protruding ears. All the expectant mothers in our family prayed for their children not to inherit that distinctive family trait. My cousin Marek just had bad luck ...

As Uncle Bandy read the sign, his dusky complexion slowly turned pale. He was about to turn on his heel and leave when I ran down to open the door and explained that it was a prank on my dad's part and we were all actually healthy. He was delighted, but still furtively looked us all up and down.

Jesus, was he excited! You would have thought it was because we were all in perfect health, but he had brought big news for my mom: "My dearest Věra, at last!" he cried with joy. "At last we Roma have a chance to make a difference again!" he added breathlessly.

He acted like he had come to tell us he'd found gold. I was still a skinny little brat at the time. The Velvet Revolution came when I was in first grade. I don't know how long after November it was when my uncle showed up, but we had already had freedom for a good minute or two.

"They're founding a Romani Civic Initiative, and we can start one here in Lenešice too!" my uncle Bandy said. To me the two of them in that moment were like the rising sun—beautiful and alive, stepping forward into a new day and a new life. My mother's hands, smeared with noodle dough, embraced my uncle's hulking arms and wiped away a tear of joy running down his cheek.

And that's how it began.

My mom sat her full-bodied frame down at the table and clacked away until she had typed up everything needed to form the group—in Czech, for short, the ROI. Soon after, there was a meeting, with almost all the Roma in the district in attendance. How could I know that if I wasn't there? Well, we had the sign-up sheets and everyone's member IDs at our place, it goes without saying. People were excited, happy, and everyone was raring to go. Uncle Pepa, my mom's oldest brother, was elected chair, my mom was voted vice chair, and my dad was put in charge of the group's finances. Some of you might be thinking, that's a nifty family business, but they were duly elected.

To this day, I still remember their first trips for meetings in Prague, and my mom telling me about Emil Ščuka: an intelligent gentleman who meant well and with any luck he could keep it going. Plus Mr. Holomek from Brno, Mr. Giňa from Rokycany, and others. I also remember our house being constantly full of cigarette smoke, since the Lenešice ROI was based at our address. Their office was in our kitchen!

It's a shame I didn't save at least one of the posters, which we hand-drew at home. It gave me the space to express myself artistically, and when I look back on it, I'm amazed my creative ideas passed quality control without a hitch. Imagine a little kid writing and doodling all over an announcement like this:

ROI Lenešice presents
A ROMA DANCE PARTY.
Come dance and listen to RYTMUS 84.

Rytmus 84 was a blockbuster group. Sort of the Michael Jackson of Romani music. And guess what? They're still famous to this day, even though they don't play anymore and some of the members are no longer with us.

Or when the Lenešice crew came back from a meeting in Prague, where all the ROI representatives in the Czech Republic came together, with a vinyl copy of *Romský folklór*, released by the ROI talent agency RomArt. Twenty Romani songs, flawlessly arranged by Gejza Horváth and recorded by a cimbalom orchestra, which we played over and over again. I can still hear the songs in my head, even though it's been ages now since we last listened. It's the same for all my friends, for everyone I know from my generation. To this day, whenever I hear a snatch of those famous melodies—"Od kanastar," or "Lačhi romňi"—I feel like I've come home. Home, where no one is dead, no one is sick . . . We had worries of course, since everything that could go up in price did, the grown-ups lost their jobs, and we children felt it too, but in spite of that, every single Rom was proud. "Yes, we are the ones who make that beautiful music, and now you're all able to listen to it."

So what else did my mom and uncle Pepa dream up in support of community life? Well, for example, when there was a dance and it got to the point where the men began to shimmy their hips while the women swayed to the beat, they would announce gentlemen's choice. And to make it easier on men who were shy, they could buy a Zora chocolate bar from the organizers and offer it to the lady they were hoping to dance with. What woman could refuse a man with chocolate? It seemed like a nice idea to me, though having to tie a ribbon around every bar of chocolate wasn't quite as nice.

Eventually, my mom's voice also reached the people through the village's PA system. She gave a speech after the killing of the 21-year-old Romani man Emil Bendík, who was beaten to death in Libkov u Klatov on February 21, 1991. In August that same year, a group of "young lads" threw a brick into the clubhouse of the Hradec Králové ROI and fatally wounded 52-year-old Josef Sztojka.

Skinheads.

Part of the price of freedom. We all had to pay it. Some might object that those young men weren't actually skinheads. They started to call themselves that because they didn't know about the antiracist roots of the skinhead movement and its symbols—why they shaved their heads and wore heavy boots. In the nineties they were skinheads, but today they're neo-Nazis—they finally read up on where it came from. The internet was new at the time and there wasn't that much information.

Even some of my classmates turned skinhead. Suddenly one day the school we went to was graffitied with swastikas and slogans calling for us, the Roma, to be sent to the gas chambers. The name "Dan Landa" and the racist oi band he founded, "Orlík," were carved into the school benches. I saw it with my own eyes, and reported back when I got home: "The second you see someone in black boots with white laces, run away as fast as you can," I instructed my family. On TV they showed a demonstration of people marching against the white laces. "Those are anarchists, they're on our side!" I said, adding to my commentary. The one advantage was at least you knew right away who hated you.

In those days it was common for skinheads to attack Romani people's homes shouting "Oi to ROI!" Daniel Landa's band Orlík was even scheduled to play at our local cultural center. We were all afraid. That was the first time I heard the word *domobrana*—"militia." So my mom led a group from ROI Lenešice to the local government office and the police, and demanded police protection in front of every Romani home.

The concert was cancelled.

With freedom came fear. The fact that they could kill us, and all the president would do is come and lay a wreath on the grave, was something I just couldn't understand, no matter how much I liked and respected Václav Havel.

I'm from north Bohemia, and the neo-Nazi movement there had a lot of sympathizers. Prague was brutal, too. My cousin Marek, the one with big ears, got the daylights beaten out of him on a regular basis. Just for walking down the street. The same thing happened to my good friend Lukáš on Christmas Day in Pilsen. He ran into a gang of bald heads, they started to beat him, then kicked him to the pavement. Imagine him lying there in the muddy December slush being showered with kicks as the cars drive past on the roadway beside them. When they noticed he had a silver chain around his neck, they stopped kicking and tried to grab it. But his courage and pride came to life. With the last of his strength, he managed to get to his feet and tell them: "So now you want to rob me and you call *us* thieves!?" That earned him a few more punches. But an argument broke out among the skinheads, giving him a split-second chance to escape. Lukáš ran like his life depended on it, but the nice, well-behaved boys were hot on his heels and there was nowhere to hide. So he jumped. He jumped into the bushes and the branches held him in the air, covering him up. His heart was in his boxers as they went running past. Thank God they didn't notice him, so he waited a little longer and then walked home to the family Christmas tree, beaten and filthy, but alive.

When, in my adulthood, fate led me to film school in Písek, I stood on the bank of the Otava, thinking about 18-year-old Tibor Danihel, who was chased into the river by skinheads and prevented from coming out till he drowned. And Helena Biháriová, a young mother of four, who was thrown into the icy, flooded waters of the Elbe river and left to drown.

My mom and uncle Pepa no longer returned from their meetings in Prague excited. That whole business with the neo-Nazis and the killing of multiple Roma seemed to have taken the wind out of everyone's sails. You try your best to live in harmony with others, and it just doesn't work. You're guilty.

But of what?

"It isn't her fault she was born a Gypsy!" That's how my best friend defended me when one of my classmates called me names. As a child, I didn't know how to defend myself, I was more embarrassed than anything else, and never spoke about it at home. In my teens, it was a personal struggle, since I lived at a boarding school with a small crew of "sympathizers" on one of the floors below me. So I made up for it in my own way, by going to Most for my postsecondary studies, where there were even more of them. But there were also a lot of Roma, so the sides were equally matched.

After I completed school, I got a job in Prague. One evening I was standing at the bus station in Florenc when my cell phone rang.

"Where are you?" asked my dad.

"I'm waiting at gate 21 for the bus home."

"Quick, run and hide, it isn't safe." Children usually ignore orders or suggestions from worried parents, and I muttered under my breath, but for some reason I did as I was told, ducking into the glass-walled waiting room. From there I could see almost the whole station. As I stood there by the wall, I saw a bunch of people panic and start to run. It was weird. Then suddenly I saw. . . a group of skinheads.

One headed for the waiting room and spotted me. A Gypsy girl . . .

My heart seized up as I imagined him dragging me outside and all of them piling on me. His blue, hate-filled eyes stared through the holes in his black mask straight into mine. I said to myself, Now or never. They're going to beat my ass anyway. So I shot back a look that was just as full of hate. I was determined and wound up. And I'm sure I looked it, too.

The two of us exchanged loving looks for a while, and then he gave up. Thank goodness. To make a long story short? Listen to your parents! If my dad hadn't called, I would have been standing right out in the open.

During the 1990s, people were out of control, they thought they could do whatever they wanted. Director Vít Olmer vomited out the movie *Nudity for Sale*. Today it's hailed as a testimony of the times. But it isn't an accurate portrayal. It's works like these that make me support the view that if a minority isn't telling its own story, it's almost guaranteed to do damage. For God's sake, how many inappropriate comments and bad jokes were we forced to endure because of that film?

Eventually I met people who shared my way of thinking and point of view. I began going to protests, shooting short films, creating video installations, organizing exhibitions, and actively promoting the truth. And I do it to this day, because there's still a need.

The waters in which others were drowned haven't carried away my memories or the feeling of happiness that I was present at the birth of this chapter of history. It was a wonderful time, in spite of it all.

WHERE TO NOW?

BY MÁRIA HUŠOVÁ

"But, fellas, you do realize what this means? Some of us are going to die!"

This sentence, from the mouth of one of the respected men sitting around the blazing fire, will linger in my subconscious forever, along with everything else from that August evening of 1990.

I was listening to the evening news through the hallway from the kitchen. It was all Public Against Violence this, Civic Forum that—the popular movements that emerged during the Velvet Revolution of November 1989 were a constant topic of discussion. It seemed like no one had any idea how people were actually supposed to live now that we had freedom. Our men from the settlement went to PAV meetings, too. I admired them for that.

I loved summer evenings in our settlement. The atmosphere was festive, kids racing up and down the street and through the courtyards. The air was filled with the sounds of traditional Romani music or the pop hits of the day, or, if it was the weekend and there was a party going on or people were entertaining visitors, the sound of voices singing in unison.

I sit with the window open just a crack. I can see the flickering flames and hear people talking. Including my father. I loved listening to the stories Roma told around the fire. I pull on a sweater and go out to join them. Everyone looks serious. Some of the men take long drags on their cigarettes and pensively exhale a white stream of smoke. As they sit around the snug glow and crackle of the fire, listening to the night birds, emotions grow heavy among the men and fathers.

"But, fellas, we don't even have any firearms. Or do any of you have guns?" It's less a question than the bleak observation of a man who has never wanted to use a weapon in his life. My father's friend Gežak runs a hand through his curly hair. He always wears nice collared shirts, half-unbuttoned, that fit well on his slender frame. Even now.

"All right, we'll just have to make do with what we've got. Shovels, axes, chains . . . We have no other choice, we have to defend our children," says my father's friend Milan Mižov. He's a heavy man with a raspy voice that stands out even in a noisy crowd. No celebration or wedding is complete without his sense of humor and fun-loving spirit. His irreplaceable role is that of the svadobný pytač—in Slovak wedding tradition, the man who asks the bride's parents if the groom can marry her. I can't think of a wedding where Uncle Milan hasn't done the asking. While the engaged couple kneels in front of the parents and godparents in the home of the bride-to-be, the pytač recites a message of thanks to them on the couple's behalf. He's sort of an intermediary between the bride and groom and their families as the couple moves out on their own. Meanwhile everyone present weeps with joy, since this tradition, like our music, is very moving. But this evening Uncle Milan is deadly serious.

"The most important thing is not to sleep by the window and make sure to keep something next to your bed. A knife or . . . in case someone tries to break into your home," my father Miško chimes in. He and Uncle Gežak look almost exactly the same.

"Listen, fellas, we need to agree on a signal to let each other know if they show up. So we can come running to the rescue!" says my father's friend Štefan Štefkov, thinking out loud. He hopes the police might actually help for a change. He is stern and resolved. And it shows in his voice. In this time of chaos, however, he's worried the ground is giving way beneath the Roma's feet.

"And you need to have sandbags at home. Water won't help if they're throwing Molotov cocktails," my father adds.

As I look around, hanging on the men's every word, I realize there's something in their faces I've never seen before. A fear of powerlessness and, at the same time, an immense determination to defend the lives of every family. But there's something else besides. The worst thing of all. A realization that for some of them this might be their last night. I imagine the horror . . . fighting with skinheads who've attacked our homes. I chase the image out of my head. It's awful!

Suddenly, on the other side of the stream, we hear a cry from somebody's courtyard.

"They're coming! They're coming! They're already in Žalobín!" That's a village a few kilometers away from us. We all look at each other. Like we've been hit over the head. The men go stone quiet and hesitantly rise from their seats. I remain sitting on a tuft of grass at my father's feet.

"I hope everyone has all the essentials ready at home, in case you need to hide your women and children," says someone in a tone of voice more chiding than inquiring.

"But there's nowhere to go! The only place to hide is the woods," sighs my father's friend Miro Prichlov. He's the level-headed type. Tall, bangs combed to one side. Always walks with his hands crossed behind his back or one hand in his pocket. I stop and think, picturing us hastily grabbing a bag of food and clothes and running for the trees—we probably wouldn't even get that far. I don't want that to happen!

I glance at each of the men with concern, trying to guess what they're thinking. I look at Uncle Milan. I can tell exactly what's going through his mind. That with his weight and weak heart, he won't be able to run even a hundred meters. He's definitely scared. My father's jaw is clenched tight. I know that look. He's got a plan. He's calculating, assessing. And I'm sure he can picture himself throwing punches. He knows there's probably no alternative. Uncle Gežak doesn't like conflict. I can sense the anger eating away at his insides, how did he get himself into this mess? Still, he's prepared. He'll fight to the death if he has to. Uncle Miro Prichlov loves his wife and children more than anything in the world. It's obvious he's worried what they're doing at home right now from his hand behind his back. He keeps quietly snapping his fingers and fidgeting anxiously. He'd rather be at home with them, where he can protect them. But he realizes this meeting is important. Uncle Štefan Štefkov has always trusted the police—the Public Security, as they were known until recently. He sure could use them now! I can see the feeling of abandonment on his face because of the fact they're not there. But knowing him, I'm sure he realizes that he and his friends will have to figure it out on their own. What other options are left? They aren't concerned for their property—when lives are at risk, there's nothing more important than that. That's what we were always taught. And I can see this decision on all the men's faces. I wonder if anyone will actually come to our rescue. What if the gadjos from the village decide we need to be wiped out? Like my grandma remembered. People could do whatever they wanted to Roma when she was little. Hit them, kick them, humiliate them . . .

But I'm torn out of my dark thoughts by the sound of someone running toward us. Closing in fast. As we wait,

I can see the tension on everyone's faces. They peer out into the night, trying to see who it is. Just then one of our boys emerges from the dark. He comes to a stop, gasping for breath, under a streetlamp. Leaning his hands on his bent knees, he blurts out: "The police were here just now. They were in Žalobín too. They said it was a false alarm. But we should be on the alert. They said they can't be everywhere."

I think I wasn't the only one who was relieved. The men sit back down. I can see into our kitchen. The delicious smell of potato lokše and black Indian tea wafts through the open window. My mom is making dinner and doesn't have the slightest idea what's going on outside. I wonder if we're about to lose the serenity that emanates from our kitchen. It's a beautiful scene.

"We have to keep watch. It's true, the police can't be everywhere, and we can't rely on them anyway. We're going to have to defend ourselves. So let's talk plans. We can take turns every two hours," my father says, organizing a patrol. The men nod in agreement. Just then, Uncle Štefan utters the sentence that says it all. That speaks of the horror of the moment that has befallen us Roma yet again.

"But, fellas, you do realize what this means? Some of us are going to die!"

A moment of silence descends after his unexpected words. A terrible silence! The men stare at the ground. Turning it over in their minds.

I wait to hear what they'll say. I sit on the ground, legs bent, resting my head on my knees. I snuggle up to my father. I'm just shy of fourteen.

Until my only brother was born, I was like the son my father had always dreamed of. I followed him around everywhere, hanging on his every word. I grew up with my boy cousins, so I was in on all the mischief. I was glad to be my father's substitute son.

It's a warm, magnificently starry August night. I can feel the sweet nighttime breeze. The men sit on stools, a walnut stump, and a little bench along the fence. There are five of them. Then my father notices my bulging eyes. "You've got no business listening to men talk. Get along home," he orders me, taken aback by my presence. "These aren't matters for children."

I reluctantly obey my father's order and get to my feet. I'd rather stay awake with them. For the first time, I can see in their faces that they're afraid. I've never seen them that way before. That, I think, is what my father doesn't want me to see . . .

One year after the Velvet Revolution, the Roma found themselves in danger. A black plague of skinheads came pouring through the open gates of the democratic West to us. Baldheaded ultraright radicals. And amid the chaotic anarchy of freedom and lawlessness, the police didn't intervene in any substantial way. To our surprise, the only ones who stood up for us were, paradoxically, the punks. The same punks we were afraid of in Communist times, at least in Eastern Slovakia, since they chased Romani men, and even sometimes older women, through the streets, and more than once they beat them up. I understood it was less about the punks wanting to protect us than a power struggle, with the punks defending their territory against the skinheads. But that didn't matter to us. The important thing was, we had someone standing with us on the front line against the new evil.

It's morning. I'm taking my little daughter to the doctor's. It's been as many years now since the Velvet Revolution as Jesus was alive. This strikes me as symbolic.

There is war in Ukraine, we face an energy crisis, we made it through the COVID pandemic, only to be caught up in another: a pandemic of chaos amid the search for a new way forward. The pillars of certainty that we thought our society rested on are crumbling to pieces and change is inevitable.

We walk towards each other. He fixes my eyes with an angry glare. I refuse to budge. I may have my daughter with me, but I refuse to be intimidated. I stare back at him confidently and don't back down for even a second. The tension between us is visible, even in the gray light of an empty street on an autumn morning.

We move along. He doesn't say a word, but his hatred and aggression are clear from the curl of his lips. I'm actually a bit scared he might pull a knife from his bomber jacket pocket, but no way we are going to cross the street to make way for him. His thin legs strut along in tight black jeans and tall army boots, intended to convey his superiority. He and I are both making a show of strength.

I've never allowed myself to feel the fear of intimidation, even in the past. I've used every means available to me as a journalist to oppose it. But that courage stems mainly from the solidarity of people I'm in the struggle with. I refused to allow that long-ago August night to be repeated. And now, after years of relative safety, I see one of them again on the street! I can't even believe it. It feels like I've been stabbed in the back. It's a strange feeling, like the past and the present have momentarily overlapped.

"They're coming out of their holes again."

"Who, mommy?" my daughter asks. She's only eleven.

"Did you see the jacket on that man we passed? The one who gave us the dirty look? It's called a 'bomber' and the inside is orange. It's the jacket skinheads wear. And they also wear those heavy boots. Some of them shave their heads, but not all. If you ever see one, just stay out of his way and ignore him," I explain, in a worried tone of voice.

"But why? What's a skinhead?"

She's never heard of them. She's as pure as crystal water. She has friends of different nationalities and just thinks of herself as a person. In her life, everyone sees things that way. I parcel out the truth carefully about the contempt she might face in life as a Romňi. Whenever a situation arises where it makes sense to explain. Like now, for instance.

Out of my subconsciousness, the memory of that August evening comes alive.

I walk by her side in silence. It really got to me that he could so boldly stride down the street, proudly displaying his hate. But why should I be surprised, I tell myself. We've got fascists in parliament now. All dressed up in suits and elected by our people. Our struggle was in vain! I'm furious and feel like we've been betrayed. They're coming back out of the sewers. The times are in their favor. Is there anywhere for the Roma to run? Fascism is once again on the rise in Europe.

A FEW PRESENTS

BY EVA DANIŠOVÁ

The car tires squealed to a stop and the door opened.
"How bout it, girl, what's your rate?"
"Same as everyone else, depends what you want."
The man smiled and leaned over to let her in. Driving in silence, they passed through the village and turned off onto the first forest road they came across.
It was Květa's first day standing on the highway. She wasn't sure how to act, how to talk to a man who wanted this. Her best friend Lenka, who'd been working the spot for two years now, brought her here. Květa had come home from prison two months before and had been living with Lenka since then.
"Don't worry, it's no big deal, and it'll be fast money, stick it out a while and we'll both have plenty for rent and other stuff. We just have to make sure there's no other girls there with their pimps. We don't give anyone a cut, we're in this on our own. I can't keep on supporting you and the rent's not gonna pay itself."
Květa didn't answer, she was just trying to picture what sort of men would seek their services: elderly, fat, lonely, ugly, little dicks or big?
She spotted an attractive-looking fortysomething, fairly well-off to judge from his manners and his car. I'm in luck, she thought. She repeated Lenka's advice to herself one more time: don't give your real name, nothing personal, insist on either protection or an additional fee, keep an eye on your money, no kissing. It's a business transaction.
It's not like I'm made of porcelain, I'll survive it somehow. She took a deep breath and looked in the rearview mirror. The driver's eyes were calm, he was just paying for a service.
"So, we good to go?"
"Yeah, yeah."
"No special requests, nothin weird, I just need to let off steam, know what I mean?"
"Sure."
She was actually looking forward to it. Not counting the occasional indulgence with Fugina, her cellmate, she hadn't had any physical contact in over seven years.
He was polite, didn't talk, and paid what he owed. Even drove her back to the spot where he'd picked her up. No feeling of abuse or humiliation. Is it really that easy? Květa

wondered, stashing the money away in her dress pocket. She waved to Lenka and gave her a thumbs-up. Lenka gave her a smile and went back to chatting with the driver of a BMW with German plates.

Květa stood on the edge of the highway. Eight hundred for thirty minutes was darn good money, she thought. That was about how much she earned for a week of hard work in the factory before she ended up staying at home with her daughter. By the time Lenka whistled to signal the end of their shift at two a.m., Květa had three more paying customers under her belt. The money in her pocket warmed her heart and she was looking forward to a shower. She was happy to have something to give back to Lenka.

"So, how'd you make out?"

"Good, I think. The guys weren't bad at all. One of em was pretty old, but it went all right. Here, Lenka, I'm giving you half. I owe you."

"Don't be silly, keep it. Just give me half the rent. We'll each buy some food and we're cool, all right?"

"Sure, it'll be fine, don't worry, I won't leave you in the lurch."

Two months earlier, Květa had been sitting in front of a committee in the Světlá nad Sázavou prison, trying to convince them that once she was released, she would do her best to get back her daughter, who had been placed in a children's home. She had managed to find a job and a place to live while serving her sentence. A field worker from a nonprofit who came to see the women in prison had helped her out with it. She requested a reduction of three years in her ten-year sentence for killing her husband. Ten years wasn't actually the maximum. The court took into consideration the injuries she had suffered. A broken left leg, a fractured skull, and bruising from kicks all over her body.

After her release from prison, Květa went to visit her good friend Lenka and ended up staying with her. She blew off the job and her place in the rooming house, and now she was counting her money for the night.

"So, how long've you been doing this?" she asked Lenka.

"I don't even know anymore, once you start it's hard to stop. Did you ever imagine something like this when we were little? Remember how we used to go to camp? The golden days, right?"

Yep, the golden days, which don't teach you not to fall for the first jerk you meet and not to get your ass in trouble. I stopped believing in love and a wonderful life with someone else very early on. A few months with my first boyfriend, then a quick wedding, since I was pregnant. The occasional slap turned into regular beatings, broken furniture, humiliation, and a constant lack of money to cover the basic things. When I stopped paying as much attention to him, since I had to look after the little one, his addictions took off full force. Drugs and slot machines. A road to hell that ended in what the cops call a home slaughter.

"So what was it actually like?" Lenka asked Květa. "You don't have to tell me, but if you want to talk, I'm all ears."

"There's nothing to say. I had seven years to think on it, and believe me, I don't regret it. I'm not mentally ill, don't worry, I won't kill anyone again, I just couldn't take it anymore."

"So forget it. Let's go get a drink, what do you say?"

"Sure, let's go."

Květa laid two thousand crowns on the table in the hallway and slipped the rest into her pants pocket.

The other girls in the club could be divided into three categories: they were mixed up in something else besides; they had been forced into it; or they were moms who needed to feed their families and usually on top of that had to support a good-for-nothing guy or a pimp who screwed everything that moved, but somehow couldn't get it up at home . . .

"Hey, Lenka, who's that guy there, you know him?" Květa pointed to a tall, darker-skinned man.

"That's Prague Daddy, he watches over the meat. Don't mess with him. You're a fresh face, he might try to sign you on."

"Hell, how am I supposed to find a normal guy around here?"

"Guys are for shit. Don't even look. The good ones are all taken and stay away from the rest. Come on, I'll introduce you to some of the girls. The guys'll come soon enough, once they've had their Jacks and Jimmies. They're acting all nice-guy now, but prepare yourself for some rough stuff."

"I hear you."

"Hey, I'm Fanda, I'm from Prague, how bout you? You new here?"
"Hey, Květa. Yeah, I'm new."
"Wanna dance?"
"It's been a while. I might step on your toes."
"Good one, a streetwalker that steps on guys' toes."
"And a pimp on the prowl. So this is how it works? The girls hustle, you guys drink, and then you have fun together?"
"Yeah, you got a problem with that?"
"No problem. It's my first day, gimme a break."
"So just have fun and chill."
Květa gave Fanda the once-over and guessed he was maybe—fifty? He still radiated charisma, he must've been a good-looking guy back in the day. Who knows how long he's been in this line of work. I could try and ask, but what would be the point?
"Come on over to the bar, I'll have them mix you a drink."
"No drink for me, I need to find a ride to Prague, just a quick round trip, know anyone?"
"What do you need to do there? I can give you a lift tomorrow, no prob."
"I don't wanna say, but it's pretty important."
"I'll give you my number."
"Thanks. I'm gonna go check on Lenka." She found her at the bar, hanging out with the girls. Her drink glass was empty.
"Hey, Leni, I'm pretty tired, can we go soon?"
"Yeah, no prob. How bout Fanda, all good?"
"He's gonna take me to Prague. I gotta see probation service about my parole, plus I wanna finally go visit my little one. I feel awful. I've been home for two months now and still haven't seen her. What'm I supposed to tell her?"
"Look, girl, at this time of night, in a place like this, I can't even think about that stuff. We can talk about it tomorrow. Right now let's go to bed."
"Hey, Fanda, what time should I call tomorrow?" Květa asked as she and Lenka walked past.
"Whenever, as long as it's after eleven!"

"Stop with the secrets and tell me how come you need to go to Prague," Fanda pressed her as she climbed into his car at 11:15 the next morning.

"I was locked up and I'm on parole. I have to check in. They're gonna ask me where I work, and I don't have a clue what I'm gonna say."

"Hmm, that's no good. What you need is a contract. Hang on, I'll call my friend, he's got a cleaning agency. He might be able to give you a note saying you work there."

"That'd be awesome."

"OK, and what're you gonna do after that? You got a man in Prague?"

"No, I've got a daughter in a home there, and I wanna see her."

"Girl, you are nothing but surprises. So we'll go pick up that note and what about after? You wanna go somewhere?"

"Sure. You can pick me up at the Anděl metro station, say, four o'clock?"

"How'd it go, did the note do the trick? And how was the visit?"

"Probation was a breeze, but I didn't make it to see my daughter. I just couldn't deal with it. I was right there at the door, but I didn't ring the bell. Crap!"

"Next time. Come on, let's go get a bite."

"Look at those Christmas decorations! It's awful, we aren't even halfway through November. Listen, Fanda, you know any working girls who've got kids? How do they do it?"

"I don't. Usually the kids're with their grandmas, either that or they're in a home."

"Right. I wanna see if I can figure it out by Christmas. I can't have the little one at Lenka's, so I dunno."

"Can't help you with that, girl. Why don't I drop you off at the bus. I can tell it won't be any fun with you."

"I guess not. This whole thing has me shook."

On the way back to Sokolov, she wondered what she should do next. Stay with Lenka, or look for a different job and place to live? Staying in a shelter would be like going back to prison. She didn't have the energy to deal with it. She decided to stay put till Christmas.

"Hey, is there traffic at Christmastime too?" she asked Lenka.

"Except for Christmas Day and New Year's."

"For real?"

"Of course. There's lonely guys too."

"I need to go see my little girl in the home on Christmas Day. I wanna buy her some presents."

"Feel free. You just have to think about what you really want. Whether you can support your girl if you're working somewhere for crumbs and living in a shelter, or if she's actually better off in the home. Your parents don't give a damn about either one of you."

"Yeah, I know, I don't like either option, but I just don't know what to do. But I'm gonna see her next week for sure!"

Květa quickly got used to the money she made in just a few hours on the highway and the nightlife in the bars. A few days before Christmas, she set off to buy presents for her daughter and finally pay her a visit. As she made the rounds of the stores, for the first time in a long time she didn't have to look at how much anything cost. She wondered what to get for the nine-year-old girl she hadn't seen in seven years. The whole time that she was in prison, she'd only written her daughter four times. She never knew what to write. She didn't want to give the girl a hope that she herself didn't have. Of the hundred and fifty crowns she got each month for personal needs, there was never any left to buy her daughter a present. It was just enough for coffee and hygiene products.

Květa picked a music box with a dancing ballerina. She had always longed for one when she was her daughter's age. She actually had no idea what her child wanted. A beautiful dress, maybe? A bead bracelet and a necklace? The more she thought about it, the more she dreaded meeting her. What if she didn't recognize her? She didn't know how to explain to a child that she couldn't take care of her. Instead of looking forward to going, she had to convince herself that she needed to go. It wasn't fair to be so close and not visit her. In place of her initial joy at buying presents, now all she felt was apprehension. At long last, she worked up the courage and rang the bell at the children's home.

The caregiver opened the door and asked what she could do for her. Květa was so nervous she began to stutter. She managed to find out that the children were away, doing some activity, and to visit she had to make a request in advance and set up a time. Instead of seeing her daughter, she handed the present to the caregiver without a word. By the time she reached the bus, her cheeks were streaked with black eye makeup, running down her chin onto her neck.

She rode the bus back to Lenka's.

"I chickened out, dammit. I bought her presents, but didn't even see her. I left her there with strangers, and in the end we're both going to be alone."

"Don't take it so hard," said Lenka. "They do a beautiful job with the holidays at the home."

"Pour me a big drink. Screw it all, even Christmas."

E KARAČOŇA IMAR NADUR

EVA DANIŠOVÁ

O motoris zorales terďiľa paš o drom the jekhetanes pes phundraďa the o vudar.
„Ta so, čhaje, savi tut hin taksa?!“
„Sar avre čhajen, so ko mangel,“ phenďa e Kveta.
O murš asanďiľa u paš oda lake mek buter phundraďa o vudar andro motoris. Na vakerenas, sar džanas pal o gav, u paľis gejle perše dromeha andro veš.
E Kveta has pre trasa peršo ďives. Na džanelas, so te kerel, so te phenel le muršeske, savo kada kamel. Iľa la pre kada e baratkiňa, e Lenka, savi pre kaja trasa phirel imar duj berš. Avľa andal e bertena duj čhon pale u akorestar bešel la Lenkaha.
„Ma dara, kereha tuke sig o love, ňič oda nane, čeporo ľikereha avri u avla amen o love pro kher the pre savoro aver. Ča kampel te dikhel, kaj te odoj nane aver džuvľija the o murša, so len pre trasa bičhaven, lengere bosa. Na kampel amenge ňikaske amare lovendar te del, keraha o love ča amenge dujdžeňenge. Man nane ajci love pro chaben the predal tute u kampel tiš te poťinel o kher.“
E Kveta na phenelas ňič, ča duminelas, save murša kada kamen. Phuredere, thule, so len ňiko nane, džungale, cikneha či bareha?
Akana dikhelas šukar muršes, šaj leske has vaj saranda berš, šukar motoris, dičholas sar paťivalo, barvalo. Hin man bacht, duminelas. Mek jekhvar leperďa, so lake e Lenka phenďa: te na phenel peskero nav, ňič pal peste, kaj te les hin o kondomos, u te na, ta lestar te mangel buter love, te arakhel o love, te ňikas na čumidel. Hin oda o biznisura.
Na som sar popkica, varesar oda kerava, cirdľa andre peste o luftos u dikhľa andro gendalocis andro motoris. Leskere jakha na phenenas ňič, poťinďa peske oda, so joj kerel.
„Ta so, sal kisitimen?“
„He, he.“
„Na kamav ňič špecijalno, kampel mange ča te marel avri, achaľuves?“
„Mišto.“
Čeporo oda kamelas. Te na rachinel sar pen varekana kamavkerelas andre bertena la Fuginaha, na suťa ňikaha imar buter sar efta berš.

Has paťivalo, na phenelas ňič u poťinďa lake o love. Mek la ľigenďa pale pro than, kaj la iľa andro motoris. Na šunelas pes phujes. Kavka loko oda hin?! phučelas korkori pestar u o love garuďa mišto andre žeba pro viganos. Kerďa le vasteha pre Lenka u hazdľa o peršo angušt. E Lenka asanďiľa u dureder delas duma le muršeha andro BMW, pre savo has ňemciko značka.

Terďolas paš o agor pro drom u phenelas peske, hoj ochto šel tel o tranda minuti hin but lačhe love. Pre kajci love lake kampelas angloda, sar ačhiľa la čhajoraha khere, te kerel jekh kurko phari buťi andre fabrika. Te tosara duje orendar e Lenka šoľarďa, hoj imar hin o agor, e Kveta dži akor suťa mek avre trine muršenca, save penge poťinde lakeri buťi. Akana imar kamelas te džal ča tel o paňi andre kupeľka u andre žeba kikidelas o love. Has lošaľi, hoj la Lenkake dela vareso pale.

„Ta so, has oda pharo?"

„Džalas oda mišto, ola murša na has varesave džungale. Jekh has phuro, no varesar oda kerďam. Lenko, dava tuke jepaš ole lovendar. Kamav tuke len."

„Ma ker diliňipen, na kamav ňič, ča deha jepaš love pro kher u ela mišto. Cinaha amenge o chaben u mišto amenge dživaha, na?"

„Hin tut čačipen, ma dara, ela mišto, na mukhava tut oda te kerel korkora."

Duj čhon anglal kada bešelas e Kveta mujal e komisija andre bertena ke Světlá nad Sázavou u phenelas lenge, sar paťivales dživela, kaj te lake den pale la čhajora, savi has andro čhavorikano kher. E buťi the o kher rodelas imar andre bertena. Šegitinelas lake oleha e terenno socijalno manušňi khatar e organizacija, savi na perel tel o rajaripen, u savi pal o džuvľija andre bertena phirelas. Chudľa deš berš bertena vašoda, bo murdarďa peskere romes. La komisija mangelas, kaj la mukhen avri trin berš sigeder. Deš berš na has nekbuter. O sudos dikhelas, sar has marďi, kana pes oda ačhiľa. Has la phagľi čang, pukinďa lake o kokal andro šero the pal calo teštos la has o kaľipena olestar, sar andre late akor ruginelas.

Sar la mukhle andal e bertena avri, ta gejľa te dikhel la baratkiňa la Lenka u imar paš late ačhiľa. Pre buťi the pro kher andre ubikacija bisterďa u akana ginel upre o love vaš kaja rat.

„Lenko, u keci oda tu kada keres?"
„Me na džanav, sar jekhvar kada keres, hin pharo te preačhel. Avľahas tuke pre goďi kada, sar samas ciknore? Leperes, sar phirahas pro tabora? Oda has but šukar, na?"
He, but šukar oda has, ča akor amenge ňiko na phenďa, te na sam diline u te na paťas perše naločhe muršeske u te na peras andre bibacht. Sig na paťavas pro baro kamiben th'o šukar dživipen. Vaj keci čhon perše čhaveha, paľis siďaharas te lel e vera, bo somas phari. Varekana man čhinelas pal o muj u paľis man imar ča marelas, phagerelas sa andro kher, čhinelas mange paťiv, na has o love pre ňisoste. Sar bajinavas pal e cikňi čhajori u našťi somas ča leha, ta jov chudľa te lel o drogi the te bavinel o automata. Kada has drom andre bari bibacht, u pro agor olestar has domácí zabijačka, sar phenen o šingune, kherutno murdaripen.
„U sar oda akor has? Te pal oda na kames te del duma, ta ma de, no te kames pal oda te vakerel, ta tut šunav."
„Na kamav pal oda te vakerel. Has man efta berš pal oda te duminel u paťa mange, nane mange oda, so kerďom, pharo. Na som nasvaľi pro šero, ma dara, na murdarava pale ňikas, ča pes oda na delas te ľikerel avri."
„Ta chin pre oda u džas amenge varekaj te bešel, so?"
„Džas."
E Kveta thoďa pro skamind andre pitvora duj ezera u okla love thoďa andre žeba andre cholov.
Aver čhaja andro klubos pen denas te del andro trin grupi: ajse, so keren mek vareso aver abo len o drogi; ola so len kija vareko ispidel u jon lestar but daran, u mek aver hine terne čhaja, save penge kavka keren o love pro chaben le čhavorenge the paš oda mek den o love peskere romenge abo le bosenge, save soven maj sako džuvľijaha, ča pre peskeri khere bisteren…
„Lenko, u ko hin koda murš?" sikhaďa pro učo kaleder murš.
„Oda hin o Pražakos, dikhel peske adaj avri nevo mas. But tut leske na sikhav. Mek tut adaj na džanen, ta te tut na lel peha het."
„Som diliňi, te adaj kamav te dikhel paťivale muršes."
„O murša hin pre ňisoste, ma rode. Ola lačhe hine veradune u ola aver trade het. Av, džaha pal o čhaja. O murša aven paľis pal amende, sar pijena peskere „jacky

the jimmy". Akana keren, hoj hine paťivale, no kisitin tut pre džungaľi duma."

„Me džanav..."

„Servus, me som o Fanda, Prahatar, u tu? Sal adaj nevi?"

„Servus, me som e Kveta. He, nevi som."

„Džas te khelel?"

„He, imar čirla na khelavas. Ma ruš, te tuke uštarava pro topanki."

„Ta kada hin baro pheras, e lubňi pre trasa, u sar khelel, na džanel, kaj te thovel o pindre!"

„U o bosos, so rodel, kas chudela. Ta kavka oda adaj hin, o čhaja keren buťi, tumen pijen u paľis jekhetanes bečeľinen?"

„U so dumines? Avka oda hin."

„Mišto, me som adaj peršones, ta na džanav, sar oda hin."

„Ma dumin u ker tuke lačhi kedva."

E Kveta dikhelas pre leste the duminelas, keci leske šaj hin berš — penda? Mek has šukar murš. Ko džanel, keci berš kada kerel. Šaj lestar phučav, no pre soste mange oda avela?

„Av, cinav tuke varesavo lačho pijiben."

„Na, me na kamav te pijel, kampel mange tajsa te džal andre Praha, ča odoj u maj pale, na džanes, ko man odoj šaj lel?"

„So odoj kereha? Me tut odoj šaj ľidžav."

„Na kamav pal oda te del duma, no hin oda predal mande angluno."

„Mukhava tuke pre mande o kontaktos."

„Paľikerav tuke. Džav te dikhel, kaj hiňi e Lenka." Rakhľa la paš o baros, sar vakerel le čhajenca. Savoro andro poharis imar piľa avri.

„Lenko, imar kamav te sovel, na džaha imar het?"

„Šaj džas. S'o Fanda, mišto?"

„Tajsa man lela andre Praha, kampel mange odoj te džal pre probačka, bo man hin mek e podminka u kamav imar te džal te dikhel la čhajora. Lenko, hin mange pal late but pharo. Imar duj čhon som khere u mek pal late na gejľom. So lake som te phenel?"

„Čhaje, ta akana mange ňič kajso nane andro šero, vakeraha pal'oda tajsa, akana džas andro haďos."

„Fando, kecengero tajsa te vičinav?“ phučľa lestar, sar pašal leste la Lenkaha džanas.
„Najsigeder sar ela dešujekh ora!“

„Ta phen, soske džas ke Praha,“ phučelas latar o Fanda, sar ke leste pal dešujekh ora bešľa andro motoris.
„Somas andre bertena u mek man hin e podminka. Kampel mange odoj te džal. Phučena mandar, kaj kerav buťi u me na džanav, so lenge te phenel.“
„Jajaj, ta oda nane mišto. Kampel tuke varesavo ľil. Užar, vičinava mire amaliske, hin les agentura pro žužipen, ta tut varesavo ľil šaj del.“
„Oda bi elas mišto.“
„U so paľis Prahate kereha, hin tut odoj pirano?“
„Na, hin man odoj andro čhavorikano kher e čhajori, kamav pal late te džal.“
„Čhaje, tut hin furt vareso pro čudos. Ta džaha vaš oda ľil u paľis so, džaha varekaj?“
„Šaj džas. Aveha pal mande avka štarengero pro Anděl?“
„Sar oda džalas, has lačho oda ľil? U geľal pal e čhajori?“
„He, pre probačno oda has mišto, no pal e čhajori na gejľom. Na birinavas odoj te džal. Somas paš o vudar, paľis na brinkinďom. Chinav pre oda!“
„Ta džaha, sar aveha mek jekhvar. Av, džas te chal.“
„Dikhes, sar imar pre sako than figinen karačoňakere vududa? Sem mek nane jepaš le novembriske! Fando, prindžares varesave čhaja, save phiren pre trasa u hin len čhavore? Sar oda keren?“
„Na, me ajse na džanav. Hin oda avka, hoj le čhavoren mukhen paš o babi, abo hine o čhavore andro čhavorikane khera.“
„Čačes. Kamav oda mira čhajoraha varesar te kerel, kim na ela e Karačoňa. Ke Lenka laha našťi dživav, ta na džanav.“
„Ta pre kada na džanav so tuke te phenel. Ela feder, te tut ľidžava pro autobusis, dikhav, hoj tuha pheras na ela.“
„Na, na ela, hin mange andro šero ča kada.“
Pal o drom andro Sokolovos duminelas, so dureder kerela. Te ačhel paš e Lenka, abo te rodel e buťi u tiš o kher? Te bešel pro azilos, oda sar te avel pale andre bertena. Na has la zor pre oda te duminel. Phenďa peske, hoj dži Karačoňa ačhela paš e Lenka.

„Šun, u pre Karačoňa tiš phiren pre trasa?“
„He, ča pre Viľija the pro Nevo Berš na.“
„Čačes?“
„Ta varesave muršen ňiko nane.“
„Kampela mange pre Viľija te džal pal e čhajori, vareso lake cinava.“
„Sem šaj džas. Ča mišto dumin, so kames. Či džaneha te bajinel pal e čhajori, te kereha varekaj vaš čepo love u bešeha pro azilos, abo či lake na ela andr'oda čhavorikano kher feder. Tiri daj th'o dad pal tumende na bajinen, nane tut ňiko.“
„He, me džanav, no nane mange pre dzeka či kada, abo kada. Na džanav, so te kerel. Oka kurko pal late čačes imar džava.“

Pro love, save sig zarodelas paš o droma, the pro raťakero dživipen andro bari, maj sikhľiľa. Tel varesave ďivesa imar ela e Karačoňa, ta gejľa te cinel varesave darunki u kamelas te džal pal e čhajori. Phirelas pal o sklepi u na kampelas lake te duminel pal oda, keci love sa mol. Duminelas, so te kidel avri eňa beršengera čhajorake, savi imar efta berš na dikhľa. Sar has andre bertena, irinďa lake štar ľila. Šoha na džanelas, so lake te irinel. Na kamelas lake te irinel, hoj sa ela lačho, bo joj korkori oleske na paťalas. Chudelas andre bertena predal peste šelthependa koruni pro čhon u olestar lake ňič na ačholas. Has oda ča pre kava the o sapuňa.
Kidľa avri e škatuľkica, savi bašavel, u sar la phundraves, khelel andre e baletka. Ajsi kamelas, sar has cikňi. Phenelas peske, hoj na džanel, so lakeri čhajori kamel. Šaj oda hin šukar viganos, mirikle the vareso pre meň? Sar pre late buter the buter gondolinelas, buter the buter daralas, sar la dikhela. Sem na džanel, sar dičhol avri, na prindžarela la. Na džanelas, sar le čhavoreske te phenel, hoj pal late na džanel te bajinel. Na has la ňisavi loš la te dikhel, korkori peske rakinelas, te pal late džal. Nane čačo te avel ča koteroro latar u pal late te na džal. Has lošaľi, sar gejľa te cinavkerel, aľe akana imar ča daralas. Agoreste rakhľa e zor u brinkinďa paš o vudar andro čhavorikano kher.
Phundraďa lake e učiteľka u phučelas latar, so kamel. Has ajsi nervozno, hoj lake na džalas mišto te del duma. Zahakľinelas. Paľis lake phenďa oja raňi, hoj

o čhavore odoj akana nane, bo hine avri, u kaj lake kampel te mangel, kana avela. La čhajora na dikhľa. Imar na phenďa ňič. Diňa la raňake sa, so lake cindžas. Kim džalas pro autobusis, čuľonas lake kale apsa pal o čhama dži pro kirlo.

Gejľa pale pal e Lenka.

„Bengenca, mukhľom la. Cinav lake o čački u aver ňič. Mukhav la odoj avre manušenca u andro agor avaha so dujdžeňa korkore."

„Kveto, ma rov, andro čhavorikano kher lenge kerena but šukar Karačoňa."

„Čhiv mange paľenka. Čhandav pre savoro, the pre kaja Karačoňa."

THE HOUSE ON ŠTĚRKOVÁ STREET

BY KVĚTOSLAVA PODHRADSKÁ

In 1968 we moved from Slovakia to be near my grandma and grandpa on my mother's side in Ostrava, in the Czech lands. At first my parents bought a little house for 25,000 crowns, then my dad and his oldest brother Feri set about building a large family home in Nová Ves. They took out a loan of 60,000. Our dad was an outstanding brickmason. He had hands of gold, I loved to watch him weave the wicker baskets that we used to store our apples and potatoes. He didn't know how to read or write, and my mom only completed four grades of primary school, since when the war came, she wasn't allowed to go to school anymore. I had ten siblings, and we all had to pull our weight. I remember how much I looked forward to my first payday at the dairy, where I started work after trade school, spending all day picking bags of milk off of the conveyor belt and putting them in blue plastic crates. I was going to buy myself my first pair of jeans.

"So, čhaje, where's your pay?" my dad asked when I came home from work, rapping the table for emphasis. "Well, eat up and tell me, how much did you get? Cause we need to buy cement."

"What cement? I want to buy blue jeans, I need to dress nice when I go to work." I pushed back against my dad, but he just smiled.

"What, are you walking around naked? You've got responsibilities to us now. You're an adult and we need every crown. Now give us all your pay and there'll be no more talk about it," he declared, and I burst into helpless tears. Without even finishing eating, I angrily handed over the 1,000-crown bill. I sulked still for a few days, but once I saw the cement at home and my dad pouring out the floors, I realized they really needed that money. My parents were truly doing what they could, and God knows there were plenty of us. They were building a home so our family would have a refuge it could call its own.

The revolution didn't bring any great changes in our lives at first. There was a large garden around our home, and my dad's dream of a big farmstead finally came true. He got some rams and young bulls, who grazed over the summer, and in the fall it was time for us to get to work on the slaughter. We all continued to gather over the weekend, but we had less and less time together.

My brother Jozef was employed at a manufacturer of concrete prefab units for sewage shafts. One day the director of the company approached him to ask if he knew how to lay interlocking paving stones, saying he had work for him, but at his home. Jozef happily agreed and did the work so skillfully the boss asked him why he didn't make his living doing that. "I don't have the startup capital," my brother explained.

"I'll lend you ten thousand crowns, go ahead, buy some tools and whatever else you need and I'll give you your first order," the boss proposed, and my brother did as he was told. He took care of the paperwork and launched a construction business. My other brother also opened a business in that field, but he didn't have startup funds, so he took out a loan from the bank and put up our house as collateral. That was common in those days. Like lots of other enterprising Roma, he got into excavation and demolition work. Both brothers got their firms off the ground and took on other relatives to help with the work, since the two of them couldn't do it just on their own. They were both trained brickmasons and like everyone else around at the time, they wanted to live better and, most of all, provide for their families. They got used to working seven days a week, no matter what the weather. Sometimes there was only work enough for four, but sometimes for as many as twenty. Things went well to begin with, there was plenty of work and not much competition. The orders came pouring in for excavation jobs, pavement reconstruction, laying cobblestones, and later, renovation of bathrooms and other residential spaces as well. It wasn't always easy money. Sometimes, after paying their employees' wages and settling up with the subcontractors, there was barely enough left to survive. There were times the clients didn't pay at all or only paid the deposit, and when it came to the rest of the invoice, they just made excuses or looked for some pretense to avoid having to pay. Their competitors also took jobs that were underpaid, ruining prices for everyone else.

My father's death in early 1997 had a huge impact on my mom and all my siblings. Gone was our precious, ever-smiling dad Gabriel, who had kept the family together and treated everyone fairly. In retrospect, the only consolation was that fate spared him what befell us that year.

In the spring, we had to limit our farming to growing fruits and vegetables and breeding poultry. After my dad's death, we had to give up on livestock completely, tending to the animals without him was more than we could handle. In April and May, it rained a lot more than usual. In early July, it just lightly drizzled at first, but then the rain intensified without letting up. On Monday, July 7, it rained less, but the water had nowhere to soak into, the soil was saturated, and the rivers flooded all across northern Moravia. Ostrava City Hall declared a flood emergency. Over the course of the morning, the water overflowed the banks, and soon it was streaming past our house. The inhabitants of Nová Ves watched, helpless, as the water level rose uncontrollably. The local firefighters warned people to safeguard their homes with sandbags. After two hours the situation had deteriorated, and our neighborhood had turned into a giant lake. The river Odra runs past Nová Ves on one side, and we were separated from it by a deep ditch along the levee, which the river broke through at a spot known as U Hrůbků. That was before anyone knew the water managers were increasing the flow through the dam at the Šance reservoir in the Beskydy mountains, which was enough to flood half of Ostrava, and that water was headed straight for our homes.

People tried to make it home from work and save what they could. The only people home at our place that morning were my mom, my sister Nataša with her kids, and our sister-in-law's kids. None of them had any idea what was hurtling toward them. People tried to secure their homes, then eventually realized, as the water level rose, that their lives were at stake and it was no use trying to save their property.

My sister Nataša, whose flat was on the second floor, called for my mom to come up from the ground floor and join her, and my mom wisely took her handbag with her documents inside. The fourteen children were so scared they didn't make a peep. They all sat there at Nataša's, and in my brother Ladislav's flat, which had a balcony, waiting to be rescued. As water rushed into the rooms downstairs, they could hear the thuds of the furniture being smashed apart. My mom just sat there praying for God to save the people at least.

The firefighters announced over loudspeakers that the first boats were on their way and first to board would be elderly people and children. The others were to relocate to the highest floor possible, even the roof. Everyone agreed that my grandma and a few of the youngest children would go first. They climbed into the rescuers' boat and sailed out of the flooded neighborhood to dry land, where there was a bus waiting to take them to the dormitories at the Technical University of Ostrava, where the city had set up an evacuation center.

With evening approaching, the water level rose to seven meters and there were still a lot of people who needed help. Including several children at the flooded home of the Duždas on Štěrková Street. After several hours, another boat reached them and more children were able to board from the balcony. It was extremely stressful for them, as well as very dangerous. They were glad to be rescued, but at the same time seized with dread. They were abandoning the home they had grown up in, and didn't know if they would ever be able to go back again.

The water climbed to eight meters. Our house was underwater, only the roof poking up above the murky surface. My siblings, the last ones in the family still left, had taken shelter in the room under the rooftop, waiting to be rescued. Just before midnight, they too left behind the ruined house, climbing out through the window. When I was finally reunited with my sister Nataša, she said in a heartbroken voice through her tears, "I'm just glad Dad didn't live to see this."

The whole family ended up in temporary accommodation and no one knew what would happen next. All we had was the clothing that we'd been wearing that day. We were glad to be alive, but the reality that we had lost everything else began to weigh on us. No one ever saw the cars that had been parked outside our house again. We stayed at the rooming house for a month, until the waters receded. As soon as it was possible, two of my brothers asked the firefighters if they could go and have a look at our house.

They rowed over and discovered that the structure was unstable and it was obvious the house would have to come down. Just like the twenty other homes in Nová Ves. We were afraid to share the news with our mom, knowing there was something going on inside her she didn't want to talk about. She was still mourning the loss of her husband, and now she had also lost the home he had built. One blow after another. All she would say, every now and then, was: "We have nothing, not even a needle to sew with."

As the start of the academic year approached, the evacuees had to leave the university dorms. Our family found itself in a rooming house in Zábřeh, where we had to stay for ten months. Our mom took it hard, seeing us fall that far. My sister Nataša tried to find a way out and, sure enough, good fortune smiled on her. The municipal office of Nová Ves found them alternative accommodation through an arrangement with another municipality. In a two-story house, not far from ours. Not everyone could live there, there was only room for three families. But the other two also managed to find accommodation, and that put my mom at ease. Everyone had to get used to living without our garden and domestic animals, which had died during the flood.

My brothers refused to give up so easily on the family seat, with its five flats. We started looking into how to raise the funds to repair it. But one long-ago mistake caused us to lose our home forever! When we were submitting our application for compensation for damages, we discovered we had no insurance for our property in the event of a natural disaster! No bank would lend us the money to renovate our home, which my brother had put up as collateral. The debt had piled up, so the bank kept the house and eventually broke it up into building plots and sold it off.

Seven years after the flood, my sister Nataša still lived with her children in the replacement flat they had been given in Svinov. But the town stopped allowing people who weren't from Svinov to live in public flats, so they were given a two-month eviction notice. Not even the municipal office in Nová Ves had an alternative place for them to live. They weren't the only ones affected by this catastrophe.

My youngest brother managed to sell at least our home's front yard, which wasn't subject to forfeit. He immediately put down a deposit on the debts of the previous tenants of a publicly subsidized flat, as the rental agency required, so the family could finally settle down.

"How much did you have to pay?" asked my mom.

"Sixty-five thousand crowns, to RPG Byty Ostrava. They're the company that owns the flat, so you'll be renting from them," my brother said, adding, "A rental in a third-floor, two-bedroom flat on Skautská Street in Poruba, it's ready to move into now."

"You did it! And there's still money left over for furniture. We also have that flood money, and little by little, we can put together a whole new home," my mom happily summed it up.

"That's just a short way from Dělnická, the popular eleventh district, where all the Roma live, everyone knows that part of town. Some of Mom's siblings even live there," Nataša pointed out.

So began the next and last stage of the Dužda clan's move away from Nová Ves. Mama Margita could visit with her brothers and sisters in Poruba, and started to feel all right again.

Eventually, part of the family set out for a new life in England, where they made their home for a while. But that's another story.

YOU'RE LIKE ME

BY MARTIN KANALOŠ

Starting in preschool, I spent summers in the village with my grandma. She had a big house with a garden and I was always perfectly happy there.

"I brought little Martin here for you to babysit," said my dad, greeting his mother-in-law as I went running over to her. "Be a good boy and don't do anything to make your grandma mad," he said as he left, unloading my knapsack full of clothes and a bag of food we had bought along the way. Then he waved goodbye to me from the car and off he drove. In front of the house, my grandma had a plastic table with chairs where, during the day, she would sit outside and read. She set me down in one of the chairs, placed a yogurt in front of me, and went inside to get a spoon. She returned with a spoon in one hand and a Mickey Mouse mug of colored pencils in the other. She knew how much I liked to draw.

"I haven't got any paper, but wait till you see what I do have." My grandma brought me over some paper food trays. "You can draw on the other side of these."

She read out loud from her magazine: "They say here McDonald's and Donald Duck have nothing to do with each other. Interesting." Then she went to open the gate, since my aunt was supposed to come by with my cousin around lunchtime. The neighbor's dog Buckshot appeared in the gate. He had pointy ears and a shaggy coat of dark-brown fur. He was a peculiar dog. My grandma liked to say he had the manners of an English gentleman. He would always wait out in front of the gate for our dog Astor, and never set foot in the garden, even when we lured him with a párek or called for him to come. He just stood there till his sidekick emerged from the house, and then the two of them set out on their wanderings around the village. Astor was a wire-haired dachshund, but he didn't look like a dachshund at all. I decided to draw the two of them walking down the road.

At noontime my aunt arrived, and she and my grandma got lunch ready. We had tzatziki, then after lunch a siesta, which meant my grandma and my aunt sunned themselves while my cousin and I kicked a ball back and forth. That afternoon, we headed for the nearby pond. There wasn't any beach there, just a meadow where we spread out our towels. I really liked the pond. I'd seen so many neat things there. One time I saw some boys fish a crayfish out of the pond.

My cousin and I swam doggy paddle, and my cousin said he would teach me to do the breaststroke. He started swirling his arms around on the surface, and in my eyes it was a perfect rendition of the breaststroke. He swam like a fiend, so I tried too. As my cousin and I chatted, we got farther and farther away from shore. Suddenly we saw a very strange phenomenon in front of us.

"Are you standing on top of the water, ma'am?" my cousin called out to the woman.

"Not at all! I'm standing on a rock out here. I know every inch of this place," the woman called back in a kind voice. We were duly impressed. Then we swam back to shore, dried off, and went home.

In the meantime my grandma hadn't been idle, baking a sponge cake with cherries from the garden. She settled onto a lounge chair and my cousin and I sat at her feet.

"I like it when you're tanned," my grandma complimented us, stroking our dark-skinned backs while we ate cake.

"How about a slushie?" she asked.

"Yay!" my cousin and I squealed in excitement. She hoisted herself up from the lounge chair and a minute later returned with glasses and straws.

"I made some apple juice and put it in the freezer!" she boasted. The miracles of our grandma's freezer by that point were well known to us. The freezer stood opposite the stairs on the second floor, quietly purring away. A few times, my cousin and I had tried in vain to open the lid, then one day we put all our effort into it and it was like discovering a treasure chest. Ice cream, popsicles, frozen fruit and dough! We knew we couldn't take anything without our grandma's permission, but now we could rest easy, knowing what was hidden inside.

"So late already!" my aunt yelped, looking at the clock and rushing my cousin to get dressed. My grandma packed some cake for my uncle in a tin, then we walked them out to the road and waved goodbye until their car had vanished around the bend.

Then my grandma went inside for her gardening shears and started to trim the withered roses while I strolled barefoot around the garden. I tried to climb the massive cherry tree. Its lower branches were solid and not that high off the ground, but I wasn't strong enough to pull myself up. I walked to the corner in the back of the garden. The neighbors' house was on the opposite end of the plot and their German shepherd was always there to welcome us whenever he caught a whiff of us by the fence. Luckily, there was tall grass growing there, which made it hard for him to poke his snout through the pickets and get to us. This time, though, he wasn't there, and I spread the grass apart to see if there was anything interesting to discover. One time I saw a blindworm on a rock. I tried to catch it but ended up with just the tail in my hand and the rest of the worm crawled away. This part of the garden was teeming with bugs, but all I found this time was our ball, which had rolled over here while we were playing. I picked it up and went to kick it around in the middle of the garden.

"Martin, honey, time to come home," my grandma called to me from the window, and I realized I hadn't even noticed that she had stopped working on the flowers ages ago. I dropped the ball and ran back to the house. It always had a nice old smell inside. The floor was covered with soft rugs, smooth against my bare feet. I sat down on the sofa and watched TV with my grandma. *The Troops of St. Tropez* was on, and my grandma and I laughed up a storm. Astor nuzzled up to us and started to lick my feet. It tickled like crazy, so I picked Astor up and put him next to me, to let him watch too.

When the movie was over, my grandma made the bed in the room upstairs and laid out my pajamas. I burrowed into the duvets along with my stuffed animal. It was a character from my favorite cartoon: a black-and-white tomcat with a red nose. One time I went to sleep in the room alone and got really scared. Then my grandma remembered she had something for me, and brought me the tomcat. I held him up in the air and pretended he was talking to me. As my eyes started to close, I gave him a big hug and imagined what it would be like if the tomcat from the cartoon actually existed. I stared up at the ceiling, which was paneled with wood like the rest of the room. Only the dim light of the streetlamp fell through the window. Every night the moths and mosquitoes swarmed all over it. It was so quiet, I could hear their wings clink against the glass. Little by little I fell asleep.

That night I had a dream about my grandpa. I never met my grandpa. He died before I was born. I knew him only from the photos that my grandma had up around the house. In one of them he was dressed in a suit and looked like a movie star. In my dream, which took place at the pond, I couldn't see his face, though. I was on the shore and he was in the distance, standing on the rock. The sky was white and everything around us was bright and shiny. I couldn't see my grandpa's face either, because it was shining so brightly.

"Grandpa, look, I know how to swim!"

"Nice job!" my grandpa praised me.

"There's something else I wanted to tell you!" I shouted to him from the top of my lungs. But my grandpa just kept drifting away, waving goodbye.

I woke up. It was morning. Astor lay on the bed next to the wall, on the other side of the room. "Get down!" I was afraid he would dirty the covers with his paws and my grandma would get mad. She was already sitting outside at the table, reading. I didn't tell her I'd had a dream about my grandpa. I didn't want her to miss him. After breakfast I drew again. I drew a picture of my grandma reading, and the whole garden behind her, with the cherry and apple trees. Then I got the idea to draw a picture of Astor. I tried to imagine what he would look like if he was a cartoon character. He would have big eyes, a big nose, and walk on his hind legs. I took a stab at drawing him like that, along with a few other characters. And I just kept drawing until my grandma set a plate of spaghetti down in front of me. After lunch she jammed a baseball cap on my head, to keep me from getting sunstroke. I walked out to the little square outside the gate and gathered pebbles.

I was startled by a truck driving up. It stopped right in front of the house where no one lived. On my last holiday, this strange family lived there, with Rottweilers who barked and growled at everyone who walked by. A couple of men got out of the truck and started carrying furniture into the abandoned house. I realized that someone was moving in. I watched as they unloaded everything from the truck bed, but after a while I got bored. I walked down the road along our fence, picking little white balls off the bushes. My grandma said they were called snowberries. I would throw one down on the asphalt and stomp on it. The berries made a nice cracking sound, which I really liked. Then I picked a whole fistful. Talk about a bang! I was overjoyed.

"What are you doing?" I turned to see who the small voice belonged to, and saw a girl standing there, about the same age as me. Suntanned, with big brown eyes and long black hair in a ponytail.

"I'm popping balls," I said, and demonstrated how I did it. When I picked the next ball and threw it on the ground, it rolled over to her and she crushed it with her shoe. We both looked at each other and smiled.

"Tereza!" someone called.

"I have to go now, see you." She dashed off toward the house where they were moving in.

I ran back home to my grandma, but found her standing by the fence. She was also watching what was going on. She squinted off into the distance, then turned around, took me by the hand, and we walked back into the house, where my grandma took the flour and sugar out of the pantry, and eggs and milk out of the fridge, and mixed them all together.

"What are you doing, Granny?" I asked, resting my nose on the kitchen counter.

"I'm baking a bábovka. Go outside and have a snack. There's melon there for you."

When my grandma came out of the house again, she was carrying a bábovka on a plate, and walked right past me, out the gate. I ran after her, but then decided to play secret agent and spy on her instead. I crept along, hiding in the ditch, as my grandma stopped and handed the bábovka to a lady who looked like a larger version of the little girl I had spoken to. The only difference was her face looked sad and tired. It was probably her mom. The two of them had a chat. I couldn't hear what they were talking about, because of the noise from the men moving the furniture. But then the moving truck drove away and I overheard the lady telling my grandma:

"You know how it is, neither of us could find a job, everywhere they turned us down. They practically spit on us.

My husband went off to England and left me here on my own with three girls. Our parents went back to Slovakia. What was I supposed to do? They need women for the factory here in Habartov. I just hope we can hang on till my husband saves up enough for us to make the trip over and join him."

"It'll be fine, you'll see. If you need anything, just stop by."

My grandma told the lady goodbye, and was only a few steps away when she was stopped by the neighbor with the mean German shepherd.

"Did you see we had Gypsies move in?" the woman said, piercing my grandma with her gaze.

"You don't miss a thing, do you?" my grandma sighed, rolling her eyes.

"They're going to rob us for sure."

"You better believe it, and you'll be first in line." My grandma waved her hand dismissively and continued on her way. Her neighbor stood staring like a moonstruck owl and hissed something in reply.

"Martin, honey, don't kneel there like that, you're going to get dirty. Come with me. Your mommy will be here soon!" I'd been exposed, but on the other hand I was glad my mom was coming. She arrived after lunch, but instead of running over to her, the way I usually did, I hid.

"Where is Martin?" she asked.

"Running around the garden somewhere. Come sit down. Some new people moved into that house where the Seillers used to live. Poor woman, all alone with three girls, let me tell you. They've got nothing."

I couldn't stand it and came out of my hiding place.

"Well, hello there, little boy," my mom said, running her fingers through my hair as I took a sweet roll from the plate. My mom and my grandma went to the room upstairs and gave me permission to watch TV. It was afternoon and all that was on was detective shows and soap operas. Lucky for me, my grandma had cable. But I had to click through about a thousand channels to find the one with cartoons. When the show I was watching was over, I looked out the window and saw my grandma coming home with my mom, carrying an empty crate. I hadn't even noticed they'd left. I dashed out the door and ran up to them.

"Where were you?"

"Don't ask so many questions," my grandma said, brushing me off. "Curiosity killed the cat. Come on, let's go make dinner." An unpleasant discovery awaited me when I went to bed. I couldn't find my stuffed tomcat. I searched everywhere. Under the duvet, under the bed, even in the wardrobe. I ran around the room in a panic, until my mom asked what I was looking for.

"My tomcat."

"I gave it to that family that just moved in. You've got plenty of toys at home."

"But I kept it here to help me go to sleep."

"So you'll bring some other toy."

"But it was mine!" I shouted, and buried my head in the pillow. It felt like a terrible injustice and I was furious. I got a headache from holding in my tears and couldn't breathe because of the pillow. My mom tried to soothe me, but it was no use. I was mad at her and it took me ages to fall asleep. I couldn't stop thinking about how they'd taken away my toy.

I was still sulking the next morning at breakfast. I wasn't hungry at all.

"Are you still mad I gave away that stuffed animal?"

"No," I said, even though I was. "I'm going out."

"Don't go to the pond!" my mom called after me, but that was exactly where I was headed. I was already out of the village when suddenly I saw three girls walking toward me. They all looked the same. Suntanned, with long black hair tied in a ponytail. The only difference between them was their height and age. The tallest and oldest one was in the middle. She was about two heads taller than me and was holding hands with the smallest girl, who may have been about two. She could scarcely walk. The third girl was the same height as me. She was the one I had popped the berries with the day before. Then I noticed what she had in her hand. I froze. It was my stuffed tomcat!

"That's my tomcat!"

"No, it's mine," the girl said, hugging the cat to her body and showering him with kisses.

"You're drooling on him!" I yelled, horrified, and tried to grab the toy away. But the older girl intervened and shoved me so hard I almost fell.

"Leave her alone!"

"But it's mine!" I objected.

"No, it's ours! It was a present to us. Each of us gets it for an hour at a time, and it's my turn now," the girl from the day before shouted at me, and the three of them went along their way.

I knew I didn't stand a chance, so I just stood there staring at them. They kept turning around to look at me and making comments to each other.

I sat down on a stump by the side of the road and waited for the wolves to come and eat me up, or that wild boar that my uncle tripped over when he was out gathering mushrooms. It made me feel sad. I propped my elbows on my thighs, head in my hands, and sat there like that till I heard the sound behind me of twigs cracking in the bushes, and decided I'd better run back home.

At home, my grandma and my mom were fixing lunch. I took a peach from the table and went to sit out on the fence. I sat there, eyes glued to our new neighbors, frowning in their direction. But they couldn't see me anyway. They were mowing the grass. The oldest one, that is. The one who was as old as me was painting the fence, and the youngest one was running around the yard.

I came up with a plan to sneak in there, grab my stuffed toy, and run back home. When I was done eating the peach, I figured I would at least throw the pit into their garden, but I didn't come anywhere close. I hopped down off the fence and slowly made my way toward their house, trying to act like I was headed somewhere else. As I walked past them, I did my best not to look, but I was curious whether or not the girl would notice me. She had a can of paint in one hand and a paintbrush in the other. She might not have noticed me if I hadn't been staring. The whole time she kept an eye on her work, but suddenly she spotted me through the fence poles. She had the most piercing gaze. I didn't know what to do, so I stuck my tongue out at her. She did the same to me. I turned to go back home. My mom was calling me in to eat.

After lunch, we went to the pond, but I had never been so bored there in my life. I splashed around the shallow part, since my mom was afraid I would drown. If only she knew how far my cousin and I had swum! But my cousin wasn't here now. Nor was the lady we'd seen standing on top of the water. For a split second, the thought flashed through my mind that it would be great if the girl who was the same age as me knew how to swim and could come to the pond with me. But I immediately dismissed it. Forget her, she had my stuffed tomcat!

That night I was expecting to dream about my grandpa again, since I had gone swimming, but no such luck. I chalked it up to the fact that my tomcat was gone. The next morning at breakfast, my mom and grandma kept chatting away until my ears buzzed, so when I was done I got up and went out to sit in the secret alcove next to the gate. It belonged to my grandma's house, but you could only climb into it from the street and a grown-up could scarcely fit. No one disturbed me when I was here. I sat in the corner, peeling the plaster off with my finger. Then you could take the piece of plaster and draw on the pavement with it, like it was chalk. The problem was the plaster broke right away and the pictures weren't as clear as when you drew them with chalk. I thought about what kind of decorations I would make when someday I brought chalk.

I heard footsteps coming down the road toward our gate. A small, dark-haired head poked into my hiding place. It was the girl who had my tomcat!

"What are you doing here?" she asked.

"What's it to you? What are *you* doing? You aren't allowed in here!"

"I don't want to come in anyway. I have to go home. I just got back from doing the shopping. Me and my sisters are hungry."

"So why doesn't your mom give you something to eat?"

"My mom's at work. She has the morning shift."

"So who's watching you?"

"No one."

"Your family's weird."

"You're weird. Sitting here by yourself, not talking to us." And with that she ran away. I climbed out of the alcove and followed her as she ran, bag of groceries in hand. Watching her, I started to feel kind of sorry for her. I don't know why. I sat down on the step to my hiding place and replayed what had just happened over and over again in my mind. "You aren't allowed in here," I had shouted at her. I could see the frightened look in her eyes like she was standing right in front of me. Now I felt bad about it. Her mom was at work and she was home alone with her sisters. Meanwhile I always had my grandma, and now my mom as well. Maybe I shouldn't have been so mean to her.

I returned home for lunch and after lunch I went to lie down in the bedroom upstairs. I collapsed onto the bed, feeling sick about the way I had behaved. It was true I lost my tomcat, but that little girl deserved more, after all. All things considered, she was a nice girl and I'd been truly nasty to her, kept running through my head.

"Are you asleep up here? I thought you were outside. Come on, it's dinnertime." I went downstairs. We had bread with homemade spread. I could hardly keep my eyes open.

"You seem a little woozy," my grandma said. "Are you sick? Are you running a temperature?" She put a hand on my forehead. I didn't have a fever. After dinner we watched TV, but I didn't see a thing—my head kept drooping. My mom ran a bath for me, washed me up. That woke me up a bit and I managed to watch TV with my grandma a little while longer, till she started to fall asleep too, so we all went to bed.

When I woke up in the morning, it was nice outside and I felt better. I got dressed and ran out of the house.

"Well, it's about time you got up," my grandma declared.

"Where's my mom?" I asked.

"She went with your dad to buy groceries. They'll be back soon. Have a sip of tea, get some liquid in you." I slurped down two mouthfuls and my mom and dad appeared at the gate, carrying bags of groceries. I ran out to greet them, hopping and skipping with joy.

"Look what we brought you!" said my dad, taking out a box of cereal that I adored and only rarely got to have. I studied the box, which was covered with cartoon characters. I loved the way it looked. I also loved that there was always a toy inside. I carefully opened the box and dug my hand around inside. I felt something plastic and pulled it out. A figure of my favorite tomcat! I stood it on the table, happy as could be, and looked at it all through breakfast. After breakfast I played with it out in the garden, pretending it was the actual cartoon character.

My mom's voice jolted me out of my fantasy. "Look who

came to see you." I turned around and the little girl from the neighbors' was standing at the gate. I put the toy in my pocket and ran over to her.

"Hi, do you want to come kick the ball with me?" she said, holding out a red-and-yellow-striped ball.

"Sure!" I said, and the two of us ran over to the freshly mowed lawn. We kicked the ball back and forth, and I was amazed how good she was and how far she could kick. She laughed the whole time.

"What's your name, anyway?" she asked.

"Martin. What's yours?"

"Tereza."

"That's a nice name." We kicked the ball for a little while longer, then Tereza suggested: "Now let's throw it!" She picked up the ball and threw it to me. I had to jump in the air to catch it.

"Make a basket with your hands," I advised Tereza. She was having a hard time catching it.

"Like this?" she asked, and I gently tossed her the ball.

"Awesome!" I said, praising her.

"How about we roll it now?" she said after a while.

"All right, but I know somewhere better. Follow me." We ran out the gate and climbed into the alcove. We sat down facing each other and rolled the ball along the ground. It came at me really fast. I caught it and rolled it back so it came spinning toward her. Tereza laughed, the sound echoing through the hiding place like a cave.

We were so absorbed in playing, we didn't even notice that the sky had clouded over and it had begun to rain. We didn't stop until the wind began to sprinkle us with raindrops, and we sat silently watching the water fall from the sky. I looked at Tereza and Tereza looked at me. I touched my hand to her cheeks and she did the same to me. We looked into each other's eyes, not saying a word.

"You're like me," I said.

AFTER-WORD: THE UNTOLD STORIES OF CZECHO-SLOVAK ROMA

BY KAROLÍNA RYVOLOVÁ

As far as memory can reach, the stories of the Romani people, popularly and incorrectly referred to as "Gypsies", have been written by others. This is partly because of the Roma's reclusiveness, which encouraged the surrounding societies to perceive them as exotic and to invent stories about them, and partly due to the Roma's exclusively oral tradition. The historical lack of their own authentic body of literature contributed to the birth of the "literary Gypsy", a stock character moulded by humanity's fears and projections, marked by stereotypical properties such as wanderlust, revolt, love of freedom, and identification with nature on the one hand, and shiftlessness, deviousness, inability to plan and unrestrained sexual desire on the other. These features both reflected on and impacted the mainstream populations' prejudices against and attitudes towards the Roma.

It was not until the early-to-mid 20th century that the first writers emerged among the Roma in Central and Eastern Europe. And in Czechoslovakia, a country which was firmly embedded in the socialist Eastern bloc, it was even later. Despite some early undertakings by the pioneer of Romani writing in Czechoslovakia Elena Lacková (1921—2003; e.g., the play *Horiaci cigánsky tábor* [The burning Gypsy camp], written in Slovak in 1949 and thematising the genocidal persecution of the Slovak Roma at the hands of Slovak fascists during World War II), the first concentrated efforts to produce letters of their own in their mother tongue did not take place until the late 1960s as one of the side effects of the arising Romani movement.

THE LAST BREATH OF PRAGUE SPRING

It is a historical paradox that the first chiefly Romani organisation in Czechoslovakia, The Gypsy-Roma Union (Svaz Cikánů-Romů, henceforth the GRU or the Union), was officially founded in the Czech part of the country in August 1969 (its Slovak counterpart operated quite independently). It was almost a year to the day after the country had been invaded by the Warsaw Pact troops in August 1968 and a period of political stagnation and repressions — the so-called normalisation (i.e., of pre-Prague Spring status quo) — had begun. Because of its untimely nature, it is sometimes described as "the last waft of Prague Spring".

Despite the organisation's incorporation in contemporary political structures — it was officially listed among the parties and organisations of the National Front — and against the communist nomenclature's expectations, the Romani leadership of the Czech GRU soon started voicing demands for the recognition of Romani nationhood. As these were unwelcome and in direct clash with the state policy of assimilation of the Roma, in effect since 1959, the window of opportunity for Romani emancipatory activities and the formation of their intellectual elite turned out to be extremely short-lived. The GRU was forcefully disbanded by the communist cadres in April 1973, and all cultivation of Romani cultural heritage and semblance of political organization of the Roma was officially discouraged and persecuted until the Velvet Revolution in 1989, which marked the end of forty years of communist rule.

Nevertheless, while the organisation lasted, an internal Union newsletter called *Románo ľil* (The Romani paper) was issued for its members, and it was thanks to this news outlet that the foundations of Romani literature in Czechoslovakia were laid.

THE IMPORTANCE OF MINORITY PRESS

Between 1970, when the first issue was released, and April 1973, when the Union was disbanded, sixteen issues of *Románo ľil* were printed. The brochure generally communicated to its readers the minutes from both GRU and the Central Committee of the Communist Party meetings and at least initially hailed the Roma's indivisibility from the people of Czechoslovakia and the Party. This information was often followed by specific tasks ensuing from the meetings for the GRU, and in the spirit of the day, resolutions by the GRU to meet and exceed these Party obligations.

The remaining pages of each issue were filled with reports from Romani community events across the Czech lands, such as football matches, Romani dances and arts competitions, and occasional news pieces informing the readers of Roma-related affairs. In time, longer treatments of more serious topics followed, covering essential periods of contemporary Romani history such as the Romani Holocaust, Romani partisans' involvement in the resistance movement, or the story of the experimental Romani school in South Bohemian Květušín. In the writing of these articles, the first Romani journalists gradually emerged, some of whom later also successfully tried their hand at creative writing.

At the end of some issues, there was a brief literary supplement introducing short poems, fairy tales, stories, and songs by Romani writers. To start with, they were mostly in Czech, but gradually the balance tipped in favour of contributions in Romani, increasingly published without translation, a process which had been facilitated by the formulation of the spelling rules of the so-called Slovak Romani. Writing for the first time in one's mother tongue, when that language was primarily oral and one had acquired literacy in Czech or Slovak, was a mind-blowing experience which many of the writers later reflected on as their personal change of paradigm.

Interestingly, the same preliminary codification of the most widely spoken dialect of Romani in former Czechoslovakia, developed by the non-Romani Indologist and Roma studies scholar Milena Hübschmannová (1933—2005) and her team of native experts, is used in Czechia to this day with only slight alterations. Needless to say, there can be no literature without language codification.

THE FEMINIST AND THE TEACHER

Of the pool of writers whose works appeared on the pages of *Románo ľil* between 1970—1973, some contributed regularly and practically went on to become household names in the new era, others appeared only a handful of times and have not been heard of since. Importantly, some re-emerged as the editorial staff of *Lačho lav* (Good word), the first ever Romani monthly produced between 1990—1991, thus affirming their talent and dedication to the Romani cause, heralded by their previous work for the Union's newsletter. Together, these early writers experimented with languages and form, drawing on traditional Romani folklore but taking it to new communication levels, and in doing so, managed to convey an important message: that the Roma can also write, and that writing in their native Romani is possible.

Let us take a closer look at two writers whose engagement with the Union and its newsletter helped shape both the emancipation movement and Romani literature per se. In the very first issue of *Románo ľil* (1/1970), there appeared a traditional Romani fairy tale *O Romovi a černé paní* (The Rom and the dark lady, in Czech) by Andrej Giňa (1936—2015) and an untitled commentary called after its opening statement *Bičhavav le Romňenge* (My word to Romani women, in Romani) by Tera Fabiánová (1930—2007). The first would become one of Giňa's typical renditions of traditional storytelling, by means of which he intentionally and conscientiously mapped out the wealth of Romani folklore, which was, due to a mix of relentless state assimilation policies and the social mobility of the Roma, quickly disappearing by then. The second was an emotional appeal to Romani womanhood to not give in to traditional patriarchy but rather to educate, cultivate, and emancipate themselves.

Contemporary witnesses maintain that Tera Fabiánová's bold revolt against age-old norms written in Romani was met with great enthusiasm in the community. She spoke frankly about the hardships of Romani women, instantly becoming their role model, but also paved the way for literature written in a language which had previously been only spoken. Milena Hübschmannová testified that Fabiánová's pioneering attempt (proofed by Hübschmannová, who was already in the process of formulating the rules of written Romani) inspired countless others to experiment with written Romani. She published three more pieces in the newsletter: two more commentaries marked by strong nationalist sentiments (featured in her own column *Zadáno pro Teru* [Tera's turf]) and one short story, *Zor nane savoro* [Power is not everything], in which she criticizes and rejects the widely tolerated violence against women in Romani households. These four texts foreshadowed her main topics for the future, while proving to her fellow Roma that fundamental social issues can be satisfactorily discussed in Romani.

Andrej Giňa's only other literary piece in *Románo ľil* — *Kajso pheras pes nakerel* (Such jokes are out of order [3/1972]) — published solely in Romani, recounts a true story of young Romani boys who played a practical joke on an old-timer and frightened him to actual death. Giňa adopts a mentoring tone at the end, condemning the boys' bad judgement, but also the belief in the *mule*, the returning ghosts of the dead or revenants — so widespread among the Roma — which cost the old musician his life. In combination with several journalist pieces in the main part of the newsletter, Andrej Giňa likewise demonstrates what his future role among the Roma will be: that of a chronicler, educator, and moral authority.

DESERT FLOWERS

The cancellation of the Gypsy-Roma Union, the first ever opportunity for Czechoslovak Roma to become agents of their own destiny, was perceived as a grave injustice by the participants of the Romani movement. Their ambitious plans for the management of their own public affairs were thwarted by the totalitarian regime and the whole movement was forced underground. In broad strokes, one could say that Romani emancipation, and Romani letters with it, were paused until 1989. However, that would be an inaccurate picture of the situation. Several centres of activity and channels of publication existed even in the grim period of the nineteen seventies and eighties.

First and foremost, it was Milena Hübschmannová who refused to toe the line and tirelessly looked for outlets for Romani writing. At the time of *Románo ľil*, her expertise as an editor and translator from her employment with the Czechoslovak Radio (intermittently between 1956—1967) was indispensable for pioneering writers. She developed vibrant friendships with many of them and generally continued her role as their personal agent until the end of her, or their, days. After leaving fulltime employment at the Czechoslovak Radio, she continued as an external collaborator and never missed an opportunity to promote Romani history, storytelling or musical folklore in her radio programmes. Along with her husband, the radio director Josef Melč (1934—2002), she frequently broadcast samples from, and even entire Romani literary works long before they eventually came out in print.

So-called "handbooks of methodology" became another ingenious channel of dissemination of Romani letters, parading as educational materials for social work among "the Gypsies" and issued by Houses of Culture (*kulturní domy*) with sympathetic and complicit staff. These low-cost, not-for-sale prints came out in small numbers, were only available through the grapevine, and these days are considered a rarity. To name just one, in 1979 a collection of Romani poetry entitled *Romane giľa* (Romani songs), was released under the auspices of the House of Culture in Prague 8. This was possible thanks to Vladimír Sloup, a friend of Hübschmannová's, who was employed there. It features poems in Romani by six writers, among others the above-mentioned Tera Fabiánová and Elena Lacková. Thematically, they draw on their shared past in Slovak settlements and traditional Romani folklore and in general do not engage with contemporary life and issues, thus enabling the beauty of the Romani language to shine in its more antiquated form with few neologisms and loan words. More similar volumes came out especially in the second half of the nineteen eighties.

M. Hübschmannová also successfully integrated specimens of Romani folklore — songs, puzzles, fairy tales, and oral history — into her various textbooks of Romani. For instance, the serialized codification of the Romani language from 1971 was published as *Základy romštiny* (Elementary Romani) in 1973 and its students were expected to practise by translating proverbs and tales. Some of the same literary material was reprinted in 1976 in the textbook *Cikánština: Metodický materiál pro učitele cikánských dětí* (The Gypsy language: A methodological handbook for the teachers of Gypsy children). Hübschmannová used the textbook in her courses for the so-called "Gypsy curators", social workers especially appointed for field work in Romani communities in the respective districts of Prague. Due to the job's unpopularity, it was often dished out to rebellious citizens as a form of punishment, thus generating a particular milieu of people with strong convictions and minority sensitivities. The course was held under the patronage of the Prague-based Jazyková škola (Language School), where Hübschmannová taught Romani and Hindi on-and-off between 1975—1990. This school turned out to be an essential hub for the networking and emancipatory activities of politically engaged Roma and non-Romani activists who mingled in her various classes, sometimes as students, other times as instructors. One particular course that made history was Romani for the Roma (1989/1990), where Romani speakers learnt the rules of Romani grammar and spelling, impossible to acquire from the mainstream educational system. The participants, most of whom would soon join the reborn Romani movement following the November 1989 revolution (e.g., Emil Ščuka, Jan "Láďa" Rusenko, Vlado Oláh, or Margita Reinzerová), brought their original pieces of writing, which were delivered in front of the audience, discussed, and translated. Many a Romani poem, short story, or narrative originated in these classes.

Finally, it must be stressed that not everything was achieved solely thanks to the remarkable production skills of Milena Hübschmannová. Following the declaration of glasnost (openness) and perestroika (restructuring) by Mikhail Gorbachev's USSR in the mid-nineteen eighties — the two pillars of political and economic renovation which ultimately led to the disintegration of the Soviet Union — Romani grassroots activities gradually also started to gain force. One platform of Romani self-determination became the folk song-and-dance groups dubbed ZUČ (Zájmová umělecká činnost [Amateur Creative Activity]). At this late stage, not only the capital of the country, but also many regional towns became centres of frantic nationalist activity in preparation for the political changes which were already detectable in the society. Perumos and Khamoro in Prague but also Romen in Sokolov or Amare neni and Čercheň in Rokycany became natural and vital centres of Romani culture and emancipation.

As early as 1982, the above-mentioned Emil Ščuka (*1957) with his Sokolov group Romen staged his original play written in Czech with some Romani dialogues and traditional folk music, entitled *Amaro drom* (Our journey). It was received enthusiastically by both Romani audiences, who were delighted by hearing Romani on the stage, and sympathetic members of the Czech public. During 1983, the play toured the country to considerable acclaim, becoming a symbol of anti-establishment sentiments. Ščuka also founded his own minority magazine, masquerading as a Socialist Youth Union's periodical. Although the first issue of *L'il* (The paper, 1986) was never followed by another, its pages were jam-packed with written material penned by prominent members of Romani intelligentsia.

Last but not least, there was a significant link to Czechoslovak political opposition. Starting from the Charter 77's Document No. 23 "Postavení Cikánů-Romů v ČSSR" (On the situation of the Czechoslovak Gypsies-Roma) from 1978, Czechoslovak dissent was showing tentative interest and support for the Romani cause. In the late nineteen eighties, several exile and samizdat volumes included samples of Romani writing, thus incorporating Romani heritage into the fabric of live counterculture.

UPRE, ROMA!

The Velvet Revolution from November 1989 — as a result of which the dissident and playwright Václav Havel (1936—2011) became the president of democratic Czechoslovakia and the first free general election since 1946 was held in June 1990 — saw the population of Czechoslovakia determined, optimistic, and above all unified. The fact that on November 25, 1989, Jan "Láďa" Rusenko and Emil Ščuka stood on the Letná hill stage in Prague facing a crowd of 800 thousand people, declaring that the Roma, too, are proud Czechoslovak citizens and patriots, while being welcomed by "Long live the Roma!" in a thundering unison, seemed to mark the onset of a new era. As movingly described in Věra Horváthová Duždová's "The Nineties", the Roma across the country embraced the opportunity to "make a difference again".

Romani political representation formed the Romská občanská iniciativa (aka the ROI, Romani Civic Initiative) and local branches quickly sprang up; between 1990—1992, as many as eleven Roma MPs represented minority interests in the Czechoslovak parliament. For a time at least, euphoria reigned and progress was noticeable on multiple levels of Romani public affairs, including Romani literature and publishing.

In January 1990, the first issue of *Lačho lav* — a Romani monthly largely based upon the lessons learnt from *Románo ľil* — was released, soon to be followed by a score of other Romani periodicals (*Amaro lav, Romano gendalos, Romano kurko, Romano hangos, Romano nevo ľil, etc.*). They carried literary texts not only from the generation of the GRU writers, but also by promising new talents. In November 1990, Margita Reiznerová (1945—2020), a rising poet from the Perumos song-and-dance group, became the chairwoman of the new Romani Writers' Union and a year later she founded Romaňi čhib (Romani Language), the first exclusively Romani publishing house. In October 1991, the department of Romani Studies was opened as part of the Indology Institute of Charles University in Prague with Milena Hübschmannová as its head, actively supported by members of the Romani intelligentsia, who frequented their classes as native instructors and contributed their literature as teaching materials. And last but not least, a Romani dictionary (*Česko-romský a romsko-český kapesní slovník*) was published by the State Pedagogical Print (SPN) in 1991, which became an indispensable companion and common point of reference not only to the students of Romani, but also to Romani activists, journalists, and ultimately writers.

BREAK FROM TRADITION

In the four years of its existence, the Romaňi čhib publishing house released eight titles by six Romani writers. In terms of genre, they ranged from traditional and/or artificial fairy tales to short stories. In terms of size, they were thin brochures, not wholly dissimilar from small prints. Gejza Demeter produced a collection of classic Romani ghost stories (*O mule maškar amende* [The dead among us]); Margita Reiznerová penned a modern myth about the origin of the Roma (*Kaľi* [The black one]); Helena Demeterová sprinkled her traditional folk material with miniature accounts of her dreams (*Rom ke romeste drom arakhel* [The Rom always finds the way to other Roms]). However, what was crucial for the development of modern Romani letters was *Mosarďa peske o dživipen anglo love* (She ruined her life because of money) by Ilona Ferková (*1956).

In her opening text of the same name, Ferková radically departs from the folk tradition and ventures to tell the story of a contemporary *Romňi* who, in order to conceal her inordinate spending from her husband, undergoes sterilization in exchange for financial compensation. The husband condemns her, as in his eyes, she has lost her value both as a woman and a human being. It is not only a reflection of the eugenic practise of the sterilization of Romani women by the paternalistic state, common in communist times but sadly reaching well past the transition period. It also marks a change of paradigm in Romani writing, where the focus has been shifted from the essentialist conflict between us and them — the Roma and the *gadje* (the non-Roma) — to the more subtle dramas taking place in the intimate realm of the Romani home.

Ferková's next volume of stories *Čorde čhave* (Stolen children, Společenství Romů na Moravě 1996) is dedicated entirely to social realism, sparing neither the meddling state authorities who control and penalise Romani families by committing their children to care, nor the blundering Roma who, in the face of the new, tumultuous times, succumb to alcohol and drug abuse, violence, gambling, and prostitution. In 2018, a collection of short stories bound by Kaštánek, a Romani bum who tells stories in exchange for beer and rum in a small-town bar, was released by KHER (*Ještě jedno, Lído! Kaštánkovy příběhy z herny* [I'll have another one, Lída! Kaštánek's stories from the gambling parlour]). And most recently, Ferková followed it up with *AMEN* (Us, KHER 2023), young adult fiction about a friendship of four working-class Romani girls on the backdrop of the nineteen sixties in Rokycany. Ferková is one of the most prolific Czech Romani writers to date. She combines social criticism with genuine empathy and a sense of humour stemming from Romani oral tradition. She also consistently works in Romani.

FROM SMALL PRINTS TO DIGNIFIED VOLUMES

The Romaňi čhib publishing house was not the only outlet of Romani writing at the time. Not long after the revolution, several other titles of the small-print type were released by various occasional and/or short-lived prints.

First of all, it was a collection of eleven contemporary Romani poets and fiction writers entitled *Kale ruži* (Black roses) in 1990, only the second anthology of Romani literature since the UGR times. Great service was done to Romani letters by the art-historian Oliva Pechová (1927—2005), the owner of a now defunct and little-researched household print Apeiron, who in the course of 1991 published three canonical Romani titles: Tera Fabiánová's *Čavargoš* (The tramp), a story of a stray dog who is taken in by a Romani boy; Andrej Giňa's *Bijav* (Wedding), a collection of three long realistic stories set in the traditional Slovak Romani settlement; and a collection of classic Romani proverbs, *Goďaver lava phure Romendar* (The wise words of the old Roma), an indispensable handbook of Romani folk maxims for all journalists, script-writers, and the like. Tera Fabiánová's autobiographical children's book *Sar me phiravas andre škola* (How I went to school) was published by ÚDO press České Budějovice in collaboration with the Moravian Roma Association in 1992.

As the millennium beckoned, small but quality mainstream publishing houses such as Argo, GplusG, Signeta, Dauphin, and particularly Triáda started to add Romani letters, both local and foreign, to their niche portfolios. Although it was a handful of titles in total, the status of the publishing houses combined with the meticulous layout and graphic design of the books lent these Romani writers previously unknown prestige. To name some more prominent Czech Roma, it was for instance the short-story collection *Trispras* by Gejza Horváth (GplusG 2006), a poetry collection *Suno* (Dream) by Margita Reiznerová (Triáda 2000), Roman Erös's mystical novel *Cadík* (Dauphin 2008), but most importantly Elena Lacková's memoir *Narodila jsem se pod šťastnou hvězdou* (A false dawn: my life as a Gypsy woman in Slovakia; Triáda 1997). No other book has had such a tremendous impact on the popularization of Romani literature in mainstream Czech society.

Triáda publishing house is the most consistent non-Romani publisher of Roma-related titles to date, which has over time published such milestones of the Romani literary canon as Andrej Giňa's collected works *Paťiv* (Honour, 2013), Erika Olahová's horror tales *Nechci se vrátit mezi mrtvé* (I don't want to go back among the dead, 2004), or Josef Serinek's memoir *Česká cikánská rapsodie* (The Czech Gypsy rhapsody) from 2016, a testimonial to Romani involvement in anti-fascist guerilla resistance, with commentaries by the historian Jan Tesař.

Although the literary development of the nineteen nineties may have seemed rapid and revolutionary, the truth is that the early stage of the post-November Romani publishing industry suffered from numerous problems. Due to the lack of funding, grassroot titles often had an unappealing low-cost appearance riddled by unfortunate mistakes, with elementary graphic design and illustrations by self-taught artists. A major obstacle turned out to be distribution. Many of these early works were published in DIY conditions by various interest groups, NGOs and obscure presses, therefore not making it into official circulation in bookshops and libraries. Moreover, readers were glutted with formerly unavailable literature by dissident, exile, and foreign writers. As groundbreaking as the stories written by the Roma may have appeared at the time, they were nothing but a drop in the ocean.

Also, the initial atmosphere of optimism and hope present in the general society as well as in the Romani communities gradually soured. Romani political representation was plagued by internal struggle; the Citizenship Act following the peaceful division of Czechoslovakia into two separate countries in 1993 created lasting problems for Slovak Roma with long-term residency in the Czech Republic, but without the documents to prove it; the mechanisms of capitalism quickly pushed the Roma to the margins of the employment and housing markets, and ultimately the society. By far the worst tragedy of the nineties, at least as far as the Roma were concerned, was the dramatic rise in ultra-right nationalism which swept across the liberated Europe.

In 2005, Milena Hübschmannová, the initiator, editor, and translator of, and crucial production force behind, much of Romani literary activity, tragically died in a car accident. Temporarily, the Romani movement and its literature ground to a halt.

TOWARDS NEW INDEPENDENCE

The period after Hübschmannová's unexpected demise produced two contradictory trajectories: on the one hand, writers of a certain renown and experience, Hübschmannová's direct disciples such as A. Giňa, I. Ferková, V. Oláh, or E. Cina, fell silent. They were not only mourning their mentor's passing but also felt they had nowhere else to turn with their new texts.

On the other hand, several new writers emerged and managed to find publishing opportunities without Hübschmannová's freely donated editorial service and outside of the Roma Studies' sphere of influence. The boldness of such an act — to successfully pitch one's own literary work without institutional support — can only be understood in the light of the low degree of literacy among the Slovak Roma migrating to Bohemia, Moravia, and Silesia in the decades after WWII.

In *Kde domov můj* (Where is my home; Divus 2005), the self-obsessed recidivist and con-artist Zdeněk Perský departs from the rules of Romani solidarity and creates a self-portrait glorifying his criminal feats and promoting himself to a role of a criminal mastermind and guru. Irena Eliášová won well-earned recognition for her short novel *Naše Osada* (Our settlement; Liberec Regional Scientific Library 2008), a surprisingly mature piece of writing about a little Romani girl who observes the relations between the Roma and the non-Roma with a great deal of humour and acumen. Roman Erös received Mácha's Rose for his debut *Cadík* (Dauphin 2008), a story of a fumbling Romani man looking for his place in life, loaded with Romani and Jewish symbolism. It is noteworthy that all three newcomers continued in their literary efforts following their debut, although Irena Eliášová has been by far the most consistently present on the scene. Most significantly, her sentimental historical novella "Slunce zapadá už ráno" (The sun sets in the morning) about the forbidden love between a Romani woman and a *gadjo* farmer, written in Romani, gave its name to a collection of four Romani women writers' texts published under the same title by Václav Havel Library in 2014.

THE HOME OF ROMANI LITERATURE

A change of pattern regarding Romani letters arrived in 2010 when the NGO Romea, the online minority news service, made a public call for unpublished pieces of writing by Romani writers to be submitted for publication. In a space of four months, as part of the project Šukar laviben le Romendar (Beautiful words from the Roma), as many as thirty-six new stories and poems by sixteen writers were released. The contributors were both experienced and "green", and while the very successful project lasted, they read each other's works and commented in the comments section underneath, thus shaping the outlines of a literary community. The follow-up photo-exhibition of the writers' portraits by the project's head Lukáš Houdek Lačho lav sar maro (A good word is like bread) transferred the project from the internet to the public space and attracted a lot of media attention.

In 2012, this overall generation of interest and energy led directly to the foundation of KHER, a publishing house specialising in Romani letters. Lukáš Houdek, Iva Hlaváčková, Zdeňka Kainarová, and Radka Patočková, former Roma Studies classmates and Romea colleagues, did not want to lose this momentum and wanted to create a space where Romani writers could freely publish and Romani literature could be freely read. Starting off as an exclusively digital platform operated by volunteers in their free time, KHER gradually transformed into a regular small publishing house, releasing an average of three titles a year, while also delivering a wide scope of activities such as literary readings, lectures, presentations, and creative writing workshops.

The Romani word KHER means "home", "house" or "room". KHER's mission is to be the home of Romani literature where Romani writers find support and publishing opportunities while also having a say in editorial planning and related activities. Since the 2018 release of I. Ferková's *Ještě jedno, Lído* — the very first hard-copy book published by KHER — the press has come a long way, with the current volume being the twentieth title. In response to growing interest of foreign audiences, and particularly Romani readers living abroad, it brings a selection of seventeen short stories by contemporary Czech and occasionally Slovak Romani writers, which portray the richness of Romani life while inadvertently mapping out the twentieth century in the history of Czechoslovak Roma.

Nonetheless, KHER is by no means the only platform upon which Romani literature is nowadays showcased and appreciated by the public. Be it the Roma-Studies journal *Romano džaniben*, the numerous minority media such as *Romano vod'i*, *Romano hangos* or the Radio programme *O Roma vakeren* (The Roma talk), the literary and cultural journals such as *A2*, *Plav*, *Tvar* and *Host*, or the leading mainstream media like *Respekt* weekly and *Deník N* daily — thankfully, the instances of well-deserved attention being paid to writing by the Roma are too numerous to mention.

THE ANTHOLOGY IN YOUR HANDS

The current selection addresses certain important social and historical themes which are recurring in Czech Romani writing for their universal relevance to the lives of the Roma. The two opening stories by Zlatica Rusová ("Brave Romani Women") and Květoslava Podhradská ("Run for It, Margita") discuss the so-called "unknown holocaust", that is the persecution of the Roma during World War II. They are both set in Slovakia as this is where the writers and their families come from, but let it not be forgotten that the reason why there are so few accounts of the suffering of the Czech and Moravian Roma in the same period is that the Romani population of The Protectorate of Bohemia and Moravia — the Czech lands occupied by Nazi Germany during World War II — was almost entirely wiped out.

Eva Danišová (in "My Dears") and Olga Fečová (in "Open-Sky Flat") touch upon the hardships of newly arrived Slovak Roma in the Czech lands after the war. People were poor, underprivileged, and uneducated, but their move to Czechia offered wonderful opportunities to those brave of heart and ready to persevere. Both narrators deliver their often hard-to-believe stories with a lot of humour and kindness.

If Danišová and Fečová speak about the early days of Romani migration, then the next batch of writers depict the times of relative peace and integration, when the Roma have already successfully settled in and were enjoying a moderate degree of prosperity. This is not to say that the socialist state pampered the Roma or treated them fairly — far from it. They were only tolerated insofar as they accepted their belonging with the working class and the radical divorce from any idea of Romaniness in favour of becoming Czechoslovak citizens with dying ethnicity.

In "Going to the Movies", Ilona Ferková offers a nostalgic and funny reminiscence of childhood tricks used to get to the pictures. In "My Wonderful Family", Markéta Šestáková talks about the shenanigans her husband's mother and father used to play on each other. In "The Way We Used to

Live", Michal Šamko paints an idyllic portrait of his growing up in a Czech village. In "Going to Grandpa's", Emil Cina reminds the reader that at some point, Slovakia ceased to be the Czech Roma's home but instead became a holiday destination, where they visited their distant relatives once a year.

"Čukča's Great Misfortune" by Gejza Demeter and "A Few Presents" by Eva Danišová show that the communities are sometimes plagued by internal problems and instances of pathology. After living a relatively good life in socialist times, Čukča is a selfish man who has forgotten about in-group solidarity. Danišová's heroine, a Romani mother released from prison, longs to relieve her daughter from care but instead accepts the life of a sideroad prostitute, where she has been forced out of necessity. Květoslava Podhradská's "House on Štěrková" brings yet another example of a good life sent to ruin, this time by the floods of 1997.

Maria Siváková's "That's Capitalism for You", Věra Horváthová Duždová's "The Nineties", Stanislava Ondová's "Inside the Bubble", Patrik Banga's "Žižkovite", and Mária Hušová's "Where to Now?" all depict — to varying degrees — the initial elation following the Velvet Revolution and the subsequent disillusionment and rapid social fall of working-class Roma in the wake of the post-Velvet transition. The rise in ultra-right violence in the nineteen nineties is particularly interestingly portrayed in Hušová's story set in a Slovak settlement, which is a psychological probe into the minds of the Roma fearing the pogrom looming over their community.

The selection is symbolically closed by "You're Like Me" by the up-and-coming Martin Kanaloš, whose story explores ethnic identity with unusual subtlety, offering a glimpse of how Romani literature may develop in the not-so-distant future.

The reader will find that the stories run straight from the heart. Far from being simplistic, they speak in everyday language of the essential values that every human being holds dear: family, home, community, solidarity, friendship, compassion and mutual support.

GLOSSARY OF CZECH, ROMANI, & SLOVAK EXPRESSIONS & PHRASES

C= Czech
R = Romani
S = Slovak

bobaľki (pl., R) — a traditional Romani Christmas dish consisting of sweet dumplings doused in milk, sugar, and ground poppy seeds

bábovka (sg., C) — a popular homemade cake, round, with a hole in the middle and ribbing on the outside. In English, variously translated as marble cake, Bundt cake, or sponge cake.

čhaje! (R) — girl!

chiža (sg., R) — a wooden shack (from the Slovak *chyža*)

chlebíček, chlebíčky (sg., pl., C) — a traditional Czech appetizer or snack: small oval slices of white bread spread with butter or mayonnaise and garnished with a variety of toppings, including ham, salami, cheese, eggs, pickled fish, and/or vegetables

dikh! (R) — "See!" or "Look here!"

gadjo, gadjos (sg., pl., R) — the Romani word for a non-Romani person or people; in the north-central Romani dialect, spelled *gadžo* (masculine) *gadži* (feminine), and *gadže* (plural).

goja (pl., R) — a traditional Romani dish consisting of roasted pig intestines with a spicy potato filling ("Chaľomas goja!" = "I could go for some goja!")

halušky (pl., S) — a dish popular among the Roma found in many Central and Eastern European cuisines, including Slovakia's: thick, soft noodles or dumplings served with salty cheese, fried bacon, cabbage, or sauerkraut

jarkos (sg., R) — a brook or stream

klobása (sg., C) — a dry, hard, spicy sausage

kozara (pl., R) — mushrooms

lokše (pl., S) — thin potato pancakes, baked on the stove with no fat

marikľi, marikľa (sg., pl., R) — a pancake, or flatbread, made of flour and water and baked on the stove

OPBH (C) — abbreviation for the Communist-era *Okresní/Obvodní podnik bytového hospodářství*, or District Housing Management Company

paťiv (R) — honor, respect, merit, and social standing: an essential concept of Romani cultural identity

párek (sg., C) — a frankfurter-like sausage

pásky (pl., C, R) — a dish consisting of three sheets of leavened dough, spread across the surface of a pan and filled with walnuts, sweet curds, raisins, and plum jam

panelák (sg., C) — short for *panelový dům* ("panel house"), *panelák* is the colloquial term for a large block of flats constructed of prefabricated concrete, common in the former Czechoslovakia (now the Czech Republic and Slovakia). Paneláks are usually grouped together in what is known as a *sídliště* in Czech and *sídlisko* in Slovak ("housing estate").

plňimen armin (R) — stuffed cabbages

Rom, Romňi, Roma (m., f., pl., R) — an ethnonym referring to the diasporic people of Indo-Aryan descent originating from northern India, incorrectly and offensively known as "Gypsies"

romipen (sg., R) — "Romaniness": a set of positive cultural norms that define Romani identity

sídliště (sg., C) — a housing estate of *paneláks* (see above)

svadobný pytač (sg., S) — "wedding asker," the person who asks the bride's parents if the groom is permitted to marry her

tu hercona! (R) — "you actor, you!"

vajda (sg., R) — a Romani mayor or community leader

zajda (sg., R) — a strong and colorful canvas sheet used to carry things on one's back